THE BRANCH AND THE SCAFFOLD

Books by Loren D. Estleman

Kill Zone
Roses Are Dead
Any Man's Death
Motor City Blues
Angel Eyes
The Midnight Man
The Glass Highway
Sugartown
Every Brilliant Eye
Lady Yesterday
Downriver
Silent Thunder
Sweet Women Lie
Never Street
The Witchfinder
The Hours of the Virgin
A Smile on the Face of the Tiger
*City of Widows**
*The High Rocks**
*Billy Gashade**
*Stamping Ground**
*Aces & Eights**
*Journey of the Dead**
*Jitterbug**
*Thunder City**
*The Rocky Mountain Moving Picture Association**
*The Master Executioner**
*Black Powder, White Smoke**
*White Desert**
*Sinister Heights**
*Something Borrowed, Something Black**
*Port Hazard**
*Poison Blonde**
*Retro**
*Little Black Dress**
*Nicotine Kiss**
*The Undertaker's Wife**
*The Adventures of Johnny Vermillion**
*American Detective**
*Gas City**
*Frames**
*The Branch and the Scaffold**

*A Forge Book

THE BRANCH AND THE SCAFFOLD

· A NOVEL OF JUDGE PARKER ·

LOREN D. ESTLEMAN

FORGE®

A Tom Doherty Associates Book
New York

This is a work of fiction. All of the characters, organizations, and events portrayed in this novel are either products of the author's imagination or are used fictitiously.

THE BRANCH AND THE SCAFFOLD: A NOVEL OF JUDGE PARKER

A Forge Book
Published by Tom Doherty Associates, LLC
175 Fifth Avenue
New York, NY 10010

www.tor-forge.com

Library of Congress Cataloging-in-Publication Data

Estleman, Loren D.
The branch and the scaffold / Loren D. Estleman.—1st ed.
p. cm.
"A Tom Doherty Associates book."
ISBN-13: 978-0-7653-1599-1
ISBN-10: 0-7653-1599-8
1. Parker, Isaac Charles, 1838–1896—Fiction. 2. Judges—Fiction. 3. Outlaws—Fiction. 4. Frontier and pioneer life—Fiction. 5. Fort Smith (Ark.)—Fiction. I. Title.
PS3555.S84 B73 2008
813'.54—dc22

2008034553

First Edition: May 2009

Printed in the United States of America

0 9 8 7 6 5 4 3 2 1

This book is dedicated to the men who rode for Parker;
and to the memory of Douglas C. Jones, who wrote about him.

I

A DREAM OF JUSTICE

This reasonable moderator, and equal piece of justice, Death.

—Sir Thomas Browne
(1605–1682)

ONE

TWO long blasts on the whistle, each bent in the middle by the wind on the river. It seemed to be shrieking his name.

"Well, they'll know we're coming." Mary Parker took her fingers from her ears.

"I think they know already."

Spotting the crowd on the dock, she drew in little Charlie and huddled closer to her husband. "Have they come with baskets of flowers or buckets of tar?"

"They're empty-handed. Come to see the carpetbagger."

"How soon can you prove them wrong?"

"Soon. I have my predecessor to thank for heightening the contrast."

"They cried for his impeachment."

"I studied his record. He's fortunate they didn't dangle him from his own scaffold."

"I should think a town with a fort would be an orderly place."

"The fort is closed. The town has thirty saloons and one bank. I am the order."

When the steamboat bumped against the hempbound pilings, the crowd eased back to allow the hands to erect the gangplank and bear trunks and portmanteaux to the dock for passengers to claim. Some newcomers were greeted and borne away amidst jabber, others escaped interest, looking for porters and transportation. Most of those gathered watched as Isaac and Mary Parker and their small son alighted. They saw a man in excess of six feet tall and two hundred pounds, wearing a sandy Vandyke beard, a soft hat, and a duster to protect his gray suit from cinders, accompanied by a large woman near his age in gloves, a cape, and a hat secured with a scarf under her chin. Patent-leather shoes showed beneath the hem of her skirt. The boy, in necktie, cap, and knickerbockers, had a high complexion and kept close to his parents, although not from fear; he intercepted the curious glances of strangers with his father's level blue gaze.

"Your honor?"

Parker lifted his chin to confront the stranger. He was a man close to his own thirty-seven years, pale-eyed and neatly barbered, in a frock coat too heavy for the season, but he gripped Parker's hand with a dry palm.

"You're the first to address me so."

"William Clayton, chief prosecutor." He bowed to Mary and acknowledged the child with a nod but no interest. "Welcome to Fort Smith."

It was a hot Sunday in early May. The family and Clayton boarded a waiting phaeton, sat with hands folded while the Negro driver and a porter secured their luggage, and rode down a broad street harrowed by hooves and carriage wheels to a fine dust that rose in clouds like flour and cast a scrim over a town built largely of unpainted wood, with neither sidewalks nor lamps to illuminate the streets at night. The saloons were shuttered for the sabbath, but wagons and horses lined the hitching rails, and stragglers from the dock dodged heavy oncoming traffic to run alongside the phaeton, staring at the occupants. Clayton tapped the driver's shoulder with his stick and he picked up the pace, leaving the rubbernecks behind but raising still more dust. Mary drew a handkerchief from her sleeve and held it to her nose and mouth.

"Isaac"—her voice was muffled, but still she lowered it a notch—"we've made a great mistake."

He patted her other hand. "No, Mary. We are faced with a great task. These people need us. We must not fail them."

Clayton spoke, distracting Mary's attention from a row of bright petticoats fluttering from a second-floor balcony like the flags of many nations. "No school yet, Mrs. Parker, but we hope to remedy that by the time the lad's old enough."

"He's seen our nation's capital and much of the continent in between," she said. "His education began early."

"How soon may I inspect the garrison?" asked Parker.

"Directly you're settled in. You'll welcome the early start. Many of the prisoners have waited months for their cases to come to trial, and eighteen are charged with capital offenses. If you can convene by the end of this month at the earliest, you just may clear the docket in time for Independence Day."

"As late as that?"

"Judge Story kept an untidy desk."

"I've heard it was worse than that."

"That's the popular view, but I wouldn't cast it about up at the courthouse. It's a Democratic stronghold and, begging your honor's pardon, you're an appointee of President Grant. Moreover—" He faltered, cleared his throat.

"I'm a turncoat. Everyone's aware of my original party affiliation, Mr. Clayton. The decision to switch has given me unique insight. I intend to keep politics out of my courtroom. I'd as soon hang a Republican as a Democrat."

"Isaac!"

He glanced at his son. "I'm sorry, my dear."

"People hereabouts would pay to see a thing like that," Clayton said.

"I understand they did."

"Judge Story suffered from sloth more than greed, although he had a chronic case of that as well. In fourteen months he managed to run up an expense bill of four hundred thousand."

"The taxpayers should be grateful he didn't show more initiative."

"At this point it's impossible to distinguish between simple attrition due to gross negligence and bald-faced theft. The Eighth is a big jurisdiction: all of the Western District of Arkansas and the Indian Nations, including places few white men have ever set foot on, and them that have you wouldn't want to meet out in the open. Prussia's smaller. A great deal can pass unnoticed in a responsibility that size. If Story was half as corrupt as he was incompetent, he could have made the Tweed Ring look like a First Street pickpocket. It will take most of the month for an honest man to begin to make sense of it all."

"Please be prepared to plead your most pressing cases a week from tomorrow."

The prosecutor's eyes flickered, the irises scarcely darker than the whites. "I don't see how you can do it, and neither will you once you've had a look about."

Three-year-old Charles Parker tugged at his father's sleeve. "Papa, when may we see the gallows?"

"It's the damnedest assignment any man ever undertook, or ever will," Clayton said. "All your judgments are final, hanging and all, with no appeal between you and Almighty God—not counting the president, who considering the human offal you'll be passing sentence on wouldn't touch it with a poker. It's instant history; and if you do it the way it needs to be done, it'll be the death of you."

"Are you attempting to frighten me off?"

"No, sir. A man ought to know what he's harnessing himself up to. My motives are less than Christian. We're to be partners, and a thing done no more than halfway by the one must be done one hundred and fifty percent by the other. I'm ambitious, but I ain't suicidal."

Parker's face registered disapproval of the deliberate lapse in grammar. His wife and son were unpacking in the Hotel Le Flore. Judge and prosecutor were seated in what was to be his chambers, a small square room barely large enough to contain a black walnut desk the size of a dining table, three tufted-leather chairs, shelves, and a credenza, with nary a horizontal surface not piled high with papers and bursting portfolios bearing witness to the disorganization of the previous administration. The curling leaves seemed to defy gravity, scaling the walls from floor to ceiling, their yellowed corners stirring in the breeze through the open window. Notwithstanding that, the air was stagnant, redolent of tobacco long since chewed and expectorated, and murky with the exhaust of the cigars the pair was smoking. A revolving bookcase leaned drunkenly to one side, stuffed with mustard-colored bound case histories with the hangdog look of children neglected and forgotten. A mausoleum of justice overlooked; a dead plant in a dry pot.

"Equal and exact justice," Parker said, when that image came to him. "Jefferson's words. If we can keep them in mind, we can dispense with everything else."

"Jefferson was a Democrat."

"What of it? Lincoln was a Republican. Together they freed millions. In any event, this is an oasis in the political desert. I explained that once." The judge broke two inches of ash into a heavy brass tray that performed double duty as a paperweight. "Thank you for the tour. My family and I will establish quarters in the commissary. Will you have someone see it's made ready as soon as possible? I don't wish to burden the electorate with a hotel bill any larger than is necessary."

"I'll attend to it. What did you think of the jail?"

Parker repressed a shudder. He'd served in Congress and fought with the Home Guard under Rosecrans, but the atrocities he'd witnessed were little more than an anteroom to the dungeon beneath his feet, separated into two sections by a stone wall that extended up through the ground floor, with prisoners sprawled on rough concrete, some in shackles, buckets for sanitary use. The stench was a permanent fixture. The rest of the building, two brick stories that had sheltered officers during garrison days, devoted half the surface level to court proceedings, the rest to the handmaidens of justice.

The judge addressed a different subject, somewhat to Clayton's surprise; the attorney had placed him as a humanitarian, who would at least inquire about the possibillity of constructing a proper jail. "The scaffold," he said. "Is it as sound as it appears?"

"It would take a charge of powder to dismantle it. It's been struck once by lightning and survived."

This arrangement was visible through the window at a distance of three hundred yards. It stood fourteen feet high on the site of the old powder magazine, extended for twenty feet, and supported a twelve- by twelve-inch beam suitable for hanging a dozen condemned men simultaneously.

"So far it's served only one," Clayton went on; "a half-breed named Childers, who slit an old man's throat for his horse. Old Judge Caldwell commissioned a substantial example of architecture to inspire fear in the territory. He underestimated the highwaymen's resolve. Here in town they call it Sam Grant's wash line."

"Who is responsible for it?"

"Jim Fagan, whom you'll meet presently. He's U.S. marshal, and your chief law enforcement officer. I believe he assigns a man from time to time to apply whitewash and inspect it for termites."

"The executioner should see to that."

"At present we've no one in that particular post."

"We should. I want to see personnel records on everyone who serves this court."

"I recommend you requisition a shovel." Clayton swept an arm along the mountain range of paper that surrounded them.

Someone knocked. Parker raised his voice, inviting the visitor inside. The door opened, admitting a small, narrow-gauged man in a blue uniform with a Sam Browne belt. He looked at the judge briefly, then at Clayton, and removed his forage cap. Strands of silver glittered in his broom-shaped whiskers and a shelf of brow left his eyes in deep shadow.

"Sir, we had a disturbance. I feared you may have heard it."

"What sort of disturbance?" asked Parker, before the prosecutor could respond.

When the man hesitated, Clayton said, "George Maledon, meet Judge Isaac Parker. Maledon's a deputy sheriff, helps out downstairs."

Maledon faced Parker. "Man threw his slops at a turnkey. I had to bust him." He patted the pistol on his hip.

"You shot him?" asked Clayton.

"No, sir, I used the other end. Doc Du Val says he'll live."

"Very well. We don't want another incident so soon after the last." To Parker: "Maledon shot an escaping prisoner last month. A single ball through the heart from a rifle."

"What is your experience?" Parker asked.

"Before this billet I was a policeman in Fort Smith five years."

"Would you consider resigning from the county and accepting a position in charge of executions in this district?"

Two tiny points of light guttered deep in the other's skull. "I would for a fact," he said. "Your honor."

TWO

"Oyez! Oyez! The Honorable District Court of the United States for the Western District of Arkansas, having criminal jurisdiction of the Indian Territory, is now in session."

The tenor voice of Court Crier J. G. Hammersly, a short-legged man with a rooster chest, rang like a temple bell in the eternal twilight of the courtroom.

Parker, looking no more and certainly no less in authority seated behind a brawny cherry-paneled desk in his black robes, snapped his gavel. "The court is ready for the first case."

And, by God, thought William H. H. Clayton, *it is.* The big regulator clock on the wall above the heads of the jurors twitched one second past eight A.M., Monday, May 10, 1875; eight days after Grant's new appointee set foot on dry land from the narrow Arkansas, like Moses from the mountain. At the time, his chief prosecutor had not thought the thing possible; but he'd learned a parcel about the man's character during the past week and would not repeat the mistake.

The clerk, Stephen Wheeler, baby-faced and without vocal inflection, rose and glanced down at the docket on his writing table. "The United States *versus* Daniel H. Evans. Charge, murder."

Evans, young and clean-shaven, was careful in his appearance. The suit and shirt his attorney had provided for him had evidently been selected by the client, for the collar and cuffs fitted him as if they'd been made to his measure and the coat lay smooth across his shoulders. He stood accused of having murdered a nineteen-year-old boy in the Creek Nation for his boots. When apprehended, the defendant had been wearing an uncommonly fine pair with hand-tooled tops and high, sloping heels, nearly new. He'd been tried before the previous judge, but the jury had disagreed on a verdict, and he'd been returned to jail. In the meantime the father of the slain youth had come forward, and in the presence of the jury he now identified his son's boots by some horseshoe nails the boy had driven to secure a faulty heel. Evans, who'd been jubilant and answered Parker's occasional remarks to him with polite banter, remained silent and pale throughout the man's testimony.

"The United States *versus* James Moore. Charge, murder."

Moore, whose deep sunburn had had little time to fade since his capture, plucked at his moustaches and glared at the witnesses against him, who identified him as one of the territory's leading horse thieves. While fleeing a citizens' posse led by two of James Fagan's deputies, the desperado had shot and killed William Spivey, the first federal officer to give his life in the service of the Eighth District court. On that occasion Moore escaped, only to be arrested by two more deputy marshals when he abandoned horse stealing for cattle rustling. A partner testifying against him gave evidence that Moore had been traveling with the owner of a herd, intending to murder him to gain possession, when he wandered into the deputies' hands. Shackled during the journey to Fort Smith, the defendant had boasted of having killed eight men.

"The United States *versus* Edmund Campbell. Charge, murder."

A Negro native of the Choctaw Nation, the heavy-shouldered Campbell had drunk himself into a fury over a hasty remark made by a neighbor, Lawson Ross, gone to Ross's house, and butchered the man and his common-law wife. He stared at the floor throughout the trial with angry eyes in a sullen face.

"The United States *versus* Smoker Mankiller. Charge, murder."

Unfortunately named for his present circumstances, the Choctaw sat broad and motionless at the defense table, not understanding a word of the evidence against him in English. For no reason ever given he'd borrowed a gun from an acquaintance named William Short and shot him to death with it. He'd been overheard proudly acknowledging the act, but since his arrest had changed his story, blaming it on two brothers named Welch.

"The United States *versus* John Whittington. Charge, murder."

The defendant was visibly ill, sallow-featured and shining with perspiration. The eighteen-year-old son of the victim in the case, John J. Turner, confirmed that he'd seen Whittington stab Turner's father along the Red River in the Chickasaw Nation, and had subdued and held him until help came to bring him to justice. Whittington and the elder Turner had been seen drinking in a low saloon on the Texas side of the river, where Turner had paid the bartender from a swollen leather poke. It was determined that on the way back home, the man under examination had bludgeoned his companion with a makeshift club, then brought his knife into play when the other had refused to stay down. When arrested, Whittington had had a large sum of money in his pocket.

"The United States *versus* Samuel Fooy. Charge, murder."

Fooy, Cherokee on his mother's side, had confessed to the slaying of John Emmett Neff, a schoolteacher in the Cherokee Nation whose skeleton had been found a year later with a bullet hole in the skull. Returning from the tribal capital of Tahlequah with three hundred dollars in back salary, Neff had offered the farm wife who had put him up for the night a five-dollar bill to settle the fifty-cent fee. Told she could not change it, the schoolteacher had struck out on foot for a nearby store to procure the silver. Fooy, a neighbor visiting the house, had gone out after him. When the victim was identified based on his name in a book found near the remains, the rest was legwork.

The six men were tried and convicted in a little more than a month. Judge Parker's charges to the juries left small doubt as to his sympathies, and Chief Prosecutor Clayton listened in wonder as the man behind the desk instructed them which way to vote. When the foreman in the Evans case informed him of the panel's decision, Parker thanked him in a tone of satisfaction Clayton hadn't heard from him previously. At his sentencing, the young man who had coveted a pair of fine boots even unto death stood tight-faced before the cruel voice from the bench. Execution was scheduled for September 3, 1875.

"I sentence you to hang by the neck until you are dead, dead, dead!" Parker banged his gavel.

And then he wept.

Clayton stood throughout each sentencing, accompanied by his assistant, a young, ham-faced man named James Brizzolara, who at the age of fourteen had risen to the rank of colonel in the insurgent army of Giuseppe Garibaldi in Italy. The judge's tone on these occasions remained level.

"There, on the morning of September third, eighteen seventy-five, you will be conducted . . ."

". . . on the morning of September third, eighteen seventy-five . . ."

". . . September third, eighteen seventy-five . . ."

". . . September third . . ."

"By God," Clayton was heard to mutter, when the date was repeated a fourth time. "By God."

On the sixth and last, young Colonel Brizzolara whispered to his superior, "They'll not make mention of Sam Grant's wash line after this. What do you think they'll call the infernal machine now?"

" 'Parker's tears.' " Clayton smoothed a cigar between his fingers.

Ropes were not difficult to obtain in Fort Smith, where cattle outfits from Texas stopped to lubricate their throats and replenish their equipment before swimming the herds across the Arkansas to the railroad depot. George Maledon, however, was particular, and incurred the impatience of clerks in half a dozen saddleries before settling on two hundred feet of the best and thickest hemp to be found east of El Paso. He procured linseed oil as well and spent hours working it by hand into the fibers until they were as pliant as a gentlewoman's hair and would glide around the coarsest neck until the gargantuan knot fixed itself beneath the mastoid bone behind the left ear and snapped the cervical vertebra like a stalk of celery; to the knot itself he applied pitch to prevent slipping. He'd paid close attention to the process when John Childers was hanged for killing a peddler, and obtained the technical information from Dr. Ben T. Du Val, who stitched up the prisoners when they got into fights and had timed Childers' moment of death against his heavy pocket watch for the official record. Forty-five, Bavarian-born, Maledon had been raised in Detroit, served with the First Arkansas Federal Battery during the rebellion, and been a city policeman before accepting a position as deputy sheriff of Sebastian County and a part-time appointment as deputy U.S. marshal to legitimize his service in the Fort Smith jail. He'd slain a man during an escape attempt and thought no more of it than he had of shooting Confederate rebels.

Two-hundred-pound sandbags manufactured for the purpose of damming the banks when the Arkansas River swelled in the spring were tied to ropes, and Maledon spent the weeks leading to the executions industriously, testing the single twenty-foot trap and the ropes' tensile strength several times daily. Soon, the *squee-thump* of the apparatus became as much a part of the sounds of Fort Smith as the creak and rattle of wagons and the tintack pianos in the Silver Dollar, the House of Lords, the Last Chance, and the whorehouses in the Row.

From time to time, as the settlement on the river entered the smothering heat of late summer, the little man paused to mop his brow and watch the steady stream of traffic turn up the dust on Garrison Avenue. Dust and traffic both grew heavier by the day.

A former military man who had taught tactics and strategy at a seminary in Pennsylvania, William H. H. Clayton stood absolutely erect at the window in Parker's chambers. From one angle showed Maledon's mighty engine of human destruction, from another the incoming tide of carriages, buckboards, and riders on horseback. Wheels locked hubs, mules balked, curses flowed.

"They've been coming in all week," the prosecutor said. "The hotels and boardinghouses are filled. The price of tent canvas has gone up three times in three days. I don't know how many more our little hamlet will hold."

"It's good for trade. Why should the saloons be the only ones to profit?" The judge, in shirtsleeves and the black waistcoat he wore to church, sat behind the desk reading sworn affidavits. On Sundays it was his habit in this his first season on the bench to accompany his wife and son to Methodist services, dine with them at noon in the stone commissary where they had taken up residence, then report to the courthouse to bring himself up to date on the docket.

"There isn't a farmer in the state who's stayed home to bring in the harvest," said Clayton, "nor a civilized Indian in the territory who hasn't pawned his watch to make the trip. They've all read about the grand exhibition, or had an account read to them if they don't know their letters. Something about it appeared in the *New York Herald* last week."

"Splendid. A public judgment followed by public punishment is the swiftest way to clear the foul air left by Story and his cronies."

"The Eastern press seems to hold that the fate of these men should be private."

"An execution carried out in secrecy is no better than lynching from a dry branch."

"You ought to write that, and set the record straight. The journalists have all convinced themselves we're savages out here."

"They'll write what they please regardless. I used to see them on Capitol Hill, scribbling in their grubby little blocks before they'd been in to meet with their subjects. They have their forum and I have mine."

Clayton observed Maledon at work. The scaffold was visible from every building in the garrison. "How much more must he test? The man is a fanatic."

"Fanatics have their uses. I'm confident he'll serve this court well."

"No doubt. He's committed. I confess I preferred having him in the basement. The faces in the jail are milder."

"I didn't reassign him for his looks."

Spectators began entering the garrison at dawn. By ten o'clock, the hour scheduled for the execution, the grounds of the old powder magazine were no longer visible for the bodies that had pressed themselves in around the scaffold. Others perched like pigeons on porch roofs and hung like fruit from trees. Deputy marshals and guards from the jail, armed with revolvers and carbines, kept the central structure clear. The songbird colors worn by the women from the Row showed brightly among dark suits, overalls, and gingham dresses, and the stooped shoulders of the Reverend H. M. Granade drew a question mark at the top of the gallows stairs beside the brief apostrophe of George Maledon, turned out in a new suit and a gray slouch hat. His hands hung at his sides, within reach of the lever that opened the long trap by means of a simple gear. It was difficult to tell where his tangled beard ended and black broadcloth began. His eyes hid beneath a mantel of bone as substantial as the scaffold itself.

Parker's stolid figure stood framed in a ground-floor window of the courthouse. It was not seen to move.

On the stroke of the hour the condemned, escorted by deputies led by Marshal Fagan, shuttle-stopped their way from the jail, wrists shackled and irons on their ankles. They climbed the stairs and assumed their places on the paired planks of the trap, nooses stirring before them in the breeze from the river. Granade read aloud a pious statement dictated by John Whittington, the knife-murderer, then led the crowd in a hymn. Asked by Fagan if they had anything to say, only two of the men in shackles spoke: Boot-fancier Daniel Evans looked out over the crowd and said, "There are worse men here than me." James Moore, the horse thief, said good-bye to an acquaintance in the audience. Maledon left his post to adjust the black caps and fuss with the nooses. When at length he was satisfied with their placement, he returned to the lever and pulled.

Dr. Du Val, standing beneath the platform, inspected the six men for pulses, waiting two minutes for each with watch in hand. At the end of the month he would collect two dollars per man for this service.

He nodded. The man in the window turned away.

THREE

The day of a hanging was not a holiday at the courthouse. Sessions took place daily except Sundays and Christmas and were not suspended even on Independence Day, when Parker directed the windows be shut to reduce distraction from early fireworks explosions. On September 3, while the bodies unclaimed by relatives were being laid to rest in a plot behind the building, the judge signed witness- and juror-fee vouchers in his slashing hand, instructed clerk Wheeler to handle them with dispatch, and summoned James F. Fagan into his chambers.

The U.S. marshal's round Irish face retained its high color as Parker spoke. His hands hung at his sides. He considered crossing one's arms an indicator of weakness and standing with one's hands in one's pockets a breach of etiquette.

He listened with increasing wonder and no expression on his features. The judge was a man of clarity, who employed none of the ambiguous turns of phrase that Fagan had expected from a former member of Congress. When Parker stopped, he said,

"Bringing the deputy census up to two hundred's a tall order. Washington pays two dollars per prisoner and six cents a mile one way. The nigger that cleans the spitoons in the Hole-in-the-Wall clears more than that Saturday night when the herd's in. Then there's the privilege of getting killed, like poor Bill Spivey."

"They're entitled to collect rewards offered for fugitives not wanted for federal crimes, so long as those activities don't interfere with their responsibility to this court. An enterprising man can shelter and clothe a family on much less. And this court isn't interested in what becomes of the chattel of the criminals they're forced to kill in the course of duty."

"They're fortunate if whatever it brings pays for the burial. Up to now they've been responsible for that if there's none else to stand the cost."

"So they'll remain. I don't intend to encourage the vigilante compulsion."

Fagan scanned the large-scale territorial map pinned to the wall behind the desk, divided into the five nations. "Two hundred deputies to cover seventy-four thousand square miles of raw country. It might be worth twenty dollars to the undertaker just to avoid the hazard of dragging some murthering scum all the way back along the Canadian without a citizens' posse for support."

"I can't challenge their discretion without witnesses to the contrary."

"You're safe enough there. If they won't peach on the killers, they sure won't come forward against them what killed them."

Parker thunked a dilapidated leather portfolio onto the marshal's side of the desk. "I've reopened the files on unsolved murders and other felonies extending back five years. Here are warrants for the arrests of the better known transgressors. Tell your deputies to bring them back alive or dead."

"Won't that encourage the vigilante compulsion?"

"You said yourself we won't be inundated with applicants. If we can't attract them with gold, we'll offer them a feudal system of independent action. That should appeal to the sort we require."

"Men like that are sure to have paper out on them somewhere."

"I don't insist upon appointing men of character, although if there's graft in the business it had better be small enough not to reach my ears. I detest men of violence, but that's what's needed to keep the peace in a place outside the jurisdiction of every local court. It's been let fester too long while men have sat here who by all that's decent should have been in shackles downstairs."

"If it's killers you're after hiring, you might consider going down there for your recruitment."

Parker gestured with folded spectacles. "Cowards and back-shooters. Child molesters. Wife beaters and whiskey smugglers and howling lunatics. Animals who slew whole families of samaritans under their own roofs. I want the jail population to increase, and Maledon not kept idle. That means saturating the territory, and I can't do that with sixty men. Begin with the rangers in Texas. Find out who's restless and like to resign. Make contact with county sheriffs and city marshals who have worked with your office and whose performances meet your standards. Review every county election and city appointment over the past year, discover who lost by a hair or because he was unpopular for any reason other than corruption or incompetence. There's a limit to the first and I won't tolerate the second. Send the wires and this court will assume the expense."

"Is it your intention to strip every Western community of its protection?"

"That is not my intention, although it will likely be the result.

My needs are more pressing. I don't want drunks and gamblers like that preening man Hickok, or bushwhackers like the gang in Dodge City. Such men are timid when they become separated from the pack. Pin that star on men of swift judgment and good instincts."

"It'll be the roughest bunch of hooligans this side of County Limerick," Fagan said.

Early on, as news of the sextuple execution in Fort Smith spread, rooted itself in the umber soil of the western Indian Nations, and grew into the solid stalk of legend, the men whom Marshal Fagan appointed to swell the judge's standing army abandoned the practice of introducing themselves as deputy U.S. marshals. Instead, when they entered the quarters of local law enforcement officers and tribal policemen to show their warrants, they said: "We ride for Parker."

Sometimes, in deference to rugged country or to cover ground, they broke up and rode in pairs or singles, but as the majority of the casualties they would suffer occurred on these occasions, they formed ragged escorts around stout little wagons built of elm, with canvas sheets to protect the passengers from rain and sun for trial and execution. With these they entered the settlements well behind their reputation. The deputies used Winchesters to pry a path between rubbernecks pressing in to see what new animals the circus had brought. Inside, accused felons, rounded up like stray dogs, rode in manacles on the sideboards and decks. At any given time—so went the rumor—one fourth of the worst element in the Nations was at large, one fourth was in the Fort Smith jail, and one fourth was on its way there in the "tumbleweed wagons."

"That's three-fourths," said tenderheels. "What about the rest?"

"That fourth rides for Parker."

Charlie Burns had served as jailer under judges Caldwell—a good fellow, cheerful and kind to subordinates—Story—a distracted man with eyes too mobile in his head for trust—and now Parker, whose jury, to his mind, was still deliberating—and seen a number of things that few would accept as truth if they weren't part of the record that continued to grow on shelves and in pigeonholes upstairs, like mushrooms in the damp.

Burns had shot and crippled the horse thief Orpheus McGee during an attempt at freedom, but that was all in his capacity and was scarcely worth remarking upon. Smoking his pipe near the door to the outside, he'd been surprised to see John Childers, the murderer, approach the barred window dripping wet from the river, which he'd swum across to meet the terms of his bond, and had had to argue with him to get him to report to Story's clerk instead of just bunking inside; what'd he think Burns was running, a shelter for tramps? Childers had complied and commenced his incarceration with all the paperwork completed.

And the jailer had been present that legendary day when lightning struck the great scaffold at the instant Childers shot through the trap. A Negro woman in the crowd had fallen to her knees, crying: "John Childers' soul has gone to hell; I done heerd de chains clankin'." Well, he'd worn them on his ankles and wrists, so there was nothing to that, but a man of no more than normal superstition could not help but mark that it was the gallows' first attempt at its purpose, and that a bolt singling it out at that moment was no ordinary stray. It was a moment Burns returned to often, never without a shudder and a glance skyward at the source of the shaft and another at his feet to make sure the earth hadn't opened up to offer him a glimpse of the damned man's charred shade.

He'd seen his due share of the elephant, right enough, but nothing to give him a worse turn than the sudden appearance at his post of a lady of fine breeding, done up in the height of Fort Smith fashion, with one arm through the bail of a covered basket and a bunch of cut flowers cradled in the other.

"Mr. Burns, I think? Mrs. Isaac Parker. I'm here to see William Leach."

Leach was devilish bad on a scale that ran considerably higher than the eight-foot ceiling of the jail. He'd backshot a neighbor who had just left the hospitality of the prisoner's house in the Cherokee, attempted to burn the remains, and been apprehended while trying to sell a pair of boots that had belonged to his victim, well-cobbled boots being a popular article of commerce throughout the discalced Nations (Burns himself never ventured into the territory with anything on his feet but a pair of down-at-heels brogans, coveted by none). Leach was one of six scheduled for hanging the following April; the Eastern press had begun to circle.

Mrs. Parker was a large woman of the Irish type, pale-skinned, auburn hair pinned up beneath her hat, with eyes of the judge's same frank blue. She was not a pretty woman but a handsome one, and if the rank smell that permeated the granite foundation of the courthouse and hung like a miasma to a distance of ten feet around the perimeter caused her distress, she didn't show it. It was particularly ripe, too, with the stinkpot stove in each of the two long sections burning against the February damp, drawing the stench steaming from the prisoners' rags and the piss and shit that embedded the stones. Burns had known male lawyers accustomed to every description of prison, once they stepped across that invisible line, to bury their noses in handkerchiefs soaked in Bay Rum. The jailer himself, on days like this and in summer when the air squatted on its haunches like a Kansas City mule, jacketed himself against the olfactory assault with apple-scented smoke from his pipe.

"No visitors without a pass signed by the judge, ma'am." He gripped the cherrywood bowl between thumb and forefinger and puffed the exhaust out the corner of his mouth.

Shifting the flowers from one arm to the other, she untied a reticule from her wrist, opened it, and withdrew a sheet of foolscap with a slender hand in an oyster-colored leather glove. Burns accepted the sheet through the bars and unfolded it. He recognized the judge's hand, as jagged as his lectures to the condemned. He grunted and turned a heavy key in the lock. When she placed a foot on the threshold, he blocked the entrance with his body.

"You read the letter," she said.

"Ma'am, I did. It don't say you can see Leach. This is no place for a gentlewoman. Not all the prisoners wear irons, and they won't run rusty to use you for their freedom. It places the guards in hazard too."

Fine Irish color climbed her cheeks; but she did not press the matter. She drew the checked cloth from the basket. The warm sweet odor of the fresh-baked cake inside found his nostrils through the jail's eternal fug. "Please take this and the flowers to Mr. Leach. I'll be back with more for the men who were sentenced with him."

"It ain't my place to say, ma'am, but it's too good for his like."

"That's my husband's view, but as you can see from the pass I'm a lawyer's wife. The wretch is forced to sit and listen to the fall of the trap every day. No Christian would deny him one moment of repose."

"Yes, ma'am." He took the basket and flowers.

"Don't take a crumb for yourself. The jailers' rations are more than sufficient."

"No, ma'am."

Outside, Maledon's apparatus squealed and thumped.

"That man is fond of his work," she said.

"Yes, ma'am. He took to it right off."

She turned up the collar of her cape and withdrew.

He shut the door, drew a finger through the frosting, and tasted. Leach was unworthy, but Burns's rebellion stopped there. The forces in opposition were too great.

FOUR

"Judge; a word with you after the services?"

Parker, seated next to Mary and little Charlie in their pew in the First Methodist Church, looked up at the man standing over him in the aisle. He was young, fair, and abundantly freckled, but he wore heavy handlebars and with his hat in his hands the bones of his skull showed through a haircut as severe as any in the military. The six-pointed nickelplate star of a deputy U.S. marshal rode high on his waistcoat.

"Wilkinson, isn't it?" Parker asked.

"Yes, sir. I took the oath last month."

"You can have five minutes. My family and I are attending Catholic services later."

Wilkinson registered no reaction to this evidence of marital diplomacy. Following the sermon, collection, and announcements of community activities, they reconvened on the steps of the church while Mrs. Parker, Charlie's shoulders in her iron grip, engaged the minister's wife in conversation. The judge looked tired; older than his thirty-eight years, with silver streaks in his beard and dark thumbprints under his eyes. He'd recently presided at his second multiple hanging—only five this time, after President Grant had without explanation commuted the sentence of a savage killer named Osee Sanders—and the press from the States had professed shock and disapproval as always, while sending correspondents in number to record every grisly detail.

"It's this man Diggs, who split a drover's head with an axe in the Cherokee three years ago," Wilkinson said, without preamble. "I've been reviewing his case. He was held in jail for a spell, and when no witnesses came forward they sprung him. Story was in charge. I'd like a crack at him."

The corners of Parker's mouth twitched. "If it's idleness you despise, I've a drawer full of warrants for murders more recent."

"I've a line on where he is, and the names of some witnesses. If you'll renew his warrant and draw up summonses, I'd bet my badge the outcome this time will be different."

"Don't bet what you've yet to earn."

"Earning it is just what I'm fixing to do."

Parker concentrated on getting his cigar lit evenly, then blew smoke at the steeple. "I'll review the case tonight. Come to my chambers tomorrow morning before the session and if everything is as you say I'll have Wheeler give you what you need."

"Thanks, Judge."

"Thank me after you've come back with your man, and without a load of buckshot in your kidneys."

"Isaac!" Mary Parker clamped her hands over Charlie's ears.

"I'm sorry, my dear. I didn't realize my voice carried."

"You should. You've been preaching to the back of the gallery for more than a year."

The next morning, Wilkinson closeted himself with Parker for fifteen minutes, waited in the hallway outside for another hour while Stephen Wheeler prepared the necessary documents and the judge signed them, and with the papers in his wallet went out to assemble provisions and supplies and redeem his horse from the livery. He made his last stop at the post office, where he dispatched telegrams to peace officers in Kansas, Missouri, and various parts of the Nations, and as far away as Ohio and Michigan. In the three years since the murder, many of those who could offer evidence against Diggs had scattered, including Hiram Mann, who had been struck with the same axe as had J. C. Gould, a companion on the cattle drive, and spent months in recovery before decamping to Detroit. Wilkinson instructed his informants to address their replies to Marshal Fagan.

He swam his horse across the Arkansas to the train station, where he loaded the animal aboard a stock car and boarded a sweatbox day coach for the three-hour run up the Santa Fe line to Springdale. Soaked and enervated, he considered a bath house, a saloon, and a room for the night, but the experience he'd brought to his new job warned him that when the hunt was on the hunted grew wary, and that there was no time to lose. Diggs had left two fellow cattle drovers lying in a pool of blood over a matter of twenty-seven dollars in cash belonging to the man who had died. He had friends in the Nations who considered it a reasonable transaction, and neighbors who had little cause to place more trust in Fort Smith than in men whose faces were familiar; once in flight, the desperate man had a broad choice of barns, corn ricks, root cellars, and empty cisterns to fort up in, living on provisions smuggled in to him while armies of federal men combed the hills and haystacks and thousands of square miles of tangled wilderness. Surprise was more than half the fight, and Wilkinson pocketed his star and wore the kit of a cowhand looking for cattle to start his own outfit.

The deputy had been less than straight when he'd pled his case with Parker. He'd bet his badge of office with confidence as to finding the witnesses to the atrocity, but the rumor that its perpetrator was still in the Nations was smoky at best. It didn't bear following into that alien country, where every man's hand seemed to be raised against him. Better to confirm it by way of the invisible telegraph line that ran through the nomadic bands of cowboys who rode the trails from Texas to Kansas.

In Baxter Springs, across the Kansas line, he wet his whistle at last in a bar long enough to hang a month's wash and struck up friendly conversations with others dressed as he, hands just in from the first spring drives. He asked each if he knew J. C. Gould, an old pard of his who might be persuaded to go in with him on his enterprise.

The pickings were slim. A lot of heads shook, and he wasted time and expense money buying whiskey for a jabbery waddy who turned out to know the wrong Gould. That first session wore him out worse than the train and the horseback ride combined. He camped out north of town to relieve stress on the U.S. Treasury and took up his post the next day in a different saloon, with antlers on the walls. He didn't want to raise the suspicions of a bartender about a saddle tramp with too much time on his hands and too much silver to spread around. Barmen soaked up gossip like slops and wrung it out with both hands.

There he dipped his bucket into the same dry well for hours. Gould seemed to have been one of those faceless men who drifted from camp to camp making no friends and no impression. Wilkinson began to wonder if he'd exhaust every watering hole in town, and what the clerk back in Fort Smith would tell the judge when he saw all those drinks in the column. But along toward evening, when the place began to fill up with unwashed bodies and coal-oil smoke, Wilkinson found a man who informed him of his friend's sad fate at the hands of a companion.

"They hang the son of a bitch?" the deputy asked.

The man, a Texas drover with handlebars more swooping than his own and a little paintbrush of a beard, splattered a brown ribbon into a cuspidor and drew a sleeve across his lips. "No, he got carpetbagger justice. They rubbed his kinky head for luck and set him loose."

"This Diggs is a nigger?"

"Hell yes. I rode with damn fine folk blacker'n him on the outside, but his goes clean through. It's a piece of good fortune they didn't elect him governor."

"How long ago was this?" He always sprinkled his interviews with queries he knew the answers to. It kept him from appearing eager.

"Three years, maybe more. I ride drag when I pass through the Nations and thank Christ for every mouthful of dust I swallow, on account of I know no bastard's lurking behind to crack my skull for what's in my poke."

"I hear things are different in Fort Smith now."

"Not so's you'd notice. They're hanging Christian white men while that murdering trash is drinking corn liquor on Spring Crick in front of God, the devil, and U. S. goddamn Grant."

This was new information, and Wilkinson looked down quickly at the glass he'd nursed down to plain water to dissemble his excitement. The suggestion that Diggs was living almost on top of the scene of his crime was bold even for a man who thought he'd beaten the scaffold. "What's on Spring Creek?"

"A Cherokee squaw and forty acres her pa left her. They say

the son of a bitch watches her plow all day and brags all night on killing a white man and making away with it. John Wilkes Booth should of busted a cap on that carpetbagging Lincoln before he freed his first nigger."

"Who says this?"

The drover's brows shot up. "Well, everybody in Texas."

"Not about Lincoln. About Diggs farming on Spring Creek."

"Who the hell knows? You hear talk." He leaned over the cuspidor and pursed his lips, but this time he didn't spit. He swallowed and fixed Wilkinson with mud-colored eyes swimming in blood. "Why do you want to know? What outfit did you say you was with before you went maverick?"

"The Double D."

"I know that spread. You know George Slaughter?"

Sensing a trap, Wilkinson ordered another round apiece and turned the conversation toward the drover's opinion of the quality of beef to be found in the Nations. Half an hour later, when the other left the bar to weave his way toward the outhouse, the deputy left. He was pretty sure he wouldn't be missed in the rapidly increasing population of the saloon, but on his way to camp stopped his horse often to listen for pursuers. A man who got to thinking he'd said too much to the wrong man was a contrary creature.

The next day, Wilkinson wired the headquarters of the Cherokee police in Tahlequah to confirm the presence of James Diggs, Negro, on or near Spring Creek. The tribal elders had no love for outside killers, and by that afternoon he had his reply. He took on fresh grain for his horse and crossed into the Nations at Quapaw. He wore matched Colt Peacemakers in suspender holsters crossed at his back and carried a brass-receiver Winchester that fired the same caliber and a Stevens ten-gauge shotgun with both barrels cut back to street-sweeper length in scabbards slung from his saddle, with a stubby British Bulldog in a pocket for a hole card. He shipped his ammunition in gunnysacks, rifle and revolver cartridges in one, shotgun shells in the other, and all five Bulldog rounds in the cylinder of the pocket gun. Two canteens, jerked venison, and pemmican cakes answered for his provisions; he intended to keep a cold camp, with no smoke or smell of boiling coffee to draw attention to where he stopped. Tobacco for chewing only, to dampen his craving for cigarettes and his pipe. He was new to the marshal's service, but not to the business of tracking men. In the wild they acquired animal instincts on top of their natural human shrewdness and were more to be feared than grizzlies. Poor Bill Spivey's picture hung prominently in Fagan's office for a reason.

A spring drizzle stood sentry square at the border and stayed with him all the way along the Neosho River and after it bent west and away, water pouring from the curl of his hat brim as from a gutter and sliding in sheets off his oilcloth slicker. Both items of gear failed to keep him from being soaked through; no matter how reliable a man's umbrella, when it rained he got wet. At times he seemed to be hauling the downpour with him, as if it came from a nozzle that followed his progress, a moving spout surrounded by dry. When he camped he made a shelter of the slicker with cottonwood branches, wrung out his socks, and slept until he was awakened by his own misery. It was Ozark country, carved by glaciers and sandblasted from solid rock by a billion years of dust and wind and hollowed out by the relentless rain. He picked his way down draws, leaning back on the reins, and when the path became nearly perpendicular he dismounted and led his horse, his feet squishing in his boots.

His sore luck held when the sun mocked him by breaking out

bright as fool's gold just as he entered Tahlequah and the promise of a sound roof and a change of clothes. He seemed to have spent all his good fortune in the saloon in Baxter Springs. In front of Cherokee police headquarters he left his horse standing in mud fetlock deep, went inside to show his star and his warrant, and got an updated description of Diggs printed neatly by a big Remington type-writing machine, the polished pride of the office. His man had picked up a scar on his neck since his first visit to Fort Smith; Wilkinson wondered if there was another dead man in that. He shook hands with the officer, a broad-faced full-blood with short hair and his badge, a star in a circle, pinned to blue flannel, and went out to serve his warrant, wet clothes and all. One man knowing he was in town was one too many; you never knew where personal loyalties lay.

He reached Spring Creek by nightfall and crossed at a shallow spot onto Diggs's farm, which consisted of a slant-roofed barn and house, both unpainted, some chickens, a milch-cow lowing in its stall, and rows of planted vegetables with wooden stakes at the ends. A subsistence place, supporting itself and barely; God help the odd transient with evidence of prosperity. The deputy tethered his horse to a cedarbrake and sat down with his back against one of the scrubby trees in the line to wait for full dark. He watched the dying of the light and then the orange glow of a lamp drawing on in a window. The last bird sang its sweet challenge to bash in the heads of interlopers and the first cricket struck up the band. An owl fluted. Wilkinson sniffed and wiped his nose and chewed tobacco and shifted his weight from time to time to pluck his damp trousers away from a fine case of red-ass.

When he could no longer see the toe of his boot he got up, stroked his horse's muzzle, slid the Winchester from its scabbard, and started toward the house, leaning forward on the balls of his feet and groping with one hand for unseen twigs and branches. Just inside carbine range a dog started barking, one of the yappy kind with a hysterical nature.

The lamp went out. He stopped. He'd been towing a path of silence through the crickets; they started in again, filling the night with their stitching.

He'd taken care to direct his gaze away from the light, to preserve his night vision. Now the shape of the house with its canted roof showed blacker than the sky behind it, an inverted check mark with dark clumps of trees standing well away from the perimeter. Diggs, or more likely his hardworking Cherokee wife, had made sure to clear the area of cover, forcing invaders into the open. He hoped his own silhouette wasn't as exposed as he felt.

Something moved against the foundation; his hands jerked involuntarily at the carbine. A chain jingled. It was the dog, stabbing its muzzle this way and that for a stray scent. A growling *woof* escaped its throat.

In a little while—it seemed longer—a hinge squeaked. The dog fell to barking frantically. There was a blow, a yelp, a whimper. Wilkinson saw this movement. Then something moved against the scarcely lighter oblong of the window and he made out a man's head and shoulders and something hovering above the hump of the one on the right: an axe.

Wilkinson raised the Winchester to his shoulder. A trickle of sweat sprouted between his shoulder blades and wandered down toward his belt, prickling like ants' legs. So far there had been no sign of the woman. He had little practical experience with Indians, had listened in fascination when men from the northern plains had told of the stalking properties of the breed. If she were behind him with some kind of weapon . . .

He fired. The silhouette jerked away from the window. He didn't know if he'd hit anything.

Light bloomed in the window.

"Goddamnit, douse that!"

The lamp went out, but not before he spotted the man who had shouted, crouched on his haunches in front of the far corner of the house right of the window with the axe leveled across his abdomen. Wilkinson charged him, sprinting, gaze fixed to the spot. He was within pistol range when a shape grew up out of the ground and ran straight at him, swinging up the thing in his hands. The deputy closed the distance in six strides and swung the Winchester. The barrel connected with a thump and James Diggs fell at his feet.

Parker listened, eyes half-shuttered behind their heavy lids, while the witnesses who had drifted in from East and West gave evidence against the slayer of J. C. Gould. They spoke for three days, at the end of which the jury retired briefly and then the foreman rose.

Diggs died on the scaffold December 20, 1878, beside John Postoak, a Creek who had killed a married couple named Ingley in the Creek Nation. Diggs's widow claimed her husband's body for burial on the farm that had belonged to her father.

II

A PRAYER FOR NED CHRISTIE

What though the field be lost?
All is not lost; th' unconquerable will,
And study of revenge, immortal hate,
And courage never to submit or yield.

—John Milton,
Paradise Lost

FIVE

"That man is fond of his work."

When Mary Parker's remark to jailer Burns reached the ears of its subject—as such things will—George Maledon accepted it as a compliment, not being given to analysis of those factors that may lead to a conclusion; but had he known the particulars, he would have forgiven them in the spirit of good Christian forebearance. Abstract concepts such as honor and the rule of law were alien to her gender.

He did not experience satisfaction in being the instrument of a man's early end, or in the suffering that might attend it, whatever the fellow's transgressions. He believed, along with the judge, that it was the law that executed a man, and that their partnership in the act itself was nothing more than the practical application of a decision foreordained by an efficient system of justice. Maledon aspired to apply that same efficiency toward the swift and antiseptic extinction of the life force, with minimum pain and maximum effect. It was true that a man strung from a cottonwood branch with dirty twine and left to strangle wound up no more dead than one escorted to a straight drop and a broken neck from good rope on a proper scaffold; the great difference lay in the time involved, and the shame of a constricted windpipe and twelve minutes of convulsions. He had heard horror stories of botched lynchings that had made him weep for the reputation of his life's work.

In pursuit of proof for his theory, the little man with the grizzled beard and sunken eyes had burned many bowls of black shag in his long German pipe, poring over medical texts borrowed from Dr. Du Val, with their diagrams and colored transparencies of the human spinal canal, and worn his thumbs through those pages of farm and cattlemen's catalogues devoted to the quality of obtainable hemp. The sections set aside by Sears, Roebuck and Montgomery Ward for shed and barn maintenance—specifically pine pitch and the various grades of linseed oil—he had smudged with brown iron-gall ink his own annotations in the margins. These sheets he had torn out and anchored in a stack beneath the rough clay pot into which he knocked his dottles; it was his ambition, after he retired, at some long date, to publish a working manual on his craft, with chapters covering extensively these mundane details.

Yucatan sisal was stiff and stubborn and unresponsive to treatment, and so he ordered good Kentucky hemp from St. Louis, an inch and an eighth thick, compressed to an inch after the necessary stretching with sandbags. Sears and Roebuck offered lubricants of the finest grade, which when kneaded into the coarse cord provided the acceleration required, when the trap opened and gravity took its part, to slam the great knot into the sweet hollow below and behind the left ear. (Maledon, himself left-handed, set the standard for this prejudice.) There followed that crisp report that announced the preferred vertebra well and truly split, and the nerves that carried sensation to the brain severed clean. In short, Maledon's science bore the sureness and finality of a bullet through the eye. (The heart, he'd learned through bitter experience, was a slow messenger.)

On the day of execution, Fort Smith residents observed him striding up Garrison Avenue, trailing smoke from the pipe his father had purchased in Bavaria and carrying a market basket on one arm. He was somewhat more fastidious about his dress than he was about his burden; his black suit was carefully brushed by his wife and his boots glistened with blacking, but the basket was the least bit small for its contents, and on those occasions when several customers awaited him, nooses hung out from under the hinged lids on both sides. They dangled yet again when he returned home; good rope could be used many times, reducing stress upon the court's parsimonious budget, and when it came time to remove one from the rotation, he displayed it on the wall in his private study as a memento. The papered walls of the little room were covered with nooses, each accompanied by tintypes of the men who had worn them, when the likenesses were available. His penchant for retaining souvenirs, it was rumored, had led to high words and chilly relations between the Maledons, and on one volatile afternoon a number of tintypes snatched off their hooks and cast down a well. Days of silence in the domestic arrangement had followed.

His wife disapproved of his work, changed subjects whenever it arose in conversation, and hectored him frequently about applying for another position with Parker's court. What she failed to grasp, and what he lacked the vocabulary to convey, was that she was married to an accomplished slayer of men. He'd killed for the Union, shot men as a police officer under three chiefs, and would put down permanently a total of five prisoners attempting to escape the federal jail during his residency. The fate of the first, slain shortly before his promotion from turnkey to chief executioner, had filled him with remorse; not for the life wasted, but because it had cheated the scaffold, and by reflection the engine of justice he'd sworn to maintain. It had been a factor in his immediate decision to accept the judge's offer that first day in chambers. On the four succeeding occasions, he would not hesitate to draw and fire one of the paired Smith & Wessons he wore butts-forward on the belt he strapped around his waist (he remained a deputy U.S. marshal withal, which carried the responsibility of arming himself on duty and off), aiming from instinct for the vitals, the way he'd been taught, but he considered each instance a failure. Close observers would note that just before the hangings that directly succeeded those episodes, Maledon took extra time and care adjusting the nooses, as if to atone for whatever incaution had led to the prisoners' fancy that there was a way around Parker's pronouncements other than the vertical. He was a man of principle.

Beyond question, Maledon's wife disapproved of his work; but she inspected him for lint and loose buttons whenever he ventured out to perform it, like any good helpmeet, and corrected what needed correction on the spot, disregarding his protestations that it would make him tardy at his post. She would not be seen as a neglectful wife. These attentions bound her spiritually to Mary Parker, who baked cakes and cut flowers from her own garden to brighten the last days of the men her husband sent to perdition. They took tea together often, secure in their sisterhood.

Maledon had not that respite to vary his days. He worshipped Isaac Parker but respected his office—held it in awe, bestowed as it was by hand by the man in the White House; Ulysses S. Grant, the hero of Appomattox—and did not presume to overstep the invisible barrier that separated them. Deep within him he sensed a revulsion on Parker's part for his lieutenant's physical connection with the act of killing those who'd killed. He resented this in his turn, but chose to cloak the distance thus created in a pious German conviction in the difference between the classes. Women were a race unto themselves, unified by a common uterus, while men were divided like milch cows and beef on the hoof, geldings and studs. And so, once justice had carried, these partners in its carriage retired separately to their solitary reflections, the jurist to his case histories, the hangman to his ropes and tintypes. Unlike the military, the American judicial system there on the fringe of the frontier provided no club for officers of the court to socialize, commiserate, and find common ground. Maledon had not even the experience of a democratic upbringing to express his opinions on the situation even to himself.

Both men, however, shared the same low opinion by their wives regarding certain aspects of their calling.

In truth, apart from Maledon's profession and the eagerness he brought to it, his mate had little to complain about. Tobacco was his only vice, and he confined his consumption to his study and the outdoors to preserve her linens. He attended church every Sunday, a few rows behind the Parkers, ignored other women apart from raising his hat when he passed them on the street, and did not take strong drink, nodding in approval whenever a condemned man used his circumstances to deliver a lecture on the evils of alcohol to the restless audience gathered to see him in his throes. In public, Mr. and Mrs. Maledon behaved as if they were equal to Judge and Mrs. Parker, who had the good grace not to betray the presumption. Their daughter, Annie, played with young Charlie, sometimes tormenting him according to the laws of her sex; when the new school had opened, they were among the first in attendance. Younger siblings, when they came along, would spend much time in one another's company. The children were popular with their peers. Local opinion, led by the editors of the *Fort Worth Elevator,* did not hold with the clucking attitude of the Eastern press; those institutions represented civilized America, with a uniformed officer on every corner and space on the docket to parse out punishment one man at a time. Thanks to the judge and his most loyal servant, life was orderly there on the border, so long as one avoided the saloons and brothels, and the families of the men who stood for justice commanded respect.

George Maledon *was* fond of his work. He took pleasure in it for itself alone, with no more malice toward those most directly involved than a wood-carver felt toward an unfinished piece of pine, or a painter a blank sheet of canvas. During his long, long career in the faithful service of the Eighth District Court, he would know only two exceptions, when he thoroughly savored the anticipation of bringing extinction to a fellow traveler.

Both times he would be denied his subject.

Ned Chistie was the first.

SIX

The most widely circulated photograph of Ned Christie, taken in Fort Smith in 1892, does not do him justice.

He was born September 14, 1852, in Rabbit Trap Canyon in the Going Snake District of the Cherokee Nation, and was in his thirty-third year when his life turned full round on a pivot. Indians and whites acknowledged him an uncommonly fine-looking man, six-foot-four with black hair that reached nearly to his waist and Mandarin whiskers, well filled out for one who claimed Cherokee ancestry on both sides. He belonged to the tribal legislature—the Kee-too-wah—and with his frank eyes and easy smile had established a reputation for charming sworn enemies over to his side when it came to a vote. Women admired him, but he was devoted to his wife and children and kept close counsel with his father, a man widely revered in the nation as Uncle Watt, who knew little English but had seen that Ned became fluent. The son was indiscriminate in drink, but that was a general failing in a territory where alcohol was prohibited and as easy to obtain as a tick bite. Whether boring out a barrel in his gunsmith's shop or walking along a street in Tahlequah deep in conversation with a fellow lawmaker, Ned Christie turned heads, male and female.

Without question, his picture did not do him justice; but then, he was dead when it was taken.

Christie's cabin, in a clearing just inside Rabbit Trap with miles of dense black undergrowth at its back, was a regular stop on the local whiskey peddler's route. This entrepreneur, who had served ninety days in the Fort Smith jail for mistaking a deputy U.S. marshal for a customer, carried a rawhide-bound notebook scribbled in cipher that told him when Christie was paid for his service to the electorate, and on that day turned his wagon toward Going Snake. On the afternoon whose events would bring Christie to Judge Parker's attention it was payday, and he had purchased two squat earthen jugs of skullbender, distilled from water retrieved from the Salt Fork of the Arkansas, fermented potatoes, chewing tobacco, red pepper, and turpentine, with a pinch of gunpowder to taste. Christie carried the jugs as far as his front porch, where he and John Parris, Cherokee also, sat on split-bottom chairs passing the first jug back and forth, swigging, and taking target practice on trees and small animals with a pair of revolvers the gunsmith had brought home from his shop to test their sights. Christie's wife came out to call him in for noon dinner but he sent her back inside.

"Leetle off," he said, when he'd missed the pine knot he'd aimed at and gonged the bucket hanging on his well.

"Couldn't be that snake piss we're drinking," Parris said.

"Nope. I shoot better when I see double."

"How is that?"

"I sight in betwixt the two."

They laughed loudly. Christie's wife shut the window.

Something moved in the brush. Parris closed one eye and fired. A yelp went up. A moment later a scruffy white dog slunk out into the open on three legs. The left rear was shattered and bleeding.

"Shit. That's my neighbor's dog."

"He favor it?"

"It'll follow a coon right up a tree. Did anyway."

"He don't have to know a coyote didn't get it." Parris leveled the revolver again.

Christie backhanded the barrel. The bullet went skyward. The dog picked up its pace, panting and whimpering.

"Headed home." Christie pulled at the jug.

"You're too soft on critters. We better reload before your neighbor gets here."

"I won't shoot a man over a dog. I wouldn't shoot a dog over a man, come to that."

When in due course the neighbor appeared, the two were nearing the bottom of the first jug and weren't inclined toward patient conversation. Words were said, in English and Cherokee, and when the man turned around saying he'd see about that, Parris threw the jug at his head. Fortunately it missed; when it struck the ground, it was the ground that gave.

"See if there's any left," Christie told Parris.

Deputy United States Marshal Dan Maples rode out from Tahlequah in answer to the neighbor's complaint. The pair was still on the porch drinking. The sun was setting, the cabin's front and rear windows were in line, and the red orb seemed to be glaring from inside the walls. Maples had heard gunfire, but he knew Christie and stepped down with his Colt still in its hip scabbard. He was a smallish man but built like a prizefighter. He had a reputation back in Bentonville, Arkansas, of never having picked a quarrel, while putting an end to more than a few picked by others. People of the Nations considered him one of Parker's good ones.

"Ned, that dog had to be shot again and put down. A good coon dog's worth two dollars. You ought to square it with your neighbor. We'll just forget you tried to brain him."

"That was John, both times."

Maples heard Parris suck air in through his nose. The two didn't seem to like each other that much. Liquor was the common bond.

"I'll take your word on that, Ned," said the deputy. "It don't matter who pays, just so's it's paid."

"In that case, you pay him."

"It don't work that way. It happened on your property. That makes you responsible. Is this how you handle things in the Kee-too-wah?"

"Talk American. A white man talking Cherokee makes me puke."

"Cherokee's American, Ned. It don't get more American than that."

Liquid gurgled. Maples shifted his position to put the sun out of his eyes. Black and purple floaters obscured the outlines of the men seated on the porch.

"It's two dollars, Ned. You want to make a federal case?"

Christie barked. It was a close approximation of a dog. Out hunting, he could swindle a turkey with his gobble and an elk when he snorted. "That's right, Dan. I want to make a federal case. Why don't you step up here and take me back to Fort Smith and dandle me from Parker's tears because my neighbor's got to shinny up trees by himself from here on?"

Parris laughed, a high-pitched alcoholic giggle that sent snakes up the deputy's back. He thought if he could get Christie away from his companion he could make him see reason. A man wanted to appear tall to his friends.

Maples wound the reins he was holding around his wrist. "Let's go to your neighbor's place, just you and me. We'll all sit down and come to an understanding."

Flame spurted from the porch. Maples' horse swung its head, dragging him off balance. He heard the shot and right behind it a branch cracking not far from him. He raked out his big Colt from instinct. He saw flame again, but didn't hear the shot or anything else until his horse stopped dragging him and he lay on his back in the dirt and heard the noise the crickets made as dusk settled, fading.

Thomas Boles was the United States marshal in Fort Smith in 1885. Balding, with a graying beard that rivaled George Maledon's for length if not for bristle, he'd served as a judge in Arkansas, been elected twice to Congress, run the land office in Dardanelle for President Hayes, and been appointed to his current position by President Arthur. Those who knew him for his many kindnesses called him Uncle Tom. Others, impressed by his bearing, referred to him—always among themselves, never to his face—as the Old Roman. He was forty-eight and inclined to be sanguine, but when he read the telegram from the Cherokee police in Tahlequah, he shouted for his secretary, and when the young man presented himself handed him the wire and told him to get it to Judge Parker right away.

"Sir, court's in session."

"I know that. Did you think I thought it was Sunday?"

"The judge—"

"He won't thank you for waiting until he adjourns. Give it to the bailiff and tell him to deliver it to the bench at once. Then come back here with the deputy roster. I want the name of every man on duty in the Cherokee Nation."

The secretary left, shaken by the emotion in the marshal's voice.

Parker was trying a case of rape. He scowled when the bailiff hurried up the aisle and stuck the yellow flimsy under his nose. The victim, testifying in a voice barely audible, faltered and fell silent. The reporter covering the trial for the *Elevator* noted that the man seated behind the big cherry desk, gray now of hair and beard, drew his face taut as he read. His hand found his gavel. He declared a recess of fifteen minutes and was on his way to the door when the other men and women in the room were still rising at Crier Hammersly's command.

The judge entered Boles's office in his robes and found the marshal studying a closely type-written list of names with his secretary standing over him.

"Is it true?" Parker asked. "Is it confirmed?"

Boles nodded his great round head. "I know the man who sent the wire. I thought I knew Christie, too, at least by reputation. He's been a credit to his tribe his whole life."

"His whole life is behind him. What about this man Parris?"

"I don't know him." Boles handed the sheet to his secretary. "Wire Tahlequah. Tell them to locate the men whose names I've checked and send them out to Going Snake. Start there and turn over every rock west of Fort Smith. If they don't know Parris, they're to be accompanied by someone who can identify him."

"What about Christie?" the young man asked.

"Everyone in the Cherokee knows Christie by sight. Go."

The secretary left. Parker asked the marshal the names of the deputies he'd selected.

"John Curtis, Joe Bowers, and John Fields. All good men, and they speak the lingo."

"Maples should have arrested both of them when he caught them drinking whiskey."

"If my deputies did that every time they saw it, there wouldn't be any room in the jail for murderers and rapists. The charge is a bargaining chip, to get information. Beyond that I won't comment. These men have to deal directly with the natives every day."

"Keep me informed. I don't care if I'm in the middle of pronouncing sentence."

Boles agreed. There were tears in Parker's eyes.

"I know Nancy Shell," Deputy Fields said. "I've bought a bottle or two from her myself, purely in the interest of criminal investigation."

Deputy Curtis didn't laugh. He'd been first on the scene after the killing and had pressed his ear against Dan Maples' cold breast. Inside the cabin he'd found Christie's wife with her children gathered around her like pickets, and had known before he asked his question what the answer would be. It was a waste of time trying to batter down that Indian barrier once it was in place.

He said, "Parris buys his whiskey there, when he's got the price. If I was him I'd run there if I couldn't run home."

"I'd feel better Bowers was along."

"He's with Chief Bushyhead, in case Christie takes it in his head to go back and get the Kee-too-wah on his side."

They crossed Spring Creek. Fields said, "Right around here's where Jim Wilkinson put the irons on that nigger Diggs. Parker's friends are few here."

"Well, let's see if we can cut down on the enemies."

Nancy Shell received them in her parlor. She was some part Cherokee and several parts other things, with blue eyes in a round flat face, and her house was the same. Indian rugs and pots shared space with porcelain lamps, pictures in oval frames, and what had to be the only daisy-horn phonograph between Fort Smith and Texas. She got up from her rocking chair from time to time to change the cylinder, but it always seemed to be the same tin tenor singing the same song in Italian. The presence of two tall marshals in striped suits and weaponry made no impression on her features. She'd offered them whiskey, but they'd declined. She rolled a cigarette as they spoke, concentrating on getting the flakes of tobacco arranged evenly and sliding a sharp tongue tip along the edge of the paper. She lit it, blew smoke out her nostrils, and said, "John."

She hadn't raised her voice, but the curtains stirred in a doorway and a man ducked his head to clear the frame. He wasn't as tall as Christie, but he was on a level with the lawmen, and he appeared to be unarmed.

"Good morning, John," Fields said.

"I don't know you."

"Sure you do. Last time I seen you here I said I'd arrest you next time."

"I ain't had a drop. Ain't got the price."

"Well, things have changed. We're arresting you for the murder of Dan Maples. You're to answer for him in Fort Smith, or here if that's your choice." Fields drew his Colt.

Parris turned to run. Curtis, quicker to act than his partner, scooped out his Colt and slammed the barrel across the back of Parris' head. When he hit the floor, the phonograph needle scratched the cylinder.

"You boys want to wrassle, do it outside," Nancy Shell said. "I keep an orderly house."

Curtis got a grip on the unconscious man's collar, dragged him across the floor and down the steps of the porch, and dumped him into the burned-out yard, where he kicked him in the ribs until he came to and tried to roll himself up into a ball. Curtis caught him on the forehead with a heel and he jerked out straight on his back. Fields stood on the porch and lit a cigar.

"Easy on his head," he said, tossing away the match. "Maledon needs it to keep the rope from slipping off."

Curtis went around behind the cabin and came back hauling a bucket slopping water over the top. He slung its contents over the man on the ground. Parris spluttered, cursed in English and Cherokee, and sat up, his hair plastered over his eyes. Fields left the porch, slid his Whitney shotgun from its scabbard on his saddle, and threw it to Curtis. When Parris parted his hair like a curtain, both muzzles hovered six inches away. Curtis palmed back the hammers with a crunch.

"I didn't shoot him!" Parris shrieked. "It was Ned."

SEVEN

Ned Christie couldn't believe his luck; so he waited.

He'd beaten his way through heavy underbrush, crossed a field, and torn a hole in the knee of his trousers climbing over a fence in the dark to approach his gunsmith's shop from behind, to find no light in the windows and no signs of occupancy inside. The marshals were too smart—many of them, anyway—to give away their presence by striking a match, but he had a hunter's sense about such things and felt strongly in his heart that no trap awaited him. But he'd learned about the world outside the tribe in the mission school and placed his faith in things other than his instincts. Civilized man was a trickster and could not be trusted to behave according to the laws of the spirit. He had no soul, and therefore no scent. A place that contained him was as one empty.

And so he waited, on his belly like the spreading adder, sent to kill Sister Sun before she could annihilate the People for grimacing when they looked at her. This was a story his father knew and believed, and although Ned had been spoiled against it and all the others, he thought often in their terms. Watt Christie's simple faith and the travesty in Tahlequah, where the Cherokee raised points of order and recognized speakers from the floor and comported themselves like little white men, had made of his son a mixed thing, part Indian, part snake.

After some little time, measured in shades of darkness, Ned Christie rose and crept forward, drawing his only weapon, one of the revolvers he'd taken home to test in his other life, with two cartridges unfired. That was good if there were no more than two marshals, better if there was but one. He did not want to kill marshals. The second bullet would free him from his anguish.

The shop was deserted, he found when he broke the lock on the back door and no fire came from the darkness. Sheathing the revolver under his waistband, he moved surely in the gloom, feeling for the long guns in their rack, the assorted pistols and revolvers in their drawers, and the boxes of ammunition on the shelves, which he placed on the woven rug on the floor and tied into a bundle with his belt. He moved swiftly and noiselessly. With the bundle cradled in one arm he turned to leave, then remembered the bottle of Old Pepper he kept under the counter for days when business was slow. He was sober. His head timpanned from the late effects of trade whiskey consumed hours before. He moved aside the blanket that covered the door to the front of the shop—and snatched the revolver from his trousers. He smelled a man.

"Do not shoot."

The words were Cherokee.

Watt Christie watched his son tip up the bottle with the strange characters printed on the label. He himself had no taste for liquor and resented the universal notion that all Indians were born drunks, with a raging thirst for whiskey and no tolerance for its effects. It hurt him to see Ned undermining his argument. He was proud of his son's accomplishments, but he prayed each night to the old gods to free him from his persistent devil.

They sat in chairs near the cold stove in the front of the shop with the shades drawn and a coal-oil lantern turned very low on the floor at their feet. The orange glimmer left their upper halves in shadow, but kept Watt's despair from worming into his vitals. Ned made no protest. For him the whiskey seemed to produce the same result.

"I knew I would find you here." Watt spoke in Cherokee; English was one puzzle that eluded his wisdom. "I taught you never to go into the brush without a rifle. You never know when supper might present itself."

Ned said nothing. Clothing rustled. Whiskey gurgled.

"It is all over the Nation. Parris told the marshals you shot Dan Maples."

"I did not." Ned answered him in the same tongue. "John shot the dog and Maples, and he would have shot my neighbor too if the jug was not more handy."

"You must go to the Kee-too-wah and tell them this. They will see you to Fort Smith, where your version may be told. They say Parker is a fair man, sympathetic to the People."

"So much so that he has hanged thirteen of us in ten years."

"He has hanged more of Them than he has of us. It was not always so. You are too young to remember."

"I remember when you could buy your own warrant from a marshal for twenty dollars American. There is much to be said for the way it was."

"This is not my son I hear."

"You are deceived. We only have friends in Fort Smith until

one of them is killed by one of us. They do not ask who. Any Cherokee will answer. I will not spend months in that shithole prison only to have my neck wrung like a turkey. If they take me I will not have even that choice. They beat John half to death to get that lie out of him, and they will beat me the other half. It is a hundred miles to Fort Smith and hell. I will not give *them* that choice. I will die here where I was born, with a rifle in my hand."

"Who will look after your wife and children?"

"The tribe will take care of them. Remember, I helped write that law."

"It is a good law. The white man has none like it." Watt took in air to the base of his lungs, then expelled it. "It seems years since you sat in town and made law."

"The white man's law ends where death begins. He believes in nothing thereafter, not even his angels and jabbery. He poisons everything he touches and calls it bread."

"You forget that it is a Cherokee who brought you to this pass."

"John Parris never liked me. He set himself out to make me as bad as him, and I fell in like the fool I am. Parker's marshals are not fools, but they chose him over me. There is no justice there. Even their tongue is twisted. From this day forth I will speak it no more."

"That is an unwise choice. The tongue of our ancestors is written on water. It will be forgotten in your lifetime."

"You overestimate my span. I will be dead before you sprout your next white whisker. But before then, they will know I lived."

"What can one man do against so many?"

"Others feel as I do. We will strike in number and then trickle away through the woods as water."

Watt wiped his eyes. "You say you are not a killer and yet you speak as one."

"I intend to break each of the laws I helped write. But upon your head I promise I will take no life unless mine is threatened. I will not shoot to kill, even if the man in my sights is a marshal."

"Where will you go?"

Ned drank. "Why? So you can tell your friends in Fort Smith?"

"That is unkind."

Here the translation falls far short of the original. The Cherokee language has relatively few syllables, but the arrangement is everything.

"I spoke rashly," Ned said then. "I am angry at myself. I became bewitched by the sweet scent of my own armpits and presumed to walk with my betters. I scaled a ladder like a squirrel thinking himself a man. The squirrel does not own the ladder. The man snatched it away. The squirrel fell to earth."

"My counsel now is worthless." Watt Christie unbuttoned his shirt, exposing a canvas money belt cinched around his middle. He unbuckled it and leaned forward to lay it in his son's lap. "That is every cent I have. Spend it on food, not whiskey. A man who has declared war upon the United States must keep his wits about him."

"I will steal what I need and slay what I eat." Ned lifted the belt and held it out.

Watt shook his head. "You are not as good a hunter as you think."

Which statement gave his son his first chuckle in many hours.

Deputy Joe Bowers, having satisfied himself that Chief Dennis Bushyhead and the Cherokee national council would not assist one of their own to evade the law, rode out to Ned Christie's cabin to serve the murder warrant. He did not expect to find him at home, but knew he would be lurking somewhere inside Rabbit Trap, which was a good name for a canyon that the closer a man rode to its tangled wilderness the more it looked like a place the smallest rodent could not penetrate. Yet the Cherokee had hunted it for generations, and those who had gone into private illegal enterprise had carried in their equipment piece by piece and assembled whiskey stills in clearings in the brush that had to be beaten back every few weeks to keep the forest from reclaiming lost ground. It was no place for a white man to go after dark, particularly on Parker's business, and so he'd spent the night in Tahlequah while Fields and Curtis interviewed John Parris at Nancy Shell's. In the morning, after two cups of coffee and a plate of biscuits larded with gravy—a delicacy he found best to his liking in the Nations and nowhere else—he crossed into Going Snake.

The other two deputies had advised him to wait for them, but Bowers knew Christie for a reasonable man who would go quietly to Fort Smith to clear up what he himself was convinced was a misunderstanding. Even Christie's political opponents attested to his loyalty to the rule of law. Bowers blamed drink—the universal plague in that territory—and some kind of mix-up that Parker would set right.

He found Christie's wife, fine-featured for a full-blood with enormous mahogany-colored eyes, sewing a patch onto a pair of her husband's canvas trousers in their parlor, with a bone needle and a sailor's palm on her hand; the honey locust thorns and shagbark hickory played hell with the toughest and coarsest-woven fabric—and forgetting her English when he asked where Ned was and when she expected him back. He knew a smattering of Cherokee, enough anyway to ask the same questions, but not enough to sort anything out of the rapid-fire responses she knew damn well were too much for him. Leave it to a woman to find a way to cooperate with an officer of the court and flummox him at one and the same time. He admired her, and by extension Christie; he'd never known a woman who'd pay him half the respect she paid her man. It said a great deal about the man. Very soon he'd regret such carelessness, and continue to do so every time it rained or snowed for the rest of his life.

The children were at school, but he didn't consider waiting for them an economical use of his time. Cherokee youth obeyed its parents like three-day-old whelps, at least until it reached that damnable age when it knew all that transpired in the world and at the bottom of the wine-dark sea (Bowers read Homer the way Parker read the Old Testament, frequently and with pauses to commit long passages to memory), and held all who came before it as benighted and pathetic. The deputy thanked Mrs. Christie, put on his hat, and went out to beat the brush. Christie was two dollars on the hoof and a man had to pay for his biscuits and gravy.

He'd trafficked with Indians sufficient to know why they were the best hunters of game who ever lived: a white man, armed to the teeth and away from paying work, fretted about the time and expense and the humiliation that awaited him at the hands of his peers if he returned to civilization empty-handed, while an Indian, nearly naked and carrying a bow, thought of nothing but his quarry. The difference separated the two by the span of three seconds, during which a turkey flushed suddenly and without warning fluttered either to safe harbor behind a tardy shot or crashed to the ground before its wings had chance to spread wide. Bowers was cogitating along these very lines when a high-pitched gobble sounded from a thicket to his left. *Supper,* he thought, and was in the act of unscabbarding his Winchester when a bullet struck him square on the knob of bone that stuck out the side of his left knee. Splinters of white-orange pain took away his breath, and he had to grab the horn of his saddle to keep from tumbling off his horse. The carbine fell—and added to Ned Christie's growing arsenal as the deputy raked at the flanks of his mount and galloped to safety like a wounded turkey. That afternoon a Cherokee surgeon in Tahlequah spent an agonizing hour separating fragments of lead from shards of bone, wound gauze around the leg, and pronounced Joe Bowers a lucky man.

"Lucky enough to walk with a limp until God calls me home." The patient anesthetized himself from a flask of Old Gideon.

"Lucky enough to walk at all," said the surgeon. "Ned hits where he aims."

Deputy Fields told Joe Bowers he had balls bigger than his brains, and cursed him for a pettifogging fool all the way to Christie's cabin.

"Don't go out there in hot blood, John," Curtis had said. "Wait till we get what more we can out of Parris and we'll both go. You don't want to repeat Joe's mistake."

"Joe went out there to talk. That was the mistake."

He told Curtis to stay with Parris. The surgeon was wrapping their prisoner's broken ribs, and Fields didn't trust the man enough to leave them alone; Christie had friends all over and there were poisons on the shelf sufficient to wipe out an army of witnesses who could give evidence against him. He checked the loads in all his firearms and drew a fresh horse from the livery.

That idiot cripple Bowers had learned a bit of the lingo, passed a pleasant how-de-do with Christie when Christie was sober and disposed to behave like a senator from Michigan, and thought he knew the red man. No one knew a red man but another red man, and sometimes not even him. But Fields knew the depth of the chasm between civilized man's concept of justice and order and the savage's notion of right and wrong. He determined to camp out at Christie's cabin for however long it took him to return to the bosom of his family and to tell him, over the barrel of a carbine, how the cow ate the cabbage and that there was no help for it but to plead his case in Fort Smith, wearing irons all the way. One dead deputy was one too many when manpower was short and miles were long, and now another was on crutches.

He caught both kinds of luck. It was first light when he got to Rabbit Trap, and Christie was at home, asleep next to his wife, whose instincts were even keener than his. At the first clink of a bit-chain outside the cabin she nudged him. He leapt from bed, scooped up his Winchester in the same movement, kicked wide the door to the outside, and pared a rasher of bacon off the side of Fields's weathered neck as the deputy wheeled his horse to narrow the target. Fields, caught by surprise both by the man's presence and by his sudden appearance, rode hell for leather in the opposite direction, blood flying in a rooster tail from a flesh wound that would vex him for weeks, scabbing over and breaking open fresh every time he forgot and turned his head too fast; expecting any time during the ride the sudden slam of a bullet in his back. Christie held his fire, but the memory of that nightmare flight would haunt the deputy forever, ruining him for the life of an active peace officer.

Days later, a message from Rabbit Trap reached Tahlequah by Cherokee telegraph: "Tell the marshals to stop sneaking around and I'll stop shooting them."

When word got to Fort Smith, Parker didn't weep. The deputies were still alive, through no virtue of their own, and in any case after ten years on the bench he'd heard so much harrowing testimony and dropped the gavel on men of such abiding wickedness, rapists and debauchers, horse cripplers, slaughterers of families, that nothing short of the serious illness of his wife or sons—two, now, following the birth of Jimmie—could squeeze a tear from those weary ducts. His sentences now fell with the crack of a lash, and Mary's cakes for the condemned erected a barrier that separated man and wife along the very foundation of those things each held dear. Rumors persisted of days of silence in the Parker household after a hanging.

He did not weep, but interrupted court for only the second time on news from the territory to summon Marshal Boles to his chambers.

Boles regarded him across the walnut desk the size of a dinner table, scaped with writing paraphernalia, burst leather portfolios in heaps, and cigars standing to attention in a glass jar. "Christie's no ordinary outlaw."

"They're all ordinary," Parker snapped. "Possums are less common. Our purpose is to make them extraordinary, and as rare as dodoes."

"They say he's sworn never to kill an officer of the court."

"*They* say reams of nonsense about Jesse James and his kindness to widows. If Christie took such an oath, he should have done so before he killed Dan Maples."

"I wouldn't place a great deal of faith in the word of that man Parris. His reputation gives a bad name to Indians everywhere."

"An innocent man places his faith in a public trial. Some of the worst men who have trod the scaffold put up less protest than Christie."

"One deputy is dead and two wounded. I fear we'll lose more

before he's run to ground, and that when he is he will never stand on the scaffold."

"If that's his choice we'll honor it."

Boles fingered his beard. "Is that a judicial order?"

"Don't flower it up with legal rhetoric. These are simple men, recruited by Fagan and you and your other predecessors from rough fields. Tell them to abandon the quaint conceit of taking Ned Christie alive."

EIGHT

In 1889, Judge Isaac C. Parker had commanded the Eighth District Court fourteen years, six days per week, with sessions often extending into the small hours of the morning, to be reconvened at 8:00 A.M. In that time, his dark hair and beard had turned silver, although he was not yet fifty, and close study of case histories by lamplight had left deep dents in the bridge of his nose from gold-rimmed reading spectacles. In that time also, five United States marshals had been appointed to direct the activities of deputies who patroled the Nations. It was a pork-barrel post, assigned by various presidents in reward for services rendered in electing them to office, with spoils attendant and no specific requirement beyond a talent for administration, and some were better at that than others, who left the details to a succession of anonymous secretaries and clerks. Terms in Congress, judgeships, and high rank in the military crowded these men's past professional experience, with little or no connection to fieldwork in law enforcement; the legend of the hard-riding, straight-shooting U.S. marshal was an invention of hack writers, who would also create the myth of the town sheriff. By and large these officials spent their days behind desks and their whiskers resembled those of elder buffalo, which grew them to the ground. Five marshals, with three to go before Parker's robes went up on the hook for good.

Gone was the courthouse in the barracks with its hellish basement jail. The building had been given over to jailers' quarters, and the former courtroom to the detention of female prisoners. Now Parker adjudicated from behind a high oak bench of the Eastern type in a stately three-story structure of red brick, with attic storage for physical evidence exhibited in criminal trials: stained axes, broken bottles, pistols, knives; common junk out of context, but each someone's tragedy. Pair upon pair of shoes and boots for whose possession men had been slain; a museum of lore as sordid as a reliquary from the Spanish Inquisition. The building dominated South Sixth Street near the center of town, a block from Garrison Avenue and culturally miles from the old fort where Parker had condemned forty-three men; a little less than half the number he would eventually send to the most notorious apparatus of execution after the guillotine of Paris. This structure stood where it always had, on the grounds of the old powder magazine, but with a sloping roof now to protect Maledon and his subjects from the elements and a high board fence to keep out the uninvited. No longer would crowds stream in from remote places to buy chicken legs and bottles of beer from vendors and watch men die in ones, twos, and sixes. Parker disapproved, but had been trumped by Congress in deference to public opinion in the States; he believed now as he had from the start that capital punishment was a public affair, carried out honestly and in the open, and not behind cover, like a lynching in a barn. But men more persuasive than he had been chipping away at his authority for years. His decisions now were vulnerable to appeal to higher courts, although no attorney had as yet mustered the sand to seek another opinion on his client's behalf.

Even the redoubtable William H. H. Clayton, who had welcomed the Parkers to Fort Smith and introduced himself as the judge's partner in the prosecution of criminals from the Western District of Arkansas and the great Nations, had been forced to sit out the current Cleveland administration, pursuing private practice, while another pled cases for the U.S. in his place. Disregarding loyal local functionaries who had continued to serve him since his earliest days, Parker remained the single consistent and unifying feature of the federal court on the border, with one exception; George Maledon, more grizzled and bristly than ever, still climbed the whitewashed steps of the scaffold, bearing his basket of ropes and dropping two-hundred-pound sandbags from them through the trap.

As for those who had best cause to hate and dread judge and executioner, they awaited trial and sentence in a well-ventilated jailhouse that from a distance resembled a military barracks, with full hospital facilities staffed by a doctor and male nurses. Situated between Second and Third streets, it offered food and sanitary provisions far superior to the vermin-infested meat and foul buckets that once stood in the chimney wells of the old basement. Here, shackles were rarely used, a last resort for the violent, the escape-obsessed, and the suicidally inclined. Showers had replaced the bathtubs made from half-barrels, and ablutions were encouraged, rather than offered as a reward for good behavior. However, the *squee-thump* of Maledon's responsibility penetrated to its depths as it had those of the first jail.

Fort Smith had grown, away from its reputation as a Gomorrah for cowboys from Texas to drink whiskey to the point of insensibility and sample women of a particular type, toward a place where families settled in proper frame houses, attended the churches of their choice, and sent their children to school. There was talk of spreading macadam on the streets of mud and dust, of adding a second streetcar to the line. The discharge of a firearm in the Silver Dollar or the House of Lords or any of their twenty-odd competitors brought swift investigation, jail, and a fine. Row girls were prohibited from soliciting business in the saloons—indeed, even from entering—and a 9:00 P.M. curfew was strictly enforced upon them.

Fines levied for infractions swelled the treasury and helped finance the civic improvements. What passed without comment—for it was scarcely necessary—was that Fort Smith was growing on the broad shoulders of Judge Parker. With justice come to the frontier, settlers and the merchants who lived off their trade bought lots, broke ground, and built without fear for the safety of themselves and their children. When the Parkers rode to church in their fine carriage-and-pair, women on the street nodded and men removed their hats. For visitors stopping over on their way West, the spectacle was like getting a glimpse of the royal family in London.

Throughout all of these recent developments, these sweeping advances and reforms, Ned Christie remained at large.

Four years had passed since his declaration of war, and he had not been heard to utter a word of English in all that time. Around him he had gathered a small army of men who felt as he. Youths mostly, they were in open rebellion against their stoic parents, for whom the shameful story of the Five Tribes' eviction from the Eastern states at the stroke of a presidential pen, and the corpse-strewn Trail of Tears that had led them at bayonet point to this desolate place, were tests of the People by the Ancient. For their children it was an atrocity, and Ned Christie was their avenger. They abandoned their schoolbooks and the tools of civilized trades and joined him to raid corrals of horses, shops of supplies and provisions, and wanderers of cash. The only token required for induction into this society was a working rifle and extra ammunition. "With this," Christie said, hoisting a new Ballard above his head, "I live longer."

His cabin was stacked with weapons: Winchester carbines and Henry rifles, Stevens shotguns, revolvers from the factories of Colt and Remington in America and of Deane-Adams in England, belly guns, horse pistols, hideouts, guns that loaded through the breech and through the muzzle, guns that took cartridges and ball-and-percussion guns that required powder and bullet molds and yards of wadding, palm shooters shaped like mollusks and big-bore buffalo guns lethal at both ends; knives, daggers, bayonets, cavalry swords, and hatchets for close work. Christie's wife had to clear the table of cleaning rods, parts of weapons, and cartridge-loading paraphernalia to set out breakfast. Washing day produced a bounty of live rounds, empty brass casings, and copper firing caps from her husband's pockets. The house took on the aspect of the armory of the old garrison in Fort Smith.

Officers of the court who had visited the cabin and seen the kegs of powder and boxes and wooden crates of ammunition lying about suggested wistfully that a bit of flaming pitch hurled through a window would effectively disarm the West's most wanted fugitive; but the memory of January 1875, when a pot of Greek fire supplied by the Pinkertons blew up the Missouri home of Jesse James's mother, tearing off her arm and killing the outlaw's nine-year-old half brother, stayed the hands of the law in this regard. That incident had turned the countryside in James's favor and extended his career another seven years.

But it was agreed as far away as Fort Smith that Christie's longevity depended less upon warriors and weaponry than upon the network of generally law-abiding neighbors who kept him informed of preparations to invade his territory. Their sympathy for his situation, while not inviting cooperation in his vendetta, spoke of their faith in his innocence in the death of Deputy Maples. When deputies asked them if they'd seen Christie, they were polite, they offered them cups of steaming coffee in winter and dippers of ice-cold well water in summer (jars of moonshine if they knew them well enough), and shrugged their shoulders; then when the visitors left they sent their children running to Rabbit Trap. The deputies, slowed down by the tumbleweed wagon and disinclined anyway to fire up the locals by chasing down and boxing the ears of their offspring, chewed tobacco, watched them hurdling fences and splashing through streams, and soldiered on, rifles across the throats of their saddles in case of ambush. Most often the worst they found was Christie not at home, and that was the end of the matter until next time. He slept in his cabin most nights and took to the brush when the alarum was raised.

A photograph of Christie taken about this time, in a studio in Tahlequah, shows off his lean, rangy figure to best advantage, with hair tumbling black and glossy well below his shoulders, Mandarin whiskers trailing from his chin, a clear challenge in his gaze, and about his person two Colt revolvers and a Model 1866 Winchester. Unlike the case with many a staged pose, weapons and the man appear familiar with one another. The circumstances of its creation, in the busy capital of the progressive Cherokee

Nation, with deputies searching every Native face for his features and a price of a thousand dollars on his head offered by U.S. Marshal John Carroll, spoke volumes about the nature of the man and the reasons for his legend.

Four years of assaults and escapes—hornet-stings about Parker's furious head—lulls in the fighting, brief violent brushes with the "marshals," and cold camps kept while men searched the hills, caves, and thickets for some sign of his passage, and Ned Christie's war was only a little more than halfway to the finish. But his candle was burning low.

There came to Fort Smith a tall man, by appearances born to the saddle, whose long hair, handlebars, and neat imperial moved the more literary of his biographers to compare him to D'Artagnan. At the time of his encounter with Ned Christie he was nearing forty and had settled into a practical and comfortable working uniform of corduroy trousers, flannel shirt, high-topped boots made to his measure, and a white hat with a swooping brim, a fashion just then finding its vogue after the example of Buffalo Bill Cody, inventor of the Wild West. He spoke with a gentle drawl—foreshortened when he barked instructions to his companions and commanded fugitives to come out from behind their barricades—and had three children with his wife, who had packed them up and returned to Georgia, where people placed family before duty. He'd argued against the move, but had failed to prevent it, or to persuade her to return. "You can't expect a woman to understand or respect it when manhunting has got into your blood," he told his few intimates. "I can't find fault with one who doesn't."

His name appeared in none of the rip-roaring dime novels of

the age, and when pictures learned to move, with jerks and false starts like a child's, he would not be among the first ten chosen for dramatization, nor as the medium strode, ran, and found the power of speech, the first fifty, nor yet the first five hundred. Yet in his time everyone who read newspapers and many who could not knew his reputation. He was among the best and bravest ever to grapple with the challenges of the late frontier, and in a hundred years no star has replaced his in the firmament.

He was born January 6, 1850, in Oxford, near Atlanta, the youngest of twelve children, and roughhouse was his birthright. At age twelve he'd ridden dispatch for the Army of the Confederacy, and in his twenties he'd been shot in the face by a member of the Sam Bass gang during a train robbery in Hutchins, Texas; the scar was still visible after more than ten years. This incident had decided him to bring the fight to the enemy, and he'd joined the Texas Rangers and then the Fort Worth Stock Association as a detective, slaying two fugitives before throwing in with the marshal's office in Arkansas.

His name was Henry Andrew Thomas, but he seldom answered to it. His friends and even Judge Parker called him Heck.

NINE

Heck Thomas accepted bonuses and rewards. He had a wife and children to support, even if he never saw them, and for all its hard work and risk, hunting men paid poorer than clerking. After the doctor in Hutchings dug the bullet out of his face, making more of a mess than it had going in, the superintendent of the railroad line had paid him two hundred dollars; which decision Heck laid more to the twenty thousand dollars he'd managed to hide from the bandits than for the sacrifice of his youthful good looks.

He cashed the bank draught and went looking for employment that didn't involve swaying soporific over the rails in a windowless express car, half hoping for an attempt at robbery just for the variety, then getting his wish and a pistol round in the face and a recovery fee of one percent, which was what the banks were paying for the privilege of investing what a man earned by the sweat of his brow. Mostly it was the close spaces he objected to; he'd had his fill of that sleeping three to a bed at home and sharing a one-holer outhouse with his parents and eleven older siblings.

He found such a posting, all open air and a fighting chance, with the Texas Rangers. He answered to Captain Lee Hall, a man of few words and most of them profane, whose actions against the vigilantes in Goliad and against the bushwhackers who had fled Missouri to continue their war against the Union by way of banks and trains spoke louder than words. Many were in shackles and shallow holes, and the doors of Huntsville had clanged shut on John Wesley Hardin, whose career as a marauder had been largely responsible for reforming the Rangers, who had disbanded after the Comanches surrendered at Adobe Walls. Heck had learned most of what he knew about tracking desperate men from Hall, and all of what he knew about the finer details of detective work; the captain had been one of the first peace officers to compile and consult a criminal book, with likenesses, descriptions, and personal histories of fugitives in hiding, and his lessons had taught Heck to pay attention to such things as tracks left by horseshoes recently repaired, a man's preference for ready-made cigarettes over those rolled by hand, and the difficulty of disguising the shape of one's ears or the distance between one's eyes when whiskers and windowpane spectacles altered everything else.

Of chief importance, Heck had acquired the wisdom of shooting first and shooting to kill. Most of the things that stopped a man when he was stopped were placed conveniently in the middle. It was an easy mark to hit, and the shooter's best insurance against getting shot himself.

He'd never warmed to taking orders, however, not even as a yonker riding for the CSA, and in time Hall's general lack of diplomacy in his dealings with subordinates wore thin. Heck took a handsome offer to work as a detective for the Fort Worth Stock Association, with steady pay, a free hand, and liberty to collect rewards. It came with an office, which appealed to Isabelle, his wife; she'd been riding him for a long time about his absences from home, and thought a fixed place of business meant a family reunited around the supper table every night.

It was that way for a time. In his sun-hammered room overlooking the cattle pens he kept track of known rustlers with pieces of colored ribbon pinned to a large-scale map of four counties tacked to the wall behind his desk, smoking the pipe of a settled man and moving the pins according to the latest communications made by wire and by drifters he struck up conversations with in the Alamo Sample Room; but when the pins drew near Fort Smith, he saddled up and rode out, often leaving word only with an acquaintance to tell Isabelle he'd be late for supper for a week or two.

He'd been gone longer than that, and closer to a month, when the episode took place that would bring him to the attention of Judge Parker's court. He'd picked up Jim Taylor, a friend from his express-messenger days who now rode for Parker in the Chickasaw Nation, and together they tracked Jim and Pink Lee, the notorious rustlers and road agents, to a house near Gainesveille, where Heck applied what he'd learned during his apprenticeship with the Rangers. When he and Taylor finished shooting, Jim and Pink Lee were dead. The sheriff in Gainesville saw the corpses laid neatly side by side on his porch, wrote out a receipt for the thousand-dollar reward, and handed it to Heck.

The Lees were killers, feared throughout central Texas and as far as the Nations. Heck was asked to run for sheriff of Tarrant County and offered a lieutenancy in the Rangers by Governor John Ireland, but he turned down both opportunities and asked Jim Taylor to put in a good word for him with the U.S. marshal in Fort Smith; Isabelle, left alone with the children for weeks at a time with no close neighbors, had wearied of Texas, and expressed the first of many veiled threats to find a better place, even if it meant excluding their father. (In time the veil would be lifted, replaced by an ultimatum.) Taylor said, "Christ, Heck, you don't need an introduction from me. Jim and Pink already took care of that."

Taylor was not a man to exaggerate. Heck submitted his application to the United States marshal's office in Arkansas, where such requests poured over the transom, scribbled by the sort of man who read pulp novels until his lips wore out, looking for the adventurous life of the Western lawman, and received a positive reply within a week. He and Isabelle made arrangements to send the bulk of their belongings to the Hotel Le Flore, packed bags and children aboard the Katy Flyer, and rented a house in Fort Smith, where Heck took the oath of office and received his first assignment, to accompany the tumbleweed wagon through the Nations, serving whiskey warrants and collecting army deserters and suspicious persons officially christened John Doe until they could be processed at the jail. He broke a chilly silent fast with his wife the following morning and followed the Arkansas into the Cherokee Nation.

His restless nature nettled him. In time, he grew weary of escorting the slow-moving prison van, palavering with storekeeps and paid informers, and rousting jail fodder out of low brothels, dugout saloons, and opium dens, and ferrying them back to civilization; his postman period, soul-destroying and Sisyphean in its monotony. Stagnating in Fort Smith following his testimony against a defendant in Parker's court, he presented himself to the marshal and asked for a crack at Ned Christie.

John Carroll, Thomas Boles's successor, was another grayhead who could tuck his beard into his belt, but he was of a more suspicious mien. Ambition put him on his guard; he owed his appointment to patience and loyalty to the Republican platform and equated impatience with arrogance. He interrupted Heck's carefully rehearsed request with a palm.

"Men more tested than you have taken a licking from Christie and his gang," he said. "What can you bring to the case that they have not?"

"I don't know Christie."

"You plead ignorance as a virtue?"

Heck said, "I've studied the record, and it seems to me they've all gone in with some notion that Christie's a civilized Indian, who if he won't listen to reason will at least defer to greater numbers and surrender. They don't take into account the fact that he's been on the scout for years, and thinks more like a cornered grizzly than a man of learning. I intend to do all my palavering with three good men and a wagonload of ammunition."

"Is it your aim to murder him as you did Jim and Pink Lee?"

"It will be no more murder than to hang him from Parker's tears."

"Judge Parker will debate you on that, and at length."

"I'd as lief rather debate it with Christie, after I've put a bullet in him."

Carroll had a leather portfolio flayed open on his desk. In it, Heck noted, as the marshal leafed through the contents, was a carte-de-visite of Christie, armed to the hair and daring anyone who regarded the image to try its subject. At length the marshal excavated a sheet of onionskin paper, upon which Heck could have read the iron-gall notation in hand backwards if he thought the effort worth it. In places the writer had torn the paper, so hard had he borne down upon the nib.

"That's Boles's recommendation, subtracting the legal fustian," Carroll said. "It's the official policy, though you wouldn't know it by the pattern of the investigations each time Christie's struck."

"They're all good men. It's hard to make the best choice when you've broken bread with the man you're sent to kill."

The marshal slapped shut the portfolio; Christie's picture escaped on a volume of air and drifted to the floor, from which he stared up mockingly. Heck—who was not a fanciful man—took it as a personal challenge.

Carroll sat back and laced his fingers across the base of his whiskers. "The farther east you go, the nobler Christie gets. I advise you not to read a word in any of the muckraking journals before you head out to Rabbit Trap. You can amuse yourself with them once he's dead or in custody."

Thomas nodded. He had not failed to note the order of his choices.

Heck hunted Christie off and on for three months. It seemed the outlaw had trained the owls and crickets to report on the deputy's progress in bucket-brigade fashion, for he was never at home, despite the evidence of recent repairs about the place that suggested a man in residence. Finally Heck let his beard grow out, trimmed it into a fussy Vandyke, put on his Sunday suit, and entered Tahlequah under cover of darkness. There he sought out a boardinghouse where he was unknown and introduced himself to the matron as a surveyor for the Missouri, Kansas, and Texas Railroad. He'd taken the trouble to secure a legitimate business card, but that effort was wasted because the woman was illiterate. He selected a room on the second floor back, as far away from her bedroom and parlor as the house permitted, paid cash, and met there after midnight with deputies Rusk, Salmon, and Isbell, who rode in from Vinita, tied their horses out back, and crept up the back stairs with their boots in their hands. Although none of them could know it, the scene was eerily reminiscent of Christie's meeting with his father four years earlier, with a lamp burning low on the floor to keep from throwing their shadows onto the window shade. The war had turned on its head, with the fugitive roaming free and in the open and the manhunters forted up indoors.

"I feel like we're plotting to raid a bank." Isbell, a fellow veteran of the tumbleweed wagon patrol, popped a plug into his mouth and used his foot to drag over a white enamel chamber pot for a spitoon.

"It'll get more skulksome yet," Heck said. "This time we're going in afoot."

Rusk, a former working cowhand, registered his disapproval. "I didn't put in for this job to be no dadburn farmer."

"How are you at crawling on your belly?"

"I'm a fair hand. I'm married."

Isbell and Salmon responded, but were cut off in mid-cackle by Heck's hiss. "This whole nation is Christie's ear trumpet. We're wasting our time if we don't catch him with his pants down."

Salmon said, "I was wondering about them banker's whiskers. I thought maybe this was a retirement party."

He stroked them. "I figure this is my last shot at that renegade. I been back here so many times my face is getting to be better known than Lydia Pinkham's. One more trip and he'll be in Texas while my feet are still wet from the Arkansas."

"Well, we can't have that," Rusk said. "Texas has got bad men enough without importing more. Give me a cut off that plug, Izz. If I'm going to crawl on my belly, I need something to spit in a copperhead's eye."

Isbell cut three pieces and handed them all around. "Let's concentrate on spitting in Ned's."

Which turned out to be a prophetic thing to say.

They tethered their horses to scrub in the hills with plenty of forage in reach, walked into Rabbit Trap on the far blind side of Christie's cabin, and camped cold in the brush for three days, drinking from canteens and tearing off jerked beef and venison with their teeth. By daylight, when the frogs and crickets were silent and sound didn't carry, they moved toward the cabin, crawling sometimes, scrambling hunchback like crabs other times with carbines portaged on their shoulders. When mourning doves hooted and songbirds trilled, they listened for a human echo and decided the calls were not manmade. An hour before the sun came up on the fourth day, they closed in.

Christie had assembled nearly as many dogs as weapons. They all caught the scent at the same time and exploded into barking.

Heck raised his voice above the yammer. "Make a rush for it!"

Each took a side of the cabin and drew down on a window. Heck raised his voice again. "Christie, we're U.S. marshals, and there are too many of us to fight! Surrender!"

A plank flew out of a gable in the loft. A barrel poked out and sent a hunk of lead chugging into the earth at Heck's feet. Christie levered in a fresh round and fired right behind it even as every carbine on the ground slanted upward. The deputies' guns went off almost simultaneously, a prolonged roar like a freight train hurtling through a tunnel. Glass panes shattered, pieces of bark flew off logs, bullets gonged against pots and skillets and the iron stove inside. Heck cried for them to hold their fire.

"If you intend to fight, send out your woman!"

Six shots flew in rapid succession from the gable. Heck dove for cover. As the deputies returned fire, he scuttled behind a lean-to attached to the cabin, open to the rear with cords of firewood stacked inside. Heck erected a pile of kindling using sheets of loose bark, crumpled some John Doe warrants he carried from habit, and burned through three matches before getting it all to catch. When he had a strong flame, he fanned it with his hat until it spread to the wall of the structure and fled behind a hickory tree, bullets from the gable chewing up ground at his heels.

Fire from the ground trickled to silence as the deputies waited and watched the flames. The wind caught smoke as thick as cotton batting and slung it against the gable.

Christie had a coughing fit. Isbell, backing away from the cabin's deep shade to draw a bead on the gap where Christie had knocked out the plank, spun on one ankle and fell, a slug in his shoulder.

The cabin was burning merrily now. A figure leaped out the shot-away door. Rusk and Salmon opened up on it as it zigzagged into the tangled brush that encircled the clearing.

"Not Christie!" Heck bellowed. He'd recognized Ned's son, Arch. The youth was nearly grown and resembled his father, but was several inches shorter. Heck's cry went unheeded at first, and bullets tore at leaves and branches in Arch's wake.

In the loft, Christie rubbed the sting from his eyes, but the bandanna he'd soaked from a canteen and tied around his nose and mouth kept most of the smoke from his lungs; he'd coughed merely to draw a marshal from cover, and when Isbell stepped into the early light to see if Christie would poke his head out to breathe, Christie had taken swift aim, felt the Winchester push against his shoulder, and knew before the ball found its mark that it would shatter bone and reduce the odds against him by one. But as he fired, Heck Thomas glimpsed his profile against the lightening sky and squeezed off a shot that smashed the bridge of Christie's nose and tore out his right eye.

He lay for a long time in a swoon, with smoke filling the loft and flames snapping at the underside of the floor, which seemed to be sweating beneath him as the pitch boiled to the surface. He felt hands pulling at him and grasped for his weapon, but they were friendly hands, taking advantage of the smoke and Arch's diversion to rescue him. He was borne down the ladder, blind in both eyes from the blood leaking out the empty socket, carried on the run by his legs and shoulders, and dumped without gentleness into the bed of a wagon. Someone climbed in with him, embracing him; he smelled his wife. He held tight to her with one arm and with his other hand clutched at a sideboard to keep from bouncing out when the horses were whipped into a gallop. His pain was white and red and green. Belated reports crackled, a slug struck an iron staple on the side of the wagon and sang away. Whoever was on the spring seat knew the narrow passages through the thorns and brambles like a river pilot who had memorized all the snags in the current. His passenger felt as if he were being borne to safety in the talons of an eagle.

When an account of the fight reached Parker's desk, he put his head in his hands and asked Marshal Carroll if they were to settle for taking Ned Christie a piece at a time.

TEN

Three years of skirmishes followed, but Heck Thomas, either in punishment for his failure to kill or capture Christie or because he was too well known in Going Snake to breach the outlaw's early-warning system, was assigned to other duties. Another Heck, surnamed Bruner, assumed command of the investigation, and with deputies Rusk and others fought running battles with Christie's men in and near Rabbit Trap Canyon; three more deputies and several Indians friendly to Parker's court were wounded.

Whether Christie himself took part in these fights was a subject of heated argument in the saloons of Fort Smith, where veterans of the seven-year conflict gathered to show off their scars and swap war stories. Some said Heck Thomas had broken his spirit when he took away his eye and his good looks, others that he was still recuperating. Still others insisted he'd died of his injury and that his friends had entered into a conspiracy to keep his legend alive by carrying out raids and defensive operations in his name. L. P. Isbell, retired from service with a paralyzed shoulder courtesy of Christie, said the biggest mistake the deputies ever made was to destroy the cabin, and with it the one place the outlaw was sure to return to from time to time; now he could be anywhere in the miles of alien country, crouched in ambush behind the next fallen log or perched overhead in a tree.

"Time was you could rout him out with a rifle and a plan," he said. "Now you'd be lucky to take him with the Seventh Cavalry."

Which words would be remembered in the marshal's office later.

Christie had, in fact, recovered, with the treatment of the same Cherokee surgeon who had dug Christie's bullet out of Deputy Joe Bowers' knee in 1885; and if anything his spirit was more determined than ever. He, his family, and those who remained loyal to his rebellion had withdrawn to the far end of the canyon, chosen a site high in the Cookson Hills against a wall of striated rock with a view of every approach, and hacked a path between it and a steam-driven sawmill operated by an acquaintance, who provided wagonloads of hickory logs, enough to build a small settlement. Working from sunup to sundown, and drinking himself nights into stupefaction—the only rest he knew—Christie, with a bandanna knotted diagonally around his head to keep the sweat from burning his vacant socket, dug stones from the earth with his companions to erect a foundation and notched and stacked the logs four deep. When the walls were complete and a roof added (and rethatched with damp sod on a regular basis to resist catching fire from hurled torches), the low, dark building, with narrow ports in place of windows, was aesthetically inferior to the comfortable cabin the Christies had lost, but as a fortress its fame spread swiftly. By the time the legend crossed into Arkansas, it included a moat stocked with water moccasins and a standing army of fifteen of Christie's closest supporters. In reality, time, attrition, and Native impatience to waiting had shrunken his resources to his wife and family, lieutenanted by son Arch and a whiskey peddler and petty thief who called himself Soldier Hair; and Christie was afraid of snakes.

By October 1892, President Harrison had installed Jacob Yoes as U.S. marshal for the Eighth District. Yoes, a choleric Teuton several years younger than any of his predecessors and several times more ambitious than John Carroll, assigned seventeen deputy marshals to lay siege to Ned Christie's stronghold. It was the largest federal force ever assembled against one man, and Yoes took personal command of the expedition, the only marshal in Parker's long tenure ever to take saddle in the field.

"At least if we shit the bed this time we won't be alone," remarked one Christie veteran.

As the summons to report to duty shot out over the wires, deputies Bruner and Paden Tolbert traveled to Coffeyville, Kansas, borrowed a military cannon and personnel to help them load it aboard a flatcar, and escorted the gun by rail to Tahlequah. Army engineers in Fort Gibson transferred several cases of dynamite from the powder magazine to Yoes and took his receipt.

There was no longer need for secrecy. Christie was said to feel secure in his citadel, and in any case had broadcast his vow—translated from the Cherokee—to retreat no farther: "Like the bear, I will die where I was born." Indians in all five nations, and non-Indians who lived there by their leave, observed for days as men straddling glossy, well-fed mounts passed through their settlements, weighted down with pistols and big-bore rifles and belts of ammunition, stars flashing on their breasts. These witnesses laughed as Tolbert and Bruner cursed and whipped mules struggling to pull their artillery piece out of the mud. Then it hove to, gleaming in its ugly potential, and they fell silent.

An army was on the march. Some swore they heard the roll of drums calling men to muster.

Judge Parker, more aware than ever that the eyes of the East were upon him, broke precedent and assigned a press agent to the campaign. The bespectacled little German set up his tripod in a private coach and in the same sawmill where Christie had acquired his building material and committed the solemn, droopily moustached, self-important faces of the heavily armed men to glass plates. When the magnesium glare faded and sight returned, they rocked over the rails and took to their saddles, each to his own thoughts, and all of them trained on the days ahead.

"Fat men on fat horses loaded down with iron," said Soldier Hair, conversing with Christie in their native tongue. "I bet a case of whiskey they don't make it halfway through the canyon."

Christie swigged from a bottle of Nancy Shell's stock and passed it over. "Why not make it two? That's the last of it."

His wife came to stand over them. They were sitting on the hard clay floor of the fortress with their backs against the logs, which was how they spent most of their days, with their Winchesters across their laps. Christie had lost his taste for the card games the white man played, and both had forgotten the games enjoyed by their ancestors. *Part Indian, part snake . . .*

"Supper is on the table," she said.

"Eat it and tell us how good it was." Soldier Hair giggled and drank.

She raised her skirts and kicked the bottle from his hand, cutting his lip. He cursed and grabbed for his carbine, but was impeded by Christie, who lunged across him to rescue the bottle before it emptied. By then the long Cherokee tradition of female dominance had kicked in, and Soldier Hair sat back and smeared away the blood with the back of a hand.

"You are no better than that pig John Parris." She spun on her heel.

"Who is John Parris?" asked Soldier Hair.

A few days later, Christie helped his wife onto the seat of the wagon that had swept him away from his burning cabin, handed up the smallest of his children, and sent them off to her sister's house in Tahlequah. She fixed him at length with her mahogany-colored eyes, then gave the lines a flip.

Dawn came the color of metal on November 2, with the raw-iron smell of early snow. The dogs outside were barking and had been since an hour before daylight. By then the men on the grounds had all found their positions behind trees and in the brush. Christie had given up trying to keep overgrowth clear of the fort as a waste of time and energy; it marched relentlessly, more stubborn even than Parker's marshals, and at forty, after seven years spent on high alert and with the effort of keeping his balance with only one eye, he lacked the endurance, and Soldier Hair the ambition. Arch had grown into an arrogant young rebel who considered yard work beneath him. They were a fine gang of desperadoes.

The men in the fort had traded positions at the gun ports throughout the last dark hour, but had failed to find a mark to shoot at, and Christie was unwilling to snap off at mere rustles in the brush; his neighbors sometimes took it upon themselves to stand sentry uninvited, and in any case he was reluctant to shoot one of his dogs by accident. It was his soft spot for dogs that had gotten him into this pickle, but there it was: You could change a man's station over a trifle such as a misunderstanding, but his basic nature was bred in the bone. He contented himself with waiting for a proper target, and admonished Arch and Soldier Hair to do the same.

Ironically, when the challenge came, he'd dozed off; and when Yoes introduced himself, in a bawling voice best suited to a platform bunted for Independence Day, and told him there was nothing for it but surrender, it startled him into firing a shot through his own roof. He'd fallen asleep in a crouch against the wall with his finger on the trigger.

A quarter-hour's worth of racket ensued, with repeaters and buffalo guns and the deep bellowing roar of Stevens streetsweepers clearing the woods of birds, varmints, and deer for a mile about and tearing great yellow gashes in the logs, but otherwise doing no damage to his redoubt; there was nothing stouter on the Holy Spirit's green earth than native hickory, and no better workmanship than the Cherokee. A stray pellet of buckshot found its way through a port and broke in half a washbasin in its stand, but Christie had ceased to fret about his wife's nice things. That was a bit of freedom he hadn't counted on when he'd decided to abandon the life of the little white man and ride the high country. He loved the old girl, but there were times when the dungeon in Fort Smith seemed preferable.

Arch found the first target, but as far as his father could tell by the way the man in his sights retreated into the brush without staggering, the only pain would be felt by his tailor. Christie regretted never having had the chance to tutor his son in the manly art of marksmanship; an unforgivable failing in a skilled gunsmith. To plug the gap, he sent a round after the boy's, knowing the marshal had better sense than to withdraw in a straight line. It would be an insult to himself to assume otherwise. A man rated his standing by the quality of his foes.

"Fire!"

When the cannon opened up, from a cover built of cut branches on the edge of the woods like a deer blind, Christie grinned, like a child at a medicine show, at the gout of smoke and fire erupting from a sylvan patch—and laughed loud enough to be heard by his attackers when the three-pound ball struck a log with a thud he felt in his testicles and bounded away in a reverse trajectory nearly identical to the first, striking the ground just short of the woods and bouncing into them like a sphere of rubber cast by a titan playing jacks.

"Duck!"

That set the pattern for the next several rounds:

"Fire!"

"Duck!"

"Fire!"

"Duck!"

Each time, the ball struck the logs hard enough to rattle his teeth, only to plummet back toward its source. Christie took snap shots at exposed limbs as the marshals in charge of the cannon scrambled out of harm's way. While they were reloading, he joined Arch and Soldier Hair in pestering the other marshals, using the smoke that blossomed from behind trees for a mark. Clouds of spent powder stung their eyes and a fog lay over the yard as in lithographs Christie had seen of Gettysburg.

Again the brush stirred in which the cannon was hidden; he braced himself for another blast. Then the brush parted and he saw the great blue-black muzzle for the first time, approaching the fort as if under its own power. It stuck out over the top of iron rails stacked in a square inside the wagon it sat upon, the rails shielding the men who were pushing it. As Christie drew a bead, hoping to dislodge the stack, bullets rataplaned off the logs near his gun port. He threw himself away from it. For the better part of a minute, all three defenders crouched in cover while the marshals laid down heavy fire at all the openings. Then thunder shook the earth as another three-pounder struck, harder than the others. Still the fort held.

Thirty times the logs were struck. That was more balls than had been brought, but some were used more than once because they had an accommodating habit of returning home after they had failed to stave in their target. Down on the ground, Marshal Yoes got the gunners' attention and slashed a hand across his throat. Bruner and Tolbert jumped out of the wagon and ran for the woods, unshipping carbines from their shoulders as they abandoned the artillery for the infantry. Yoes called for more fire and sent deputies Bill Smith and Charlie Copeland running to the wagon, carrying a crate of dynamite between them by the rope handles. The wagon containing the silenced cannon stood twenty yards from the fort, a miniature redoubt in its own right and the first armored vehicle in combat history.

With Tolbert and Smith hammering at the fort on one side and deputies Ellis and White doing the same on the other, Copeland dashed the sixty feet, trailing smoke from a burning fuse, and jammed a bundle of six sticks of dynamite into the space where two logs crossed at the corner, then ran a serpentine course back with bullets stitching the sod around him.

The roar of the explosion boxed the ears of marshal and deputies, pounding the ground and throwing eight-foot sections of log thirty feet in the air. Ellis, White, Copeland, Tolbert, and

Smith charged the fort under cover of the smoke and dust, levering and firing as they ran.

A gap had been blown in the wall large enough to admit a wagon. The deputies vaulted over the debris and wheeled right and left, throwing down on shadows in the haze.

A volley of shots sent them to the walls. In the lull that followed, they searched for targets, but as the fog settled, they saw they were alone. Tolbert opened his mouth to shout this information to Yoes—then flattened against the wall as more reports crackled from nowhere.

"They're under the floor!" White pointed his Winchester down and slammed a succession of bullets through the planks, new and yellow and recently erected on a framework built on the clay beneath. The other deputies joined him, riddling the boards.

Outside the fort, Deputy Marshal E. B. Ratteree saw a man crawl out through a space beneath the floor, but held his fire in the murk of smoke for fear of hitting a fellow deputy. The man saw him and shouldered his own rifle. Before Ratteree could react, his face caught fire. Momentarily blinded by a powder flare whose mark he would carry for the rest of his life, he fired back.

Ned Christie bounded to his feet, whooping and gobbling. A space of silence, and then a dozen carbines rolled thunder. He pirouetted and fell, as loose-limbed as a scarecrow.

Arch Christie escaped once again, as he had from his father's burning cabin three years before. The deputies found Soldier Hair crawling on hands and knees under the floor and had to turn him over with a foot and shove their muzzles into his face to obtain his surrender; he was badly burned and both eardrums were punctured.

Jacob Yoes's deputies slung Christie's corpse into the wagon containing the cannon and carried it a hundred miles to Fort Smith like a trophy bear. They took a door off its hinges, leaned the stiff body against it, propped Christie's Winchester in his arms, and posed with him for the little German photographer; it was the closest any of them had gotten to him in seven years. After citizens filed past to look at the man who had declared war upon the United States, Watt Christie arrived to claim the remains and took them back to Rabbit Trap for burial and the traditional Cherokee plea for the disposition of his spirit.

III

A WOMAN IN HER TIME

These impossible women! How they do get around us!

—Aristophanes

ELEVEN

Judge Parker congratulated Marshal Yoes, but had not the leisure to draw a breath of relief at the close of the longest hunt for a lone fugitive in American history. Privately he considered the expenditure of seventeen men, an artillery piece, and dynamite to exterminate one bandit an admission of desperation, and a failure of sorts. In any case, the docket left no space for reflection, and his enemies in Congress were threatening once again to slice up his jurisdiction like one of Mary's cakes for the condemned. Many of these meddlers had still been at school when he first took the bench; it was the privilege of youth to regard so venerable a fixture as an impediment to civilization instead of its instrument. The hanging of six more men in company on January 16, 1890, had revived all the old arguments, even though the private nature of the execution—attended by invitation only, with passes signed by the marshal—had drawn little fire from his old nemesis, the Eastern press. The eyes of the Union were drifting eastward, toward the robber barons of New

York, and southward, toward the Spanish situation in Cuba, and no less an authority than Frederick Jackson Turner was about to declare the frontier closed. It was at such times that a man felt the world turning beneath his feet.

The strain of defending his territory, and of his punishing schedule, had whitened his hair and beard. From a distance he appeared to be wearing a polished porcelain bowl on his head, and when he bent over his papers in court he looked like an old woman in his robes. That impression evaporated when he lifted his chin and fixed the prisoner in the dock with the cold blue stare of an experienced killer of men. Seventy-one had died by his judgment.

The number should have been higher. Presidents would interfere from time to time, to placate certain wrongheaded contributors, and his opponents on Capitol Hill, carpetbaggers to the last, had granted convicted prisoners the right to appeal his decisions to the Supreme Court, after fourteen years of allowing him a free hand. For a time, no attorney exercised this right, knowing Parker for a fair man and not wishing to incur his displeasure by questioning his wisdom. Then J. Warren Reed, a prancing peacock of a man, Parker's opposite in everything but gender (and his silk shirts and wasp-waisted clawhammer coats obscured even that distinction; also, he was his wife's intellectual inferior), took the case of his client, a thief and murderer named William Alexander, to Washington. The Supreme Court had reviewed the evidence, ruled incompetent the testimony of a key prosecution witness, and ordered a new trial. This time, Reed went on the attack, splitting the jury five to seven; and William H. H. Clayton, Parker's friend and partner in justice from the early days, rusty and out of practice from his hiatus under Cleveland, had told the judge in confidence that he was pessimistic about the outcome of the third trial. (Next month, he would drop all charges.)

When Parker himself was still awaiting word of the decision in Washington, a groundswell of cheering penetrated the window of his chambers in the new courthouse, originating in the fresh construction of the jail, and he knew he'd been defeated. Minutes later his clerk, Stephen Wheeler—brigadier general, retired, in the Arkansas State Militia, still baby-faced behind his imperial whiskers—appeared holding a telegraph flimsy. Parker merely nodded. Somehow, the news had reached the men most directly affected by the appeals process before it entered the halls of justice. Predators were the first to sense weakness in the enemy.

But Fort Smith still loved its judge. The slapdash, temporary cowtown of '75 had gentrified with brick and mortar and side entrances to the saloons for the ladies; electric lights blazed in the federal courtroom, and although Parker thought the wire the traction company men were stringing between poles to electrify the streetcar line unsightly, it was one more sign of progress, erected on the solid foundation of the rule of law. Feared and despised in the jail, hated in the low dens of the Nations, he walked the city streets unconcerned for his safety, always allowing time to stop and converse with shopkeepers and fellow members of the Methodist and Catholic congregations and to pat the heads of their children and remark upon their growth. He was elected president annually of the Sebastian County Fair Association, an office looked upon with more reverence than mayor. Representatives of the Eastern journals expecting to find an uncouth mountebank, tobacco stains in his beard and a pistol in his belt, discovered instead a dignified and benevolent old uncle with the head of a Roman senator. In interviews he was amiable and watched with sly pleasure as they hastened to record his learned theories in their grubby little blocks, knowing their editors would butcher or bury them among advertisements for cream separators and whisker balm.

At home, Parker dwelt upon his personal failures.

These came to him when his wife had retired. He'd finished annotating in his jagged hand the case histories he'd brought home and sat in the horsehair chair in his study with the lamp glowing on the Bible in his lap. Charles, his firstborn, had developed a wild streak, which he'd managed to conceal on Sundays and holy days when Parker was home, and which his mother was too gentle to remark upon even to his father. By the time Parker learned of it, it had progressed too far to reverse; but judging was his profession, he blamed himself for overlooking the evidence when it was right under his nose. Charlie had spent time with Annie Maledon, George's daughter. That had ended badly, and Parker had been too relieved to hear it was over to inquire into the details. He'd had too much respect for his chief of executions to express his disapproval, but he'd hoped Maledon would be aware of the class differences and put an end to the affair on his own. In this he'd disappointed his employer. But Fort Smith was a small town still, for all its advances, and Parker could not help overhearing rumors of other liaisons and caddish behavior, which if he had a daughter he would be sure to bring to the attention of the boy's father; but perhaps not, if the father were Judge Parker and he someone else. He hoped the boy had the character to come to a realization about himself and make the necessary adjustments. The iron was in the blood, after all; he was the son of a jurist and the great-great-grandnephew of a governor.

Young James was timid and lazy. His sensitivity came from his mother, who continued to deliver flowers and cakes to the men awaiting execution. Such a nature, determined to see decency where it did not exist, was less than equal to the challenge of disciplining a youth with no initiative or ambition. Parker himself could not remember when he'd last tasted one of Mary's cakes. The turnkeys, who could not resist sneaking samples, avowed that she had become an uncommonly fine baker through practice.

One man could bring order to a wilderness, provided he had vision and the sense of purpose the job required. One man could raise his sons to observe probity and devotion to duty and society, assuming he possessed those qualities himself and applied himself to the task. No man could do both. No man should be expected to try. Yet he had tried.

He removed his spectacles and rubbed his eyes, as if the weariness rested in them alone. The house was quiet but for the gasps of the fire dying in the stone hearth, the chimney cracking as it cooled. Mary, who had taken to drinking a glass of brandy each night to conquer insomnia, would be unconscious from the spirit's effects, and Jimmie would sleep around the clock if he didn't have to eat or get up to use the chamber pot. Parker didn't know if Charlie was even home. It was at times like this, here in the one place where a man should have the authority he reserved for the three hundred thousand people in his charge, that he gave himself permission to ruminate upon the past and find sympathy for that impossible woman Belle Starr.

Most of what was written about the West was rubbish, and more rubbish was written about Myra Belle Shirley from Arkansas than about Jesse James, Billy the Kid, and Buffalo Bill Cody combined.

The process by which a lank-limbed, crab-ridden consort of bushwhackers with a face like a log butt made the long climb from the brothels of Carthage, Missouri, to be coronated the Bandit Queen of the Border said more about the hacks who performed the ceremony than it did about their subject. To them, shut up in their whiskey-soaked furnished rooms in New York and scrawling in chair cars hurtling at forty miles per hour through the country they wrote about and never looked at, every desperado had a soft spot for orphans and kittens and every woman who strayed off the path of domesticity to follow the outlaw trail looked like the girls who modeled corsets in catalogues. The scribblers in soiled collars and beetle hats knew nothing of the conditions on the scout, and the unavailability of such refinements as face powder, dental hygiene, and soap.

Belle, at least, was real; which may have been the reason why her saga endured while the debutantes' parade of Indian princesses, Miners' Madonnas, Sirens of the Cimarron, and Buckskin Betsies, Bonnies, and Belindas had finished up back at the pulp mill. They'd sprung full-grown from the semen of their creators' pens and hadn't the blood in their veins to survive. There was no reason to believe either that at one time—say, twenty years before she made Judge Parker's acquaintance—she had not been comely. For certain her manners were those of a woman of breeding. But the nickel novelists would not have been interested in her in those days, because her story up to then wouldn't have sprung the collar of a pastor.

Well, there was the romance with Cole Younger; but a past without a spot of scarlet is a dismal thing.

She was the daughter of well-to-do Virginians in the Arkansas Ozarks, that feral land of green mounded hills and deep cuts exposing strata of granite and limestone, natural skyscrapers dizzying to behold from top or bottom, which stretching into the Nations would form the rear elevation of Ned Christie's fort.

The family moved soon after, and by age eight Myra Belle was heiress to a mercantile empire in Jasper County, Missouri: hotel, livery, and blacksmith shop, maintained by John Shirley and his sons, Bud and Preston, the girl's brothers. In that year she enrolled in the Carthage Academy for Young Ladies, where she learned to pour tea, play piano, and read and write in Latin, Greek, and Hebrew. She took to horseback lessons with decorous skill; lithographs that appeared in *Frank Leslie's Illustrated Newspaper* many years later blundered in showing a flaxen-haired hellion galloping through treacherous mountain passes astraddle. The one equestrian photograph she posed for shows a middle-aged woman wound in yards of velvet, with a plume on her hat, a pistol on her hip, and both lower limbs arranged demurely on one side. Boasted she: "I did everything Cole and Jesse and Frank did, sidesaddle and wearing a bustle."

Federal troops taught her to hate. They burned Shirley's empire to the ground in 1863, charging that the hotel had been used to harbor rebels, and shot young Bud to death for protesting. In that year, most of Missouri decamped to Texas, and Shirley, an entrepreneur despite his grief, packed up the remains of his family and possessions and followed it to Scyene, where he and Preston bred horses for sale to cattle outfits intending to drive their beeves to the hungry postwar Eastern markets. This was when Myra Belle would learn the details of reproduction among mammals, and also the various techniques employed by start-up cattlemen to swell their herds. Hair branding, the running iron, and other methods and tools of the rustling trade became as familiar to her as the embroidery hoop.

It's unclear whether she met Cole Younger at this time, or if they'd known each other in Missouri, where he'd ridden with Bloody Bill Anderson's bushwhackers and acquired the skills necessary to rob banks and trains. As the brains of the James Gang, he was too sanguine to have trotted after Myra Belle to Texas, whatever her charms at the time, and so it's likely their relationship heated up there, as did most things. Both had lost beloved family members to the Union; great romances have been constructed on common ground less firm. It's a matter of record that she became pregnant, and whether the father was Younger or Frank Reed, whom she married, is open to speculation. Reed was a former guerrilla who had plundered Kansas and Missouri with the infamous Tom Starr. Myra Belle's preferences had become predictable.

Pearl was born in Bates County, Missouri, where Reed had rejoined Starr. The murder of a man named Shannon forced a temporary move to California. There a boy was born and scarcely christened before a mishandled stage robbery sent them back to Texas at speed. John Shirley lent them money to open a livery stable, but Myra Belle ran the business while Reed worked in the field to stock the stalls with stolen horses.

This was an unwise undertaking in a state where horse thieves were regarded with less favor than common murderers. On August 6, 1874, Lamar County Deputy Sheriff J. T. Morris shot and killed Reed. His widow placed the children with her parents and took up dealing faro in Dallas, on occasion crooking the game in favor of Jesse James, who had fled the posses in Missouri to spend some Yankee gold while on holiday. The arrangement was strictly for old times' sake; Jesse had nettled at Cole Younger's equal share of notoriety for the raids they'd pulled off together, and Myra Belle remained loyal to her first love. She considered Jesse a straitlaced hypocrite who preached the Ten Commandments and kept only the ones that didn't count, and Jesse thought her a harlot and a card cheat into the bargain.

Followed a stint in Galena, Kansas, playing house with Cole's cousin Bruce Younger, a gambler in the saloons of that cow capital. (Cole was at this time beginning a life sentence in the Minnesota State Penitentiary at Stillwater for the misguided robbery of the bank in Northfield.) When Bruce's luck ran cold, she decamped to a sixty-acre farm on the Canadian River in the Nations, assuming housekeeping duties as the wife of Tom Starr's son, a man nearly ten years her junior. It was at this point that she dropped the name Myra and became Belle Starr, on the advice of a Eufala numerologist; all her life the Bandit Queen considered herself a student of the modern sciences, refusing to travel without her astrology charts and a carved wooden head partitioned off like a butcher's guide with phrenological labels identifying the seats of humor, passion, culture, perversity, and patience. (She claimed for her own part a prodigious bump of loyalty.)

It was 1880, and the last golden decade of the authentic Wild West had begun. Within two years, Jesse James would be dead, shot in the back by a Judas; Pat Garrett would bust a cap on Billy the Kid, his confederate in the Lincoln County War; and Bob, Grat, and Emmett Dalton would learn the rudiments of keeping the peace for Judge Parker before deciding to try their hands at breaking it. Buffalo Bill would soon pimp the frontier for the entertainment of paying spectators in New York, Chicago, and Europe, Jesse's brother Frank James would beat numberless charges of robbery and murder and conduct ticketed tours of the James ranch, and Sitting Bull and Geronimo would surrender to the U.S. Cavalry. A nation of dime-novel readers, their thirst unslaked, would turn their attention to Belle Starr, whose likeness in *Harper's* and *Ned Buntline's Own* bore a closer resemblance to Jenny Lind than the horse-faced matron who rose in kid gloves, a hat with a veil, and floor-length skirts when Judge Parker entered the Fort Smith courtroom. Beside her was Sam Starr, looking decidedly less comfortable in a stiff town suit purchased by their attorney for the occasion, his dark Cherokee neck cruelly bisected by a starched white collar. His black eyes sought constantly for egress, only to come to a full stop at the calm, muttonchopped countenance of George S. Winston, Parker's private bailiff, and the butt of the Army Colt revolver rising ostentatiously above a cavalry scabbard strapped to his hip. He was a Negro, and Starr subscribed to his father's fear and hatred of the fighting freedman. He was precocious in his precaution; Winston's service to the court predated Parker's, and in several attempts at escape from that room, none had succeeded.

Belle was less impressed. When the principals and spectators were seating themselves, and before Parker could snap his gavel, she spotted an old enemy, and before Winston could react, she made a beeline for the penned-off section reserved for officers and the press, seized a little man seated there by his lapels, dragged him over the oaken railing, and slashed a red welt across his face with a riding whip Winston had not thought to confiscate from her. By the time the bailiff reached the scene, the man had slumped back into his seat, a hand to his cheek, and Belle surrendered her weapon without resistance. She left Winston holding it and returned to her spot beside Sam.

It developed that the little man—Albert A. Powe, editor of the *Fort Smith Evening Call*—had written some fanciful prose upon the $10,000 reward offered for the arrest and conviction of Sam and Belle Starr, with emphasis upon Belle's amorous adventures with the outlaw aristocracy, and she'd taken it upon herself to defend her honor without awaiting her husband's intervention. Parker, a man of surpassing humor and irony despite his reputation in the Puritan East, banged for silence, waggled a finger at the codefendant, and warned her, with subterranean forces twitching at the corners of his mouth, that another such digression from the dignity of the courtroom would bring a charge of contempt, and time spent in the women's detention in the old barracks. (Observers could not help but note, as she sank into a curtsey worthy of the Court of St. James's, that Parker cupped a hand over the unseemly reaction in the lower half of his face.)

Photographs had managed to capture the ravages of time upon the protean feminine face, but such reminiscences bear witness to the powers of seduction of those who have known beauty, and the wisdom that although it will not last, the memory that it once existed will continue to reap reward in the future. On this evidence alone, her loveliness stands beside Helen's of Troy.

The month was October 1883. Parker's power was at its height. Barring presidential intervention—and Chester Alan Arthur, whose likeness belongs in *Webster's International Dictionary of the English Language* beside the phrase "political hack," offered no such illusion—his pronouncements carried all the weight of the stone tablets from Mt. Sinai. But Belle was unimpressed. Parker was a man, by all accounts a gentleman, and once a woman has taken the measure of the brutes, the higher species are tame birds for the slaughter. The charge was horse stealing, a capital offense in that place, where to leave a man dismounted was to condemn him to death. But Parker had never marked a woman for hanging, and this prejudice encouraged her to believe that her danger was not mortal. The difference was the same that favored the gambler who could afford to lose. She bet everything on the hand that God had dealt her, and counted upon the odds to rescue Sam as well.

Thank God they had not been brought up on a lesser charge.

She had known many men, in and out of the Biblical sense, and to each she had been faithful, until such time as fate and the astrological forces instructed her to shift her allegiance. For the time being, they directed her to stand by Sam. When prosecutor Clayton, a mattress-faced carpetbagger straight out of a political cartoon in the *Charleston Mercury*, berated Sam on the stand for his deficiency in letters, she sent lethal glances from the attorney to Parker, who—it seemed to her—flinched, and directed Clayton to restrict himself to the evidence. This was an epiphany. It was as if she herself were directing the trial.

Four days of this, the pendulum swinging between conviction and acquittal as the pettifogging lawyers parsed out the facts, evicted the jury while the finer points were dissected, squabbled over, and both counsels silenced like unruly children by the waggling finger behind the bench, and then Parker lectured to the panel at stultifying length and bade it retire to consider its verdict. No suspense there; had Parker simply said, "Guilty," and thanked the jurors for the waste of their lives, the result would not have been different. After a brief recess—briefer, perhaps, if the clock were not so near noon, and luncheon not promised for the deliberators—the farmer in the foreman's seat, solemn and monkey-faced in his clean overalls, stood and let fall the stones of doom.

"You will listen to the sentence of the law," Parker told the couple, "which is that you, Sam and Belle Starr, will spend not less, nor more than one year in the Detroit House of Corrections, in penal servitude for your crimes against the citizenry of the United States." Or some such babble; Belle paid little attention beyond the price.

She caned chairs for nine months, in the stone building on the Detroit River (in the language of the pavement, *up the river* would survive its source by many years). None of the matrons complained about her behavior, and Sam was as docile on the men's side. They were released on the same day, whereupon they left the Siberian Michigan wilderness for the opportunities still to be found in the Nations.

TWELVE

She saved Blue Duck's life, after Isaac Parker, Jesus Christ, and Blue Duck himself had laid it to rest. It was a thing to take pride in, even if the life itself wasn't worth a broken stay, and would likely play itself out behind walls of stone doing God-knows-what with his fellow prisoners.

Belle liked his looks and grooming. He was a white man despite the name, spent fifteen minutes each morning trimming his pencil moustache with a pair of nail scissors, used pine needles to clean his teeth, and changed his shirt twice a week. He never raised a hand to her, even when she striped his face with her riding whip for laughing when she used a mounting block to board her favorite mare.

She was still married to Sam Starr and would remain so for the rest of her brief life, but by 1884 that relationship had cooled, and she'd moved in with Blue Duck in a house in the Cherokee Nation, where they lived without an Indian residency permit, a misdemeanor in Parker's court. Deputies escorting the tumbleweed wagon carried warrants to arrest them next time their route passed near enough to take the trouble to bring them in. But before that, Belle's companion moved himself to the top of the priorities list when he got drunk on trade whiskey in the Flint District of the Cherokee, remembered an old insult, and emptied his revolver into a farmer named Wyrick. Whooping and whirling his horse, Blue Duck reloaded and snapped off a wild shot at an Indian boy working Wyrick's field, missing as the boy ran for cover. He was equally off the mark minutes later when he fired three times at a neighbor named Hawkey Wolf, frightening him seriously but causing no physical injury. None who heard of this incident could come up with a reason for the visit, so it was decided the shooter was only amusing himself on this occasion.

Blue Duck committed the additional indiscretion of boasting of the Wyrick affair over a jug of busthead in a store near Vinita. One of his listeners sent for Deputy Marshal Frank Cochran, who arrested Blue Duck and a friend said to have accompanied him on his raid. The friend was acquitted, but the jury found against Blue Duck. He was sentenced to mount the Fort Smith scaffold on July 23, 1886.

Belle Starr was in the gallery when the sentence was pronounced. Some who knew her and were not influenced by her purple press said she had dead eyes, cold as wax, but there was plenty of fire in them that day, all of it directed at Prosecutor Clayton, who had humiliated Sam on the witness stand when the Starrs were tried for horse stealing three years before, and his remarks upon Blue Duck's character during his turn in the dock had to her mind gone beyond the purpose of merely convicting him. Had Bailiff Winston not taken care this time to disarm her of the riding whip she carried everywhere as a sort of trademark, she'd have given the man a good lashing and she didn't care how many chairs she had to cane in Detroit to square things with Parker. She considered Clayton a coward who used the safe cover of the courtroom to assault men who if he crossed their path in the Nations would make him wet his drawers with a hard look.

It was a quirk of Belle's nature that she carried no such passion against the judge for condemning her man, or for any of the five times she herself stood accused before him. She thought him a man who did his job, no more and no less than that, and he seemed as quick to lecture Clayton as his opponent at the defense table whenever he strayed over some line. For his part, Parker seemed more bemused than angered by Belle's offenses against justice, and was possibly a bit starstruck by her reputation in the yellow journals. Certainly the sentences he passed upon her were milder than those he'd brought against men who had committed similar crimes. Belle considered him a gentleman, with all the contempt a woman of her background felt for that breed; she had, after all, acquired some of her most effective weapons at the Carthage Academy for Young Ladies. She took particular care selecting a dress and some delicate scent for her appearances in court.

The gavel came down on Blue Duck's case at the end of January. While he was in the old jail, listening to George Maledon testing the trap and his ropes, Belle returned to the Nations and Sam Starr.

Sam had never lost his interest in her, and had demonstrated the point by trailing a man she'd dallied with shortly after their return from Michigan and removing his face with a charge of buckshot. The outlaw wasn't as shrewd as his infamous father, welcoming her back without question. Blue Duck's blunder and conviction seemed to him sufficient cause for her affections to fade. Sam was still in this frame of mind some weeks later, when he fled a posse of Cherokee Lighthorse over some old difference of opinion and jumped his horse off a twenty-foot cliff into the Canadian River. The dive was reckoned the longest in equestrian history, and the fact that horse and rider survived and swam to freedom gave him the edge for a while over old Tom Starr.

This episode, and Starr's enforced absence thereafter, threw Belle's plans seriously out of gear. Her real motive in coming back to him was to assemble a new criminal enterprise and raise money for a brilliant lawyer to appeal to President Cleveland for Blue Duck's pardon.

Despite the stories told about her, Belle was strictly an adjunct, and no leader. She was arrested in short order after she and three men of Sam's acquaintance were accused of robbing an elderly man named Farrell and his three grown sons in the Choctaw Nation. She was said to have been dressed in male gear at the time—a man's wide-brimmed hat, high-heeled boots, and duck canvas shirt and trousers, as endemic in that country as lederhosen in the Swiss Alps—but still riding in ladies' fashion, with one knee hooked over the pommel. However, at a preliminary hearing in Fort Smith, none of the four victims could identify the woman attired in the height of that season's style as their bandit, and she was released, only to be brought in again a few weeks later for stealing horses from a ranch belonging to a man named McCarty. In restraints on the way back to Arkansas, she wept bitterly; but since that was inconsistent with the legend they'd created for her, the hack writers ignored the report. She failed Blue Duck and was certain he'd hang while she was still fighting this new charge.

But there was no sign of tears on her face when, free on bail, she entered the office of J. Warren Reed and sat in the embossed leather chair in front of his desk, resting a large carpetbag on her lap.

Reed was a vain man who wore corsets to accommodate his snug coats and pointed his handlebars with Pearson's Wax. In the woman's blue velvet dress and Sherwood Forest hat trimmed with ribbons—itself a fat two-dollar item in the proliferating millineries in Fort Smith—he saw the possibility of a substantial fee, and something to his account at the tailor's to keep himself out of small claims court. Her frank flat stare, and her notoriety, gave him no qualms. He was the kind of man who cut across cemeteries after midnight and feared nothing worse than a bruised shin on an inconveniently placed headstone. He'd determined to beard Old Parker in his den at his first opportunity, but had no intimation that the opportunity was so close at hand.

"I'm familiar with your case, Mrs. Starr," he said. "I read all the city and territorial newspapers. This rancher McCarty has a reputation for casting a wide loop when it comes to foals belonging to his neighbors. With his testimony in tatters I feel I can win you an acquittal, if not indeed a directed verdict in your favor."

The corners of her lips twitched upward in a parched, thin-lipped smile that reminded him of some portraits of Elizabeth the Great, another mannish woman who just might possibly have lived up to her reputation. "Anytime I can't twist my way around Judge Parker is time I took up lacework in St. Louis," she said. "I'm here about Blue Duck."

"Blue Duck? I'm afraid I'm not—" It wasn't often he was dismasted in his own office.

She filled him in on the particulars, with scarcely a word wasted. It occurred to Reed that she would have made a fine legal secretary. And as the details seeped into the honeycomb material of his singular brain, J. Warren Reed caught the bittersweet scent of challenge. He could not wait to tell his wife of this day. She was the only woman in the world who was more ambitious than he, and damn few men could match him for his faith in himself and his future.

"I can't promise anything," he said, once Belle had finished speaking and the regulator clock on the wall opposite his desk, a twin of the one in Parker's courtroom, had clonked twice in the vacuum. "I'll need to study the transcripts. Offhand, the fault most consistent in the judge's method lies in his summations to the jury, and the language he chooses when he pronounces a sentence of death. The first is often prejudicial—shockingly so—and there is an element of sadism in the second. I truly believe the old hypocrite enjoys the role of Jack Ketch."

"I don't know who that is, but if you can get Blue Duck clear of the scaffold, I'll pay the freight." She stood up, inverted the carpetbag above the desk, freed the catch, and dumped stacks of banknotes bound with India rubber bands onto the leather top.

Reed, managing to dissemble the pounding in his chest, didn't trouble to count the notes in her presence. He slid them together into a block, dipped a horsehair pen into a squat bottle of iron-gall ink, and wrote her out a simple receipt stating that her account was paid in full. She surprised him then by offering him a limpid hand in a kid glove—the reward tendered a gentleman by a lady of fine breeding, and not at all the hearty grasp of a woman who rode, cursed, took the Lord's name in vain, and generally trafficked in the same vices as men.

"I'm stopping at the Hotel Le Flore," she said. "You can report to me there, if I'm not tied up in court or in Parker's Dungeon of the Damned."

She demolished the government's case, as she had predicted; although she knew little of the labyrinthine passages through the American legal system circa 1886, she had the measure of Judge Parker and the drab, simple men who sat on the panel—farmers, mostly, with dirt under their nails and no conception of a lady lathed in the mills of society beyond a furtive glance at forbidden sections of the Montgomery Ward catalogue—and felt confident in the revolutionary allure of her saga reprinted endlessly on brown sawtooth paper bound between crimson-and-yellow covers; the callow public defender she'd drawn in the lottery had little to do but allow the jurors to compare his client's refined posture in the dock to rancher McCarty's slumped figure and yellow-stained beard in the witness box to secure the exchange Belle had foreseen:

"Gentlemen of the jury, have you reached a verdict?"

"Sure thing, Your Honor. We—"

"Wait until I ask, sir. How do you find?"

"We find"—the man in overalls and a rusty funeral coat consulted a scrap of paper in his horned palm—"we find the defendant not guilty as charged in the within indictment."

Parker slapped his gavel, dismissed the jury with thanks, and shooed Belle Starr from his courtroom. His calendar was filled with cases to try.

J. Warren Reed drafted and redrafted his letter to the White House, gave it to his wife to transcribe in her refined hand on good rag paper—she made improvements and corrections from her own extensive knowledge of the law—and posted it by special delivery. He sent word and a copy of the letter to his client at the Hotel Le Flore and waited. He had not met with Blue Duck and had no intention to seek a personal conference. The man had nothing to offer that would help obtain clemency, and much that could prevent it. Anytime an attorney for the defense could work the system without soiling his cuffs on an actual defendant was cause for self-congratulation.

Grover Cleveland's situation was complicated. His Republican rivals, who had been slow-roasting him for two years over his personal morals, were sharpening their blades for the congressional elections in November, the railroads were pressuring him to pressure Congress to assign them rights-of-way to build more spurs in the Indian Nations, and his support among his fellow Democrats was eroding. Many of them were sworn enemies of Isaac Parker, who had deserted the party a dozen years ago, and their diatribes on the grisly situation in the Eighth District had been reported at gassy length in the columns of the *Congressional Record.*

Reed had known all this when he'd composed his plea, and also that Cleveland had robbed Parker of a record-setting, scaffold-testing eight-man hanging on April 23 of that year by commuting the sentences of six of them to life imprisonment in Detroit. Once the presidential pen had been whittled to so fine a point, an experienced petitioner had but to strike before the momentum slowed. Within two weeks of its posting, his letter brought Cleveland's reply, signed in his heavy hand. Blue Duck was ordered to be transferred from the jail in Fort Smith to Menard, Illinois, there to begin a life sentence in the federal penitentiary.

If Reed expected one of Belle's rare George Washington smiles when she returned to his office in response to his note, he was disappointed. Her skirts rustled across the floor in a straight line and she leaned forward to rest both hands atop his desk, the famous riding crop in one.

"Blue Duck is no good to me behind bars," she said. "I need him pardoned."

The lawyer was amused. "My dear madam, what you're asking has happened only once, and the man was convicted of rape, not murder. Chester Arthur had already been defeated for the Republican nomination, so he had nothing to lose. This president's friends and enemies take a dim view of killing farmers. They need their votes."

"I don't follow politics. It isn't a ladies' game. How much have you got left from what I gave you last month?"

"It isn't a matter of what's left. I'm paid for my time, and the amount of that I'll need to reopen the case, interview witnesses, and establish grounds for a presidential—"

"Draw what you need from what's left. I'll be back with more." She walked out, the crop under one arm like a folded parasol.

THIRTEEN

Sam Starr, fresh from the legend of his twenty-foot plunge into the Canadian River on horseback, rode the same splendid animal between tall stacks of September corn smack dab into the same Cherokee Lighthorse officers whose pursuit had led to that stunt. This time, Starr charged straight into them Missouri guerrilla fashion, his reins in his teeth and Colts barking in both hands. They parted, giving him the right of way, then wheeled their horses and took out after him. A slug killed the most celebrated horse since Comanche of the Seventh and Starr was captured, only to be rescued by confederates from the farmhouse where he was being held for the tribal council.

Informants told Belle that the Lighthorse and marshals both had had their fill of Sam Starr and his like and were recruiting a small army to kill or recapture him and burn down the homestead on the Canadian that Belle had named Younger's Bend, where criminal gangs were known to congregate. Without a base of operations, her plans to raise funds to pay Lawyer Reed were worthless. She advised Sam to surrender to the marshals, who would give him a fairer hearing through Parker's court than he'd find before the Cherokee council. Sam was disinclined to reverse the policy of a lifetime, and their debate on the matter was overheard, some said, as far as Going Snake; which was scarcely possible, but then business in the Nations showed small regard for the laws of man and God. In any case, Ned Christie had begun his campaign against the United States, and if the row reached his ears in Rabbit Trap Canyon he ignored it, because he had more personal concerns to occupy him. But Belle's temper was waspish, she had a mule's own disposition, and Sam's people-handling skills were restricted to others of his gender. On October 11, Deputy Marshal Tyner Hughes watched in wonder, drawing his pistol and working his jaws on a plug in his cheek, as the most wanted man in the Nations rode up to him in front of the jail, stepped down, and spread his coat to show he carried no weapons.

Many years later, when Parker was dead and buried and oil had been discovered in the State of Oklahoma, men who as children were present on that occasion, and some who weren't but claimed the distinction anyway, told of the day the great Sam Starr, wearing the butternut coat and sweat-stained campaign hat in which his father had ridden with Captain Quantrill and Bloody Bill Anderson, trotted a fine sleek racing stallion straight up Garrison Avenue while every marshal and Indian policeman was scouring the Cherokee for him and calmly handed himself over to the mercy of Parker's court. The members of the Eastern press who had come to interview them in their newfound wealth waved aside such ancient history;

they were more interested in why an old red man in a moth-eaten blanket had decided to buy himself a private railroad coach with no tracks to run it on.

The coda to the affair was anticlimactic. Starr was arraigned, posted bond out of Belle's tight budget, and rode back to Younger's Bend, scratching his head, to await trial. He considered the law a contrary critter and harder to predict than a badger.

Belle remained behind in Fort Smith, where Parker one day beckoned her to join him in his chambers. She hesitated, but the absence of an armed escort assured her she was in no trouble, and the tea service on his desk bespoke hospitality rather than incarceration. She watched him fill the delicate cups with his fine pink hands, as hairless as an old woman's and calloused only where the fingers gripped his pen, and wondered if he had brewed the tea himself; there was something spinsterish in the judge's manner that escaped his demonizers back East.

They sipped. Belle noticed that the judge preferred his justice strong and his tea weak. He cleared his throat, cleared it again; his Adam's apple dented the careful crease in his cravat. He appeared ill at ease in a social situation; one, at least, in which his gavel served no purpose. "You know, perhaps, that I am president of the Sebastian County Fair Association." His manner begged an affirmative reply.

"I don't come to Fort Smith often, and not usually by my choice," she said. "You could claim you ran the fire brigade and I couldn't contradict you." She was enjoying his discomfort.

"I can't claim that distinction. As one who has the honor to attest to the former, I hope to persuade you to play a part in the festivities."

"I've never been good at raising hogs. When one gets big

enough to consider showing, I slaughter it. Sam is partial to ham steak."

"I don't judge livestock. I haven't the credentials." He betrayed something of the impatience he reserved for audacious attorneys. "Would you consider leading a mock raid on a stagecoach, purely for the entertainment of spectators during the event?"

She rotated her cup in its saucer. Had she been drinking, she felt she would have choked.

"It's a grotesque spectacle," he hastened on, oblivious to her reaction, "one I should not have given my assent to five years ago, when such atrocities were far more common and carried out in deadly earnest. However, I suppose it's a signal of progress that we should put forth the thing as an attraction instead of something to be eradicated."

"I've never robbed a stagecoach. I wouldn't know how to go about it."

He smiled in his beard. The man had a sense of humor, rare enough in his position and remarkable in his circumstances, which she knew to be unique in its challenges from high and low. "It needn't succeed. The object is to provide noise and color, with blank cartridges and the usual theatrical claptrap on the order of Buffalo Bill's extravaganza. Your"—he tasted the word—"notoriety will draw customers. If you're concerned that I'm asking you to play the clown, I must tell you I'm placing my own dignity on the line as well. I've agreed to be a passenger, and Mr. Clayton has consented to accompany me, along with one or two other officers of the court."

Belle reflected later that she must have been singularly in possession of her poker face. Any light that appeared in those lifeless eyes at that news would surely have caused Parker to reconsider the invitation.

She set her cup and saucer down on the desk with a thump. "I'll do it. I never could resist a fair."

The exhibition was gay even by the standards of that jaded city, where until recently inebriated cowhands had ridden their string ponies up the steps of the Two Brothers Saloon and recalcitrant Comanches had terrorized visiting tenderheels with their scalping knives and a snootful of Old Pepper. Covered wagons clogged the streets, bearing all the comforts of home for those who had arrived too late to book rooms in the hotels, the girls in the Row worked double shifts, and vendors prowled the boardwalks, selling ice cream and cotton candy for prices that would have made the dollar-an-egg merchants of Creede and old San Francisco curse the lost opportunity. Patent-medicine showmen burst the hinges on their strongboxes with banknotes before they were sent on their way by city policemen, a Frenchman spent a night in jail for sorcery on the evidence of a demonstration of pictures that moved. A bicycle salesman from St. Louis made his case for the obsolecensce of the horse. Opium dens on First Street exhausted their inventory and substituted pipes filled with loco weed scraped from the soles of boots fresh from Texas. From his window on the ground floor of the old courthouse, Judge Parker looked out upon the barbarism of his age and recalled his wife's early judgment: "Isaac, we've made a great mistake." Then a string of firecrackers went off with a volley that reminded him of the tense days with the Union Home Guard, spooking a horse into spilling a cartful of some vendor's baked potatoes, and he returned to his desk to review a case of rape, robbery, and murder on the Osage reservation. He burned a cigar over the explicit details. It was a wicked world.

Belle had not lied about her inexperience; holding up stagecoaches was a distinct gap in her resumé. She researched the method with all the solemnity that poor Cole, rotting away cording jute in Minnesota, would have brought to the enterprise. Quietly and without ostentation, she polished a live cartridge on the velvet of her skirts and inserted it into a chamber of her borrowed Colt among the blank rounds charged with powder and harmless wadding, singing to herself softly: "Old Bill Clayton lies a-mould'ring in his grave . . ."

On the day of the event, Belle, got up in a pulp-writer's idea of female-bandit regalia—flowing skirts, frilly lace bodice, and a cocked hat with an imitation ostrich plume of dyed turkey tail feather—trotted up Garrison Avenue sidesaddle aboard a fine sorrel stallion, and reined in beside the requisite politicians' platform draped in red-white-and-blue bunting with town dignitaries pressed against the railing in silk ties and sashes of office. She posed obligingly for a little German photographer, soon to be anointed with the responsibility of committing Ned Christie's conquerors to the graphic record, then spotted a fresh opportunity for legend. Albert A. Powe, he of the *Fort Smith Evening Call*, an unpopular local reputation, and a celebrated whipping at the end of Belle's riding whip, made the mistake of showing up, and was seized by citizens and borne, short chubby legs kicking, to within Belle's reach. She uncorked her rare, compressed smile and lent an arm to help haul him up onto the cantle. She quirted the reins across the horse's withers, and as it pounced forward, the little man threw his arms around her waist, gasping asthmatically as she galloped around the fairgrounds at a Sam Starr pace, depositing him at last in a whimpering heap in full sight of the spectators around the arena. "The pen," wrote one journalistic rival, "may indeed be mightier than the sword; but it is no match for the Bandit Queen of the Indian Territory aboard a prime example of Arkansas horseflesh." She did not fail to note that the jackals of the press tore into their own with the same relish they reserved for everyone who fell into their den.

Her scholarly studies had informed her that few successful stagecoach robberies had taken place entirely from horseback; when the crisis came, the true highwayman relied far more strongly upon his own resources than those of an animal with a brain the size of a turnip and all the courage of a journalist. As the lacquered red Concord trundled out onto the grounds, she gave the crowd its money's worth, whooping and hollering with the tame Indians from the Nations in their beads and feathers, then leaned back on the reins, leapt from the saddle with the force of the horse's momentum, and bore down on the coach, snapping the hammer on the punk cartridges and keeping count before she came to the live round with Clayton's name on it.

Live cartridges had a will of their own, and found their way despite the best intentions. But she never had a chance to put that explanation to the test of an inquest. Clayton's arrogant be-whiskered face failed to appear among the three passengers sharing the facing seats with Judge Parker. She held her fire one short of the fatal round.

Clayton had bowed out at the last minute, claiming the burden of his caseload. She didn't accept it. Parker's was heavier, yet he had found time for digression in the interest of his community. There in the clamor of cheering and dust and the driver's gees and haws, her gaze locked with Parker's, as cold and blue as drift ice in the Arkansas in January; and she knew that she had underestimated the old buzzard. It was a defeat for him as well as for her, for she would not repeat the mistake.

The Hotel Le Flore, relentlessly Parisian, cloaked its dining room in tatted curtains, framed rotogravures of the French capital, the *Mona Lisa,* and the gardens at Versailles, and featured thick slices of veal swimming in champagne sauce with hearts of artichoke looking like little vaginas floating in pools of red wine. The menu was engraved in French on paper as thick as a Creek blanket, with the prix fixe appearing only on the copy handed to the gentleman. Reed's eyes went directly to the bottom, recorded the information with the crunch of an adding-machine lever inside his skull, and lifted his gaze without reaction to his client's. "How do you prefer your oysters?"

"With Blue Duck on the side." Her eyes were like open graves. She wore widow's weeds, black as fresh tar, with a veil pinned to her hat with bow-tie flourishes that looked like tiny suspended bats. He could not know that she was in mourning for her lost opportunity with Prosecutor Clayton. "What's the news? I reckon it's good, or we'd be eating greasy fish on paper down by the Arkansas."

"It's good. Escargot good, with a burgundy chablis, if they have it and you don't mind eating snails."

"I've eaten wolf's liver, still warm with the wolf studying my throat. They're a long time giving up the fight. Me, too. When do I get to take Blue Duck home?"

"Let's not get premature. There's a deal of paperwork to make out, and two or three bureaus to put their stamp on it. Let's just say for now you'll be celebrating the anniversary of the birth of our Lord with your friend, in the place of your choice, with none looking on. I don't expect Judge Parker to pray for my immortal soul come Christmas morning, but I gave up on his friendship when I came to Fort Smith."

"Does that mean you've got the pardon?"

"It does, barring unforeseen delays. Um—"

"Um," she said. "I've picked up half a dozen tongues in the Nations, but I wouldn't know how to translate 'um' for a one." She made room for her carpetbag on the linen-draped tabletop, hauled out bricks of currency, and arranged them in neat avenues between the candle and his bread plate. "Are we square?"

He looked around quickly, meeting the gazes of neighboring diners, and scooped the banknotes into his leather briefcase. "I am always at your service," he said. "You're the only client with whom I've never had to bring up the delicate subject of compensation."

"Take care I don't steal it back," said Belle.

FOURTEEN

Mrs. Lucy Surratt ignored her neighbors every day of the year but one, when the bleak winter on the Canadian River got to her and she invited them into her husband's home to commemorate the anniversary of the birth of Christ. On the Friday before the holiday, 1886, Belle Starr got tired of watching Sam drink and fret about his upcoming trial, threw him a clean shirt, and announced that they were going to the party.

She needed the change. J. Warren Reed had underestimated the stalls in Blue Duck's case, her daughter Pearl had told her she was about to become a grandmother out of wedlock, and son Ed was in jail in Fort Smith for peddling whiskey in the Nations. Belle blamed her absences from her children's side for the way they'd turned out, despite whipping them with extra enthusiasm during visits to make up for the neglect. As a result, Pearl was terrified of her mother and Ed hated her.

Sam Starr was a hostile drunk whose every brush with the law had followed a session with busthead. He was snarling when he and Belle drew rein before the Surratts' past sundown, and once inside proceeded to find fault with the punch, the close climate on the dance floor, and the way the fiddler played. When a bottle made the rounds he emptied it and hurled it at the poor musician, striking him on the neck and ruining "Jack o' Diamonds."

"Simmer down, Sam," Belle said. "We need the music."

Sam responded by wheeling their hostess out on the floor and jostling the other dancers. One lunged toward him, but was restrained by a companion. Everyone knew Sam bit when he foamed.

It was Frank West's poor timing to come in from a smoke out back just about this time. The Cherokee Lighthorse policeman wasn't wearing his uniform, but Sam recognized him from a previous encounter.

"You're the son of a bitch shot me and killed my horse that day in the cornfield."

West regarded him with oak-colored eyes. "That wasn't me, Sam. It was Chief Vann and Marshal Robberson done that."

"You're a liar." Sam drew his Colt and shot West in the neck. It was Sam's night for necks.

Blood spouting from his jugular, the policeman pulled a short-barreled revolver from the pocket of his overcoat as he fell. The powder flare caught Sam's shirt afire. The bullet shattered his heart. Male guests helped Belle load him into her carriage. The next day, a hired hand moved a cord of wood to dig a hole in the only unfrozen patch of earth at Younger's Bend. Belle laid a bouquet of dried lady's slippers on the mound.

When the report of Sam Starr's death reached Judge Parker, he told Stephen Wheeler to strike his name from the docket. The clerk noted the relief in his superior's tone. He had seen often the traces of dust on the judge's knees after he had prayed for the souls of the men he had sent to the scaffold.

The cabin at Younger's Bend yawned large and empty without Sam's larger-than-life presence. Belle missed Blue Duck more than ever, but his case was still crawling through the logjam in Washington; Grover Cleveland had troubles of his own that season, with a hostile Congress and the worst winter on the plains in a hundred years driving the price of beef through the roof and threatening another panic. On an impulse, Belle wired her children to join her, the telegram to Ed reaching him in his cell where he was finishing out his sentence. She warned Pearl not to bring her bastard with her when she came. The lessons of the Carthage Academy for Young Ladies died hard. She could abide any sins except those against social decency.

For a time after the passing of Sam Starr, a pall of peace settled upon the Indian Nations. Of all the chronic felons wanted perpetually in Fort Smith, Ned Christie now stood alone. Five years, and the health of several deputy U.S. marshals, would pass before he made his final stand. The wild West lurched a step closer to tame.

Belle meanwhile settled into the quiet life of widow and mother. Those who knew her by sight paused as her apparently dutiful son helped her down from her carriage when she went to McAlester's store for provisions and supplies; those who knew her by reputation only professed disbelief that this plain woman decked out in the pinnacle of Eastern fashion was America's own Bandit Queen. They turned again to the Valkyries borne of the fistulous imaginations of self-styled journalists, who never disappointed.

Blizzards laid claim to the prairie. Thousands of cattle froze in huddles, children lost their way, crouched, and turned crystalline scant yards from shelter. Meteorolists—a new term for readers of the Eastern sheets to wrap their lips around—cleared their throats at podiums and predicted a new Ice Age. Evangelists dusted off Revelations. Chicagoans brawled over tins of corn and peaches in markets, convinced that a cellarful of foodstuffs was all that stood between them and starvation when the snow drifted to the roof of the Mercantile Exchange. But on the Canadian, Belle Starr rocked on her front porch, drew her shawl about her shoulders, and warmed her vitals with coffee laced with brandy, obtained through the ladies' entrance to the House of Lords in Fort Smith (the skullbender they sold in the Nations tore her up inside). At forty-one she considered herself retired from the adventurous life. It was a good bargain, given her history and the lies everyone told about her; Wild Bill had made only thirty-nine, Jesse thirty-five, and poor Cole had been buried alive since age thirty-two up in squarehead country. That little fat nance Albert A. Powe had let his mercenary instincts get the better of his fear long enough to approach her with a proposition to help her write her memoirs.

She rocked and thought about that. It was a story worth telling, better than anything she'd heard about the pack of howlers that Judas Pat Garrett had published about Billy Bonney, who it seemed to her she could have set on the right path with a sound whipping the first time he'd strayed. There was war in the thing and betrayal, and Sam's twenty-foot plunge horseback into the river; she hadn't been with him on that occasion, never went out on raids except when he was unavailable to lead them, but Powe didn't know that and neither would the readers until she told them, and she wasn't about to let truth get in the way of the record. Those Missouri wildwood boys had taught her a thing or two about stretching yarn. She wondered if publishing paid better than highway work.

Seasons changed while she was contemplating the literary life.

The snows out west receded, leaving behind carcasses in heaps and scattered corpses, the spring rained hard and the summer ran hot and dry. Lawyer Reed wrote her a litany of Grover Cleveland's travails that made her wonder if he wanted her to transfer her concerns from Blue Duck to the president. Another harsh winter hammered the continent all the way to New York City. Entrepreneurs in that wicked town charged elevated train passengers two dollars a head to conduct them down ladders from their stalled positions to the street. Belle shot a deer and had to quarter it to get it up the drifted hill from the river.

Spring again, and she put in corn and potatoes and fattened a hog, whether to feed her grown children or to enter in Parker's fair she wasn't certain. She wondered if she'd have been free to slop and till if Clayton had been aboard that stagecoach. It would have made a dandy chapter, and an object lesson to cowardly counselors. She might write it regardless. Clayton had sure showed the white feather there.

Her children made her feel old. She took up with Jim July, a nephew of Sam's, and gave him harbor when the marshals and Cherokee Lighthorse sought him for horse rustling. He wasn't as loyal as Sam, disappeared for days at a time while she suspected he was seeing other women, but she was realistic about her prospects and made no scene when he returned. When during one reunion she learned he'd fled a tumbleweed wagon and hid out overnight in a ditch, she told him he ought to follow his uncle's example and turn himself in; the jail in Fort Smith was no less comfortable than a ditch, and the meals were regular. "And Sam never spent a day," she added.

"That's because he got shot."

"That didn't have anything to do with the business."

"It just seems to me a powerful lot of men wind up shot around you."

"Well, I didn't shoot them."

"Not seeing nobody else did comes to the same thing."

Belle had no answer for that that wouldn't have started the row all over. It was her first indication that Jim resented her as much as her son Ed. Of all the people under her roof Pearl was the most trustworthy, and she'd betrayed her by running off and getting with child. Belle still caught her from time to time, staring out the window and mooning over the bastard girl she'd left with friends. This domestic existence had nearly as many snares as the bandit life. Such was the course of her thoughts as she curried her mare, Venus, clawing away fistfuls of dead hair and wishing all the dying things in the world were disposed of as easily, exposing the glossy fresh growth beneath.

She heard skulking outside the barn and challenged the intruder to show himself, curling her fingers around the handle of a pitchfork leaning in a corner of the stall. When the man entered the doorframe she recognized Edgar Watson, a neighbor. He was good-looking, in a dissipated way, broad-shouldered and straight in the legs, but he had a wet mouth and bitter little eyes like buckshot, and was one of those men who trailed their pasts behind them like snails. She'd ridden with his kind, dishonest men twice over who broke common bonds with no more thought than they showed when they broke the law. It didn't do to show them one's back.

"I been wondering if you changed your mind about leasing them twenty acres," he said.

"You wasted a trip. I'd as soon let them lie fallow as let you take a plow to them."

A whining note entered his tone. "What the hell did I ever do to you?"

"Not a thing, Watson, and you won't as long as I refuse you the opportunity."

She'd had too much experience with his breed to give him specifics. Wives kept a loose hitch on secrets when there was another woman around to confide in, and Mrs. Watson was a refined Easterner who knew good breeding and trusted in it, although too late for her relationship with Edgar. Belle had learned from her that her husband had fled a murder charge in the Florida wilderness. It wasn't the killing that bothered Belle so much as the length of his flight to avoid prosecution. Where she came from, a road agent placed his faith in his neighbors and in his knowledge of familiar terrain to confuse posses and make them lose heart and turn home. A man who abandoned his neighborhood to the enemy never stopped running. She saw a field half-tended when trouble came and no money to collect from a man on the scout.

"You're lying about letting that land lay fallow," he said. "I heard you got a tenant."

"You heard right. We've entered into a contract, so go skulk about someone else's barn."

Watson produced makings from his overall bib and built a cigarette. He made as shoddy a job of it as he had his life. "He was to bust that contract, you'd have a summer's worth of brush to clear away next growing season."

"He'll keep to it. Not every man is as slippery as you."

"Trouble dogs you like a whipped hound. If Parker's men take you down for this or that, the territory will claim your spread, and there's a parcel of seed gone to crows and such and nothing to show for a broken back. Might could be he'd see reason when it's put to him and cut his losses."

"We'll see what they have to say about that in Tahlequah, and Fort Smith if it comes to that. Conspiracy to violate a signed covenant is a matter for the courts."

"I reckon the Nation and Parker's court have enough on their hands with Ned Christie and the like not to trouble me over it."

Belle lost her temper. That wet mouth and what it was doing to that sorry cigarette infuriated her sense of the social graces. "I don't suppose the United States officers would trouble you, but the authorities in Florida might."

Watson, it seemed to her, turned green. With shaking fingers he took one last slobbery drag on his smoke and dropped it onto the trodden hay at his feet, where it might have caught the barn on fire if she hadn't mashed it out as soon as he left. "The sun don't shine on the same dog's ass all day long," was all he had to say in parting.

Months passed. Her unplanted twenty grew over in weeds and juniper and she made plans to sell it in the spring. Younger's Bend was poor enough ground for crops, and with Sam's old gang scattered to the winds it was a useless space of God's forsaken earth.

Reed sent her a copy of Blue Duck's pardon, signed by Cleveland. It was months old, and she had yet to hear from the man she'd worked so hard to set free.

On February 2, 1889, she was one day short of her forty-third birthday. Her gift was Jim July's sullen acquiescence to her prodding; men were weak creatures, after all, boys at heart, and the legend of Sam Starr's bold surrender sent him over at the last. She watched him assemble the rags of his best finery, an old guerrilla shirt whose linen ruffles she'd put to the iron with care, a slouch hat without too many stains and a snakeskin band, and a fine pair of stovepipe boots, and agreed to ride with him as far as San Bois in the Choctaw Nation, thirty miles from the Canadian. They stopped for the night at the home of friends, dined on biscuits and gravy, boiled radishes, and Arbuckle's coffee strong enough to raise a blister on a bullhide, slept fitfully on a featherbed, and parted at sunup on Belle's birthday, Jim to Fort Smith and Belle back to Younger's Bend. At 3:00 P.M., saddleworn and hungry, she put in at the house of Jack Rose, a neighbor, and partook of fare similar to the previous evening's. She could not help but remember Reed's promise that she would celebrate Blue Duck's freedom over French snails and red wine.

In her physical and emotional exhaustion, her loneliness, Belle was only partly aware of Edgar Watson's presence in the yard. Everyone knew everyone else in the eastern Nations; friends were friendly with enemies, and enemies observed truces in the name of Christian forebearance. She recalled, as she saddled up for the ride home, that the men who had met to slay one another in Tombstone, Arizona, in 1881, had played a convivial game of poker the night before. This was too much complication for the dullards who wrote cheap novels, but was entirely in keeping with standards in the territories. In any case she considered Watson beneath contempt and outside serious consideration; the mere mention of Florida had been sufficient to bring him to heel. She jerked tight the cinch, mounted modestly to the side, and quirted her trusty whip across Venus' withers.

Her way led around Watson's poor farm, where a fence required her to detour through low scrub to pick up the road that led to Younger's Bend and her cabin, which stood one hundred fifty yards from Watson's house. A figure stood behind that fence as she passed. She gave it no heed other than to spur Venus into a lively trot.

The first charge struck her full in the back, tipping her from the saddle as the second raked her neck. She knew it for turkey shot, not nearly as heavy as the pellets meant for buck deer, but the force of it stunned her as she struggled to roll onto her back in the road. She knew from observation that people who fell on their faces invariably died in that position, like limp rags with one arm crumpled beneath them. The fire to survive burned fiercely within her.

Thus she had a full view of the killer who leapt the fence and poured a freshly reloaded barrel into her face and throat.

But the fire still burned. She was conscious when a neighbor brought Pearl to her mother's side many minutes after the shooter left her in a wallow of bloody mud. Belle managed to string syllables into one or two words that meant nothing to her listeners—*Open your ears!* she screamed in her skull; *Understand me!*—then coughed up a jiggerful of blood and sank into darkness.

Marshal John Carroll noted that Judge Parker moaned and closed his eyes when the word came in of Belle Starr's death. After deputies reported the details, he called for the detention of Edgar A. Watson, Belle's son Ed, and Jim July.

"Your Honor, July was on his way to Fort Smith when it happened."

"You of all people should know better than to underestimate these border raiders when it comes to hard riding. He could have doubled back, then dug in his spurs for town after the murder was done. Some men get to brooding over good advice from a woman when they're let alone."

For July's part, when the news arrived he procured a fresh mount, lathered it up clear back to the Canadian, threw down on Watson, and brought him in to jail himself. But the man never faced trial. Neighbors declined to testify against him at his hearing, and communications with Florida failed to produce a warrant for murder or any other felony. The charge was dropped, and July's action removed him from suspicion. No one was ever indicted in the death of Belle Starr.

Parker permitted himself a moment to remember a woman he would miss in his courtroom. Belle Starr had won the granite heart of Cole Younger, called Jesse James a hypocrite to his face, beaten justice in Fort Smith, yet withal maintained the outward appearance of a woman of culture; she'd read *The Iliad* in the earliest Latin translation, while Parker himself had struggled with Pope's popular version in English, ridden the High Country in the pirate tradition of Mary Read and Jeanne de Belville, and very nearly had shot the best prosecutor in the United States out from under his hat in full view of the citizens of Sebastian County; she had romanced a Texas banker, it was said, and left him with a thirty-thousand-dollar shortage in his books; a male citizen of the Cherokee Nation had been forced at the point of her gun to retrieve her hat when it blew off her head, which action she explained was a lesson in good manners. Belle had had her troubles with her grown children, as who had not, and brought two of the Eighth District's most infamous bandits to the hobble in Fort Smith. She had known how to reload at full gallop and which spoon to use when she stirred her tea. Parker's world was a more orderly place without her, and so much more drab. He wept.

IV

A FLAW IN THE SYSTEM

Revenge is a kind of wild justice, which the more man's nature runs to, the more ought law to weed it out.

—Francis Bacon

FIFTEEN

A hangman had feelings.

He was a man for all that, and fretted about bills and cracks in the cistern and whether he was a good husband and father. The pests who swarmed in to plumb his depths and make them public had paid entirely too much attention to the "hang" and none at all to the "man." But they were less than human themselves, and so when they came to call he filled his pipe and let them fondle his rope collection and dropped before them his pearls of wisdom burnished with Bavarian graveyard humor. "Haunted? No. I have never hanged a man who came back to have the job done over."

They took it all down like monkeys pretending to be stenographers and still managed to get it wrong. He read that he'd smiled grimly (a difficult expression to carry off; he'd tried before and his son had laughed at him) and said, "No, and if one ever came back to haunt me I'd hang 'em again." They compared his deep-set eyes to sockets in a bare skull; his beard was "noose-shaped," his build cadaverous. To a man they plundered the mortuary advertisements in their own newspapers for terms to characterize him. An editorial cartoonist in Baltimore had rendered a vile likeness in pen-and-ink, a humpbacked Reaper grinning in his hood with a pile of human bones at his feet; he'd thrown it in the fireplace before Annie could see it.

She'd been little then, and by God if he could turn back the clock he wouldn't hesitate.

It grieved George Maledon that his daughter had in all probability lost her innocence to the one young man in Fort Smith who did not fear him. Charles Parker was a self-loving dandy, and enjoyed an easy popularity among fellows of his own age that went no deeper than the white enamel on a wash basin, beneath which was brackish zinc. Under it they liked him no better than anyone else and professed friendship merely to declare independence of their disapproving parents. Their gibes, good-natured on the surface, bore an adumbration of contempt for themselves as well as for him. In that society, Charles alone was immune to self-loathing.

Fort Smith had grown beyond all prediction since Maledon had first set foot on the scaffold, but it was like an onion that had grown too swiftly by way of heavy unseasonal rains, with the outer layers wrapped loosely around the solid inner bulb, wherein resided the small rough town of 1875, where every citizen knew all the others and news of their least consequential actions was more current and reliable in the barbershop and around the barrel stove in the Mercantile than in the *Elevator* and the *Evening Call* combined; there, he had learned of his daughter's unchaste reputation. Young Charlie had claimed her virtue, then turned from her to fresh challenges, and rather than picking herself up from the dust and shaking it from her skirts she had continued to drag herself through it with whoever's son was willing, and with one or two who were no longer anyone's son, with wives and children Annie's own age at home. Saddle tramps she had had, half-caste Indians from the Nations, and men who had come to town to face Parker's justice for misdemeanors in the territories. She had wasted little time after her humiliation, with the result that when her father learned of her infamy, it was far too late to take a razor strop to her with any promise that it would raise any more than welts on her legs and sweat on his brow. He took it down from its hook above the basin, held it for a time, and returned it to its place, years older than when he had unhooked it.

"What did you expect?" asked his wife, when he confronted her. "Did you think she would come to you with her pain, you in your study with those nooses all around and pictures of the dead men whose necks you put them on?"

"It was the law did that. I only took out the suffering."

"Did you think the suffering began when you sent them through the trap?"

"Where is Annie?"

"I haven't seen her in days. How many days before that did you see her?"

He said no more. Since the day his wife had chucked his first tintypes and ropes down the well, he'd known it was impossible to argue with a woman on the basis of logic. You asked them a question and they responded by asking another that had no answer.

Disloyally—so he admitted to himself—he blamed his late wife for his daughter's beauty. Plain women had little to fear from predatory males, and had Annie inherited her father's bony brow or her stepmother's unornamental features instead of the wealth of black hair that glistened unfettered to her waist, the striking eyes and Cupid's-bow lips, the figure that needed no corset to lift the breasts and narrow the waist, she would have remained at home. She was also too intelligent for her gender, becoming aware at an early age that the woman whose responsibility it became to rear her from childhood cared more for their son, James; and that, together with her father's dread reputation that kept respectable suitors from their door, had forced her into the gravitational pull of young men whose histories demonstrated their lack of fear of the engine of justice he helped to maintain. Children brought up in divided households were rebellious by nature. What better way to declare one's independence than to take up with the enemies of domestic tranquility?

Of all his acquaintances, restricted as they were by circumstances to the officers of the Eighth District Court, there was one alone who might be expected to understand his plight and offer counsel. He put his forage cap in hand and called upon Judge Parker in his chambers.

Parker sat him down with the reserved cordiality he'd shown Maledon from their first meeting, in that same room so redolent with the memory of good cigars, disintegrating leather bindings, and the fading phantoms of sour mash and expectorated tobacco left by the conflicted men who had sat before him behind that great walnut desk. Reading his guest's expression with those eyes that had recorded the characters of a hundred or more defendants and hundreds more who had given evidence for and against them, the judge excused himself, and returned moments later with a stout bottle of brandy and two crystal glasses clutched in his hairless pink hand and poured them each two fingers of honey-colored liquid. Maledon, who read men as easily, and who as Parker's closest ally in the hundred years' war against chaos knew his host better even than William H. H. Clayton and the army of men who had ridden for him in the Nations, recognized this as an act without precedence. The brandy, of course, came from Mary Parker's own store, procured through the ladies' entrance to the House of Lords to bring on the sleep that would not come to her otherwise. The woman kept impossible standards, and would have been far more content wedded to a store clerk or a postal carrier, whose most important decisions did not involve the lives of men. The same was true of Maledon's own wife. He and Parker were twins from the same exacting mother, however much the judge feared and detested his chief executioner's proximity to the consequences of his pronouncements of sentence. Parker's fingers never touched their necks.

For all that, Maledon had spent less time in that room than anyone else in the district's service. There was the brief interview that had led to his promotion from turnkey to hangman, and two other confrontations, when he'd asked to be excused the abhorrent duty of hanging a fellow veteran of the Union Army, and when he'd rebelled against sacrificing his time with family to operate the gallows at night. (Much good that had done him.) Parker had agreed both times, handing the first assignment to a guard from the jail and postponing the second to a daylight hour. Parker was reason personified, distilled as purely as the spirits they shared upon this occasion. Parker for his part took a healthy sip in commemoration of the singular nature of the event; Maledon, whose lips had not brushed liquor since the early days of his service to the Army of the Potomac, dampened his moustache merely and left the remainder of the contents of his glass untasted.

"Annie—" He cleared his throat.

"Yes."

Parker, he now saw, with the rush of disillusion that comes to a disciple when the fog lifts and he sees his idol for a creature of clay, had invested all the penitence of a degraded sinner into that single syllable. In it his listener heard a paragraph of apology and confession. Charles Parker was a cross to be borne only by the lowest of God's creatures.

The silence that followed fell with the thud of a charge from a Confederate mortar. It was not to be borne, and so Parker filled it with a slap of his palm upon the stack of leather portfolios that made an impenetrable forest between him and the desk's inlaid top. Maledon did not deceive himself that the records there contained had direct application to the business at hand; it was symbolic of the towering evil that faced Fort Smith.

"Marshal Yoes's men keep a vigilant eye upon the recidivists who pass through this jurisdiction," Parker said. "I won't blaspheme so far as to say that I mark the sparrow's fall, but through them I flatter myself to say that I know rather more about what goes on in the district than the gentlemen of the press."

Maledon made no expression, his head tilted forward and his beard on his chest, as he learned that his daughter had been seen in company of late with a man named Frank Carver, at twenty-four her senior by six years. Parker's description, detailed and factual, painted a picture of the sort of young man who attracted the attention of impressionable girls: tall and slender, with barbered imperials and a taste for fine clothes, including the splendid boots that had led so often to covetousness and tragedy in the Nations, which was where he made his home. He spent money far too ostentatiously to have come by it through honest labor.

"What does he do?"

"He's pleased to call himself a gambler, but that isn't his only source of income." Parker turned his glass in its wet circle on the desk. His eyes remained on his guest. "He receives an annual allotment of eight hundred dollars from the Indian Bureau as a husband of a Cherokee with two children of Cherokee blood."

The hangman lowered his head another inch.

"His family's in Muskogee, where he's been arrested twice for possession of alcohol. His drink of choice is Jamaica ginger. You may have heard it called Ginger Jake. It's a scourge in the territory."

Maledon nodded. This was a flavoring extract obtained from ginger, intoxicating in the extreme and lethal if ingested in large quantities without diluting it with water. Banned in the territory, it was readily available across the Texas state line, where retailers and wholesalers proliferated, well aware that most of their customers transported their purchases back to the Nations for sale or personal consumption. Carver had been acquitted both times he'd been tried in Fort Smith; it was difficult to convince a jury, to whom the offense itself was a trifle, that a young man who presented so fine an appearance in court had anything in common with the sots who came through on that charge.

"Where are they now?"

"Charlie Burns, who checked Carver into the jail twice, saw them at the slip last week, waiting for the ferry. They could be anywhere in the eastern Nations by now, although I suspect not too close to where his wife and children are struggling to survive without their allotment."

"Can you send someone after them?"

Parker looked more uncomfortable yet. "At present, I've no sufficient cause to issue a warrant for Carver. Annie is past the age of consent in the State of Arkansas, so the white slavery laws don't apply. I've no doubt he's guilty of defrauding the United States by appropriating funds intended for wards of the government, but without evidence I can't authorize his arrest. Old friends in Congress are just waiting for me to make that kind of mistake. I am sorry, Mr. Maledon, truly I am."

Maledon combed his fingers through his whiskers, over and over. "I must go after them myself. If I talk to her I can make her see reason."

"You're sixty, and in no condition for such a journey. Where would you search? If you were fortunate enough to stumble upon them, Carver would be within his rights to send you away."

"You've forgotten I'm not exactly helpless without my ropes."

"Shooting down an escaping prisoner and shooting down a man in his own neighborhood are not the same thing. I should not want to sentence you to die on your own scaffold, but I will if you do murder, and there will be no phrases of comfort when I make the pronouncement. You are not a cold-blooded killer; you must disabuse yourself of that notion." The judge's expression had softened. Then it went flat. "In any case, your presence is needed in Fort Smith. There are four capital cases awaiting your attention." Parker hooked on his spectacles and opened one of the portfolios on the desk. They were acts of dismissal.

Maledon rose and went to the door.

"George."

In seventeen years, neither judge nor executioner had addressed the other by his Christian name. Maledon gripped the knob and waited.

"I'll direct Yoes to have his men maintain a weather eye for Carver and Annie. Some of them know the girl by sight, and his face is familiar in the Cherokee, but I'll see descriptions are provided. They can report how she is faring. She may get homesick in the meantime. Most runaways come back under their own volition."

Maledon left without responding. He spent the rest of the day on the scaffold, oiling the gears that operated the trap and inspecting the mortises and tenons for cracks and dry rot. He did not return home until after dark, and then he locked himself in his study without speaking to his wife. There in the company of his ropes and the faces of old customers he smoked pipe after pipe, filling the room with noxious vapors.

In March, John Thornton mounted the steps to the scaffold for the murder of his daughter in the Choctaw Nation, whom he had shot through the head, presumably in a fit of rage after she'd deserted him for a husband. The condemned man offered no words of explanation or farewell. When he dropped, the rope whizzed around his neck, the knot caught in the hollow behind and below the left mastoid, and blood geysered like water from a hydrant as the vertebra snapped clean through and the muscles of his neck, too weak to support his superincumbent weight, tore apart. Jerking, his body remained connected to his head by the tendons alone. Several officers of the court, who had reported to that enclosure many times to witness the fulfillment of sentence, never returned to see another. A few resigned. Thornton's coffin dripped blood from its seams as it was lowered into the Catholic cemetery.

George Maledon had not been present. Some said he'd refused to participate because Thornton had fought in the uniform of the Union, others that Parker's partner in punishment had lost his taste for the business. Said one, "That's like Old Scratch losing interest in snaring souls." Wagers were proposed, but no one offered to approach him for the truth, and nothing was to be gained by asking the judge to betray what went on in chambers. Deputy Marshal George S. White, whose inexperience while filling in for Maledon had produced the gory spectacle, pledged to adhere to his other duties henceforth.

Soon afterward, Fort Smith society learned that Annie Maledon and Frank Carver had left the Nations for far Colorado. No one knew just when the news had reached her father.

SIXTEEN

Eighteen ninety-two was a big year in the Nations. Apart from the scandalous flight of the Prince of Hangmen's only daughter, that twelvemonth witnessed the explosive end of the low comedy of Ned Christie's war, and in Coffeyville, across the Kansas state line, the annihilation of the Dalton Gang after three years of train robbery, some sixty thousand dollars spirited away from righteous hands, and the lowest casualty count of any of the desperate associations of the era.

The brothers—Bob, Grat, and Emmett—had first taken to the adventurous life in the service of Parker, riding with their eldest brother, Frank; then leapt the fence after whiskey smugglers slaughtered him from ambush in 1887. For a time, they had partnered with smugglers and rustlers while still wearing badges, but when warrants were issued in Fort Smith for their arrest, they fled to California, where they struck the Southern Pacific Railroad but failed to break open the safe in the depot. Back in the Nations—Oklahoma Territory, now, with Sooners busting clods on homesteads once divided among the Five Civilized Tribes—they took on four new members, including Bill Doolin, and carried away fourteen thousand dollars from the Santa Fe Limited at Wharton in the Cherokee Strip. Other raids took place in Lelietta, Red Rock, and Adair; their take now rivaled that of their distant cousins, Frank and Jesse James, who had been seventeen years at the enterprise, but that wasn't enough for leader Bob, a bucktoothed, jug-eared criminal mastermind shot through with the sin of vanity.

Under the influence of busthead whiskey, Bob proposed a shift from trains to banks, which he reasoned had the advantage of standing still, and added that an experienced band like theirs could split up and assault two such institutions at the same time, doubling the plunder and eclipsing the infamy of the James Gang forever. Moreover, he suggested Coffeyville, a town known to the brothers since infancy, as the place to benefit from their plunge into legend. He sobered up later, but having parried aside the others' arguments was reluctant to withdraw his scheme in the cold light of wisdom. His solution to the intelligent point that the residents of Coffeyville knew them as well as they knew Coffeyville involved false beards and farmers' overalls. The town met them in force with scatterguns and squirrel rifles and laid them out on a boardwalk to have their pictures taken. Emmett alone survived to begin a period of lengthy imprisonment in the Kansas State Penitentiary at Lansing. In Fort Smith, Judge Parker read the details in the telegraph column of the *Elevator* and put away early plans to hang three brothers at once.

His jurisdiction was shrinking. The new homesteads were part of the United States, with local magistrates put in place to adjudicate disputes and violations of the criminal code. Congress and the Supreme Court had assigned crimes among Indians to the tribal courts, which forced Parker's deputies to parse out complaints according to what constituted an Indian: full-blood, half, eighth, sixteenth? Mistakes were made, carrion-eaters of the J. Warren Reed stamp swooped, and the judge was brought to task in Washington. He accused the justices of splitting hairs, was quoted, and bitter invective circled about him under the Capitol dome. Open letters signed by Parker and officials in the U.S. Department of Justice appeared in the press. Reporters described the contretemps, borrowing colorful verbs and adjectives from the boxing columns. Washington whittled away at his fiefdom. Circuit courts were allowed to review all capital cases tried in the Eighth District, inserting yet another wedge between Isaac Parker and God Almighty. Colleagues helped themselves to cases that for years had gone directly to his desk, yet his docket grew no lighter: He mounted the bench every morning at eight, Monday through Saturday, and often did not descend from it until past midnight. The dark smudges beneath his eyes looked like bruises, the last brown hair on his head turned white as filament. He was fifty-three years old.

At home alone, her sons pursuing activities outside her ken, Mary Parker drank brandy to lay her cares to rest and bring on sleep. One bottle no longer lasted her a week.

Parker's men, led now by the legendary Three Guardsmen: Heck Thomas, Chris Madsen, and Bill Tilghman, rode through the Nations alongside the tumbleweed wagons and left them behind to scale the Winding Stair Mountains and the walls of Rabbit Trap Canyon, rooting out rapists and murderers and whiskey distillers, swapping lead with them, and occasionally stopping slugs. Those who failed to rise decorated the walls of Marshal Jacob Yoes's office with their likenesses.

And George Maledon worked oil into good Kentucky hemp

with his strong hands and waited for news of Annie and Frank Carver.

In Colorado, Carver found work on a cattle ranch. The wages were minimal, but he supplemented them by gambling, at which he was sufficiently adroit to show a profit without arousing the suspicions of his opponents, who tended to try suspected sharps on the evidence of circumstances alone and punish them, according to their humor or the charms of the defendant, on a scale with stripping and flogging at one end and lynching at the other. Aware of the delicacy of his situation, Carver drank in moderation and held Annie's interest with gifts and loyal attention. When after two years the ranch foreman was forced to cut personnel and Carver's luck at the tables turned bitter, the pair returned to the Cherokee Nation, where Frank boarded Annie with a colored woman eight short blocks of the house where his wife had taken in washing and sewing to support herself and their children; he did not return to his wife, however, hoping to persuade her to grant him a divorce on the grounds of desertion. This she refused to do, and since there was little honest work to be found in that vicinity and money that might otherwise have been spent at cards and dice went toward foodstuffs and house repairs, the pressure to provide income compelled Carver to ride the rails to Texas, preying upon passengers with friendly games of chance and spending most of what he won on Jamaica ginger in Texas.

Annie was not the sort of mistress who embroidered pillowcases in her man's absence and sold fresh-laid eggs to earn her board. She transferred bags and baggage to the home of another Frank, surnamed Walker, and there made sport with the Maledon name and the manly reputation of him who had forsaken respectable domesticity for her sake; so Carver regarded the situation, as Annie and Walker learned weeks later, when word reached them that Carver had returned.

In Fort Smith that season, the interruption in the Maledon family unit faded into the background as Parker considered that the Dalton episode had not so much come to an end as begun a new phase under the command of Bill Doolin, who had joined the gang in 1891 but had not been present in Coffeyville when it was torn apart a year later. While the bodies were still on display, and a surgeon was still plucking lead from Emmett Dalton, Doolin assembled a rich association of colorful nicknames in the persons of George "Bitter Creek" Newcomb, "Tulsa Jack" Blake, Oliver "Crescent Sam" Yountis, Richard "Little Dick" West, Roy "Arkansas Tom" Daughtery, George "Red Buck" Waightman, and two others, including Bill Dalton, eldest brother of the demolished family, who had forsaken the California legislature for the lure of his blood after Coffeyville had destroyed his hopes for high office. These lurid appelations crimsoned many a gray column and Western Union bulletin board as banks and trains fell to assaults throughout Kansas and the newly minted Oklahoma Territory.

But these were not the Nations of memory, where a desperado might reasonably expect to retard the consequences of his calling in the wild scrub of the Cookson Hills and the root cellars of neighbors who still held the United States to account for the Trail of Tears. The great Land Rush of 1889 had introduced thousands of white settlers into the extremities of the Eighth District, who tore up the scrub for potatoes and built ricks to store corn, not fugitives. Among them was a thirty-eight-year-old former Iowan named William Matthew Tilghman.

Tall and rangy, with swooping moustaches and eyes that went from kind to vengeful as quickly as clouds slid away from the sun, Tilghman had shot buffalo at eighteen, served as a deputy sheriff under the legendary Charlie Bassett in Dodge City at twenty-three, and divided the next ten years between his ranch near Fort Dodge and a succession of positions keeping the peace in the roughest cowtown in Kansas. When Oklahoma opened to homestead, he'd quit his job of city marshal and staked out several lots in Guthrie, whose quickly expanding population elected him marshal. Two years later he laid aside that badge and took up the simple six-sided star of deputy U.S. marshal under Jacob Yoes and Judge Isaac C. Parker.

Tilghman's experience needed tempering yet, for the territory retained a vivid sense-memory of untamed wilderness; Ned Christie was not long in his grave, and in many districts the quality of a man's boots was worth more than his life. Heck Thomas, who had failed to apprehend Christie but had since sacrificed marriage and family to the service of Parker, taught the new man the basics of manhunting in hostile country. An ordered, military approach to what amounted to enemy lines came courtesy of forty-one-year-old Chris Madsen, who had served in the Danish Army, the French Foreign Legion, and the United States Fifth Cavalry, with which he had ridden into the Battle of Warbonnet Creek and covered Buffalo Bill Cody while he slew Chief Yellow Hand and tore from his head the first scalp for Custer in 1876. A hard man with flint in his beard, a plug in his cheek, two grown children, and already a string of dead fugitives in his portfolio in Fort Smith, Madsen bridled only when younger deputies addressed him as "Pops," cuffing their ears hard enough to make them ring and unleashing a string of Scandinavian curses. His Danish accent became pronounced when he was excited, which he almost never was; a quickening of his jaws as he chewed was for those who knew him a clear indication that the moment was tense. He was a chief deputy, and even Thomas called him "Mr. Madsen." (Parker, practically a contemporary, hailed him by his Christian name.)

The people of the Nations would come to know them as the Three Guardsmen: Madsen, hard and silent on the trail; Thomas, eyes bright when he caught the scent of human prey; Tilghman, easy in his manner but cat-swift in his reflexes. A trio of killers.

In the spring of 1893, the Doolin Gang raided a bank at Spearville, Kansas, divided the plunder, and split up to hide out until posse fever passed. Entering the Cherokee Strip, Crescent Sam Yountis lost the use of his exhausted mount, challenged a farmer riding a fresh bay to surrender his animal, and blasted him off its back when he demurred. The bandit caught the reins before the horse could bolt, vaulted into the saddle, and galloped on to his sister's farm.

The killing took place near Guthrie, where Heck Thomas and Chris Madsen rode circuit for the federal court. Madsen knew all the farms in the vicinity. He collected Thomas, laid siege to the farmhouse, and shot Yountis with a Winchester when he emerged from the house and fired at Thomas, who kicked the revolver from the dying man's hand as he struggled to rise.

"Too damn bad I didn't get you," Yountis said.

"You came close enough, py golly." Madsen put his boot heel on Yountis' throat and held it there until he finished struggling.

The gang struck a Santa Fe express in Cimarron soon after, and bettered the Daltons' final adventure by dividing its ranks and holding up two trains simultaneously at Wharton. This,

Parker reflected, represented a new phase in frontier outlawry: the drive, beyond mundane material gain, to make one's own mark on the historical record and imitate in life the swashbucklery that incarnadined the popular press. Frequently, tardy raids upon hideouts abandoned by wanted men, and saddle pouches confiscated from captured bandits, yielded small libraries of tattered paperbound novels with whole sensational passages underscored heavily in pencil; blueprints for adventures yet to be undertaken, and the bar raised to first-column level. When Charley Pierce, a charter member of the Doolins, was recognized and shot to death by fellow hands on the ranch where he was hiding out, his pockets were found to be stuffed with yellowed cuttings from Texas and Arkansas newspapers chronicling the gang's depredations. Over a cup of tea while addressing one of his wife's social clubs in Fort Smith, Parker remarked drolly that it was just a matter of time before some progressive band of border ruffians applied to St. Louis for a press agent. Only Mary Parker, who maintained a barometer of her husband's passions, detected the depth of his despair over the public lionization of the element he had sworn to banish from his jurisdiction.

In September 1893, the Doolins cut loose at thirteen deputy U.S. marshals surrounding a house where they'd holed up near Ingalls. The return fire shattered windows, knocked shingles off their hinges, killed a goat, and shot away the front door, but three deputies were killed and all but two of the gang got away: Arkansas Tom, who surrendered, and a teenage prostitute named Jennie Stevens, whose horse Bill Tilghman shot out from under her as she leapt a fence toward freedom. The tiny Stevens and a friend, Annie McDougal, had been selling their favors to the Doolins for months, donning male dress to act as lookout during some robberies and stealing eggs and chickens to feed them when they were in hiding. Tilghman, exasperated at the size of his catch, spanked Stevens over his knee before placing her in custody. After a bank in Pawnee gave up ten thousand dollars to her friends, he and Steve Burke, another Parker deputy, captured McDougal, but not before she'd shredded Burke's face with her nails, knocked off his hat, and torn tufts of hair from his scalp.

"Little bitches," said Burke, upon depositing her in the women's quarters of the Fort Smith jail beside Jennie Stevens. A reporter overheard and, either misunderstanding him or in deference to decorous editorial policy, dubbed the dwarfish Stevens "Little Britches." Not to be outdone, his colleagues anointed McDougal "Cattle Annie," and the pair enjoyed a brief scarlet vogue in half-dime novels before history lost interest. Parker damned the Fourth Estate for making romantic figures out of petty thieves and cheap harlots.

The comedy was light enough, and too much so for the grim record. In one afternoon in Ingalls, the Doolin Gang had slain more men than the Daltons had managed to do in three years, and in the same gesture slaughtered more peace officers than the Jameses and Youngers combined. Parker raged at his new marshal, George J. Crump. The rewards mounted.

The gang spread out. It slew a sheriff during a robbery in Canadian, Texas; an auditor in a bank in Southwest City, Missouri (witnesses identified Bill Dalton, reformed politician, as his murderer); and returned to Dover, Oklahoma Territory, robbing the Rock Island line and shooting to pieces several innocent bystanders during the getaway. Rumor held that Red Buck was mustered out of the association for this atrocity; casualties among noncombatants played hell with romantic legend. (In Thieves' Valhalla, Jesse James played faro with Belle Starr and chuckled, stopping the holc in his head with a palm to preserve the resonance.) After Tulsa Jack was stricken dead on that ride, and Bitter Creek Newcomb and Charley Pierce fell victim to reward-conscious ranch hands, the gang was decimated. Raids spread as far as California and Iowa would be laid at its door in reporters' desperate attempts to stretch the gravy, but their editors grew restless; it was true that they wrote for morons, but morons had been known to rebel, as witness the election of Benjamin Harris to the office of president, which error had been rectified by the return of Grover Cleveland. With more pressing news streaming in from economic panic in the East and the Spanish situation in the Caribbean, and nothing fresh from the vanishing Nations, the name Doolin slipped to the inside pages, then away.

But Bill Doolin was still at large, and his final chapter would be the strangest of all, although none would know its truth for many years.

George Maledon followed the saga listlessly in the company of the dead men who shared his tiny study. His interest in criminal activity in the Nations, which he had once kept track of as avidly as a farmer tracing the path of a blight that would one day be his personal concern, had evaporated, and with it his zeal for his profession. He began to consider retirement. Then in the spring of 1895, three years since Annie had left the shelter of his roof, his wife came to him in his study to say that his daughter had been brought to St. James Hospital in Fort Smith with a bullet in her spine.

SEVENTEEN

In the Nations, Ginger Jake was known as the Great Divider: You never knew how it would affect a man under its influence, or indeed if it would affect the same man twice the same way.

Sometimes, the distillate made the drinker more the way he was when sober, creating a kind of caricature. If he was angry and given to violent outbursts, it might make him react to the smallest slight with savage blows or a weapon; if he was gentle and good-humored, he might meet the vilest insult with a jest or an offer to buy a drink for his calumniator.

At other times, a complete reversal of personality was the result. Many of the men who employed the opportunity of George Maledon's scaffold to deliver oratories on the pernicious poison of strong drink and women of ill fame before they swung were by reputation God-fearing men of good conduct who had turned bestial on the authority of Jamaica ginger. A number of their fellows had lost their lives refusing to defend themselves against assailants, imagining themselves to be more peaceful men than they were when sober, and trusting in all mankind.

Frank Carver, soft-spoken and clean in his habits, liked by men and admired by women, belonged to the most dangerous category, a changeling who depending upon the amount drunk, the strength of the mix, and the phase of the moon, might laugh off an injurious remark or horsewhip a stranger he suspected was talking about him behind his back on no evidence at all. Those who had seen him on benders had learned to give him distance or flutter on his perimeter, waiting to see which way the frog jumped before pressing their acquaintance. However, this last course was perilous, because his mood was likely to shift with the speed of a striking snake, but with less warning. There were men in Texas who could confirm that, if their shattered jaws didn't get in the way of their speech, and a divorced woman in Okmulgee with a scar that pulled her face out of line when she tried to smile.

Most of what went into the record about Carver's last meeting with Annie Maledon came directly from the written statement she had dictated before she died, eleven weeks after a round from his revolver lodged in the soft tissue of her spine, where no surgeon could get to it without causing more damage. Her last days had been spent in a state of semiconsciousness, with morphine in her veins to ease her passing over.

Carver, she said, returned from Texas while she was in residence with Frank Walker, a man known to them both, and called upon her there several times when Walker was out. Harsh words were spoken, resulting twice in threats against her life if she did not come away with him. Annie explained that by this time her former lover was in a state of constant inebriation, and that she feared to be with him, as she had seen how quickly his humor could change from affable to morose. The most frightening thing about him in this condition, she said, was that he managed to walk straight and speak without slurring under circumstances that would have reduced a man of much greater height and bulk to a gibbering idiot without a rudder; one had to know him as intimately as she to recognize the hazard.

On the night of March 25, 1895, Carver sent word to meet him on the east side of the tracks belonging to the Missouri, Kansas, and Texas Railroad in Muskogee; the note informed her that he was leaving for Texas forever and that it was the last time she would see him. She suspected his motives, but was reluctant to ignore the invitation and give him cause to change his mind. However far she had drifted from the lessons of home and family, she still prayed every night, beginning with the prayer that Carver would go away and never return. She persuaded Frank Walker to accompany her to the assignation.

Carver's appearance under the light of a tallow streetlamp reassured them both. He never failed to put on a fresh collar, drunk or sober, but his boots shone, his coat was brushed and pressed, his whiskers trimmed, and for the first time in weeks the whites of his eyes were clear. Annie leaned forward from the waist just far enough to smell the sweet scent of the pine needles Carver used to pick his teeth, and determine that there was no liquor on his breath. She satisfied herself that he had broken the shackles once again and nudged Walker, who stepped forward and shook Carver's hand.

The three agreed to bless Carver's departure with a last night on the town. In the first place they stopped, Carver immediately began drinking, and as they moved on to the next, Annie clung closer to Walker, who curled his arm around her waist comfortingly; he did not know the man well enough to recognize the signs of moral disintegration hidden beneath his clear speech and steady step. While leaving the third house of notorious reputation, Carver leaned close to Annie and whispered in her ear: "Honey, you're done for tonight. I'm going to kill you before morning."

"What did he say?" asked Walker, when she clutched his arm.

Carver produced a heavy-barreled revolver from beneath his waistcoat and fired it into the air.

"None of that, Frank," Walker said. "You'll have the Cherokee Lighthorse on us all."

Carver grinned and returned the revolver to his belt. They walked another square. Then he jerked out the weapon and fired twice at a streetlamp. The second bullet came closest, brushing the flame. When Walker opened his mouth to protest, Carver leveled the revolver at Annie, who whimpered and turned into the other man's arms. There was another report and she shuddered and sagged in Walker's embrace.

Carver fled, but returned moments later as a crowd gathered around the young woman lying in the street with Walker supporting her head with a hand. "Oh, Annie, are you dead?" cried Carver. "Who has done this?" Then he ran away again.

Annie Maledon's former lover was arrested that night in the home he was once again sharing with his wife and children and removed in shackles to Fort Smith, with the deputies in escort speculating aloud as to whether George Maledon would attend to his humanitarian duty or let Carver strangle; George White, whose blunder while serving in Maledon's capacity had led to the beheading of John Thornton, described that affair and said he wondered which was more distressing for the man in the noose. Carver arrived in Fort Smith pale and shrunken in his restraints.

Frank Walker had not been seen since the night of the slaying; rumors insisted he had a wife in Texas and had likely returned to her, but no one knew the address or if he lived there under the same name. While the prosecution was preparing its case, Carver's brother and other relatives pooled their resources and retained J. Warren Reed to plead for the defense.

In the years since his successful fight on behalf of Belle Starr's lover, Blue Duck, Reed had if anything adopted more resplendence in his dress, with velvet facings on his lapels and ornaments of fraternal affiliations dangling like tiny scalps from his watch chain; his girth had increased as well, and he had foresworn at last the discomfort of a corset. His persistent preference for clawhammer coats caused the citizens who saw him strutting the boardwalks brandishing his gold-headed stick to remark upon the way his backside thrust out his tails like a rooster's. These same observers gossiped that his remarkable wife, Viola, who had studied for the bar in West Virginia but had been balked by the barricade of her gender, was the more accomplished lawyer of the pair, and that without her application and counsel, the popinjay whose very name turned Judge Parker's gaze glacial would still be defending chicken thieves in the Appalachians. But Parker himself, while enjoying this assessment, knew it to be unfair; Reed was an aggressive debater, predatory in the extreme, and a polished thespian whose stage was the courtroom. He could charm and repel by turns, and in so doing deflect attention from the evidence most damaging to his client.

Before 1889, the Reeds of the world had been helpless against Parker's suzerainty. With no fixed system of appeal in place, the judge could turn the stampede over the facts with a snap of his gavel, a threat to consign the transgressor to the basement dungeon for contempt, and what amounted to a directed conviction during his instructions to the jury. But Washington had cut the ballocks off the old bull; such tactics were grounds for reversal, and Reed, who knew he stood no chance in Parker's court the first time around, had but to goad the old man into committing a judicial indiscretion that would earn a second trial. A baseball enthusiast, the attorney was determined to keep fouling off pitches until he wore down the fellow on the mound and belted one deep into fair territory. That had been his strategy throughout his first seven years in practice in Fort Smith, and of the 134 men he had represented in capital cases, only two had hanged. The rest had been discharged during preliminary examination, acquitted by juries, or had their sentences reduced or commuted by order of authorities higher than Parker. The letter signed by President Cleveland ordering Blue Duck's pardon hung in a frame in Reed's office opposite a steel lithograph of the martyred Abraham Lincoln.

In Walker's absence, conviction depended heavily upon the deathbed statement of the victim. Reed here was in his element: As handy as Blue Duck's isolation had proven in structuring his pardon, he valued even more the testimony of an eyewitness who could be cross-examined without its author offering a word in rebuttal. He went to work on the several inconsistencies in the rambling, agonized text, drew numerous objections from the prosecution, sustainments and warnings from the bench, and made copious notes for his request for appeal of the verdict and sentence he fully anticipated. The prosecution, less savage following the retirement of William H. H. Clayton in favor of a judgeship in the new central district in McAlester, was vigorous nonetheless, and the jury voted to convict. On July 9, Parker sentenced Carver to hang on the first day of October.

Throughout the proceedings, George Maledon, who seldom

attended court, sat in the gallery, keeping his own counsel and directing his sunken gaze toward the back of the head of the man who sat at the defense table beside Reed. He was among the first to leave when the verdict was announced.

Fort Smith society, which convened without exception to retry all of Parker's cases in the Silver Dollar, the brothels on First Street, and the sewing circles on Garrison, pondered over whether Maledon would set aside his professional considerations and select common balers' twine and a shoddy choke-knot for the man who had stolen his daughter's innocence (this against anecdotal evidence to the contrary) and her life, so excruciating in its prolonged withdrawal, with spinal fluid staining the winding-sheets; but it had underestimated the depth of his dedication to the machinery of justice. He determined on using virgin rope, and rejected two shipments of Kentucky hemp that he pronounced substandard because of heavy rains during the growing season before deciding upon the third. His discrimination in this detail rivaled those of connoisseurs of French wine, who knew vineyards and their climate with biblical scholarship. The fibers that would separate Frank Carver from this pale would be the finest in Western agriculture, and the measure of pitch and linseed as precise as a chemist's when preparing a purgative for a close family member. Like Parker, whose reversals and disappointments had honed his judicial decisions to a razor's edge, America's Executioner was devoted to the highest principles in this personal affair. He applied these same attentions to the scaffold, ordering the replacement of certain joints that appeared quite servicable on the surface and supervising the sanding down of the finish by convict labor and the application of a fresh coat of whitewash.

The infamous scaffold had by this time acquired a slant roof to protect it from rain. When viewed from behind in its high enclosure, it resembled nothing more sinister than a storage building for harnesses or grain. The black scars of that vengeful bolt of lightning at its inauguration had long since been concealed by cosmetic attention. Parker's Tears had never looked more decorous.

These attentions were lost on the Supreme Court, whose members had not forgotten the injuries inflicted upon it in public by the pen of the man in charge of the Eighth District Court. They reviewed Reed's writ of error, pared to the basics by the coolheaded Viola, considered the implications of a sentence of death carried out by the father of the victim in the case, reversed Parker, and granted the defendant a new trial. Smelling blood, Reed launched a fresh attack on four points of conflict in Annie's statement, and this time secured a victory more apparent to him than to most of those who followed the trial: While the first jury had voted in favor of Carver's execution after four short hours, the second required two full days of deliberation before agreeing upon a verdict of murder in the first degree.

Maledon, frustrated only by the protraction of justice, restretched his rope, dismantled, cleaned, and reassembled the gears that operated the trap, and made the mistake of confiding to an acquaintance that he was looking forward to this execution. The remark reached Reed, who conveyed it to certain supernumeraries with the ear of higher powers in the system. Meanwhile he filed a second writ of error. A third trial was granted. The additional time enabled the attorney for the defense to assemble a set of witnesses who offered testimony confirming Annie Maledon's faithlessness to most of the virtues. This jury ruled in favor of murder in the second degree and recommended life imprisonment.

At the sentencing, Parker hesitated, fingering his gavel, and was seen to review his prepared remarks, sliding his spectacles up and down his nose as if the words he himself had written were foreign to him; which in fact they were. He was weary, visibly so, he had a pain in his belly and a heart that beat all out of cadence with the consistency of his moral principles. Each new reversal of his decisions had plagued him with the unfamiliar malady of second thoughts and self-doubt. At length he tightened his grip on the handle his palm had polished to a high gloss, ruled in favor of the advice of the jurors, and commended Frank Carver to the custody of the penitentiary in Columbus, Ohio, for the rest of his natural life. The gavel cracked.

George Maledon that day petitioned Judge Parker for his retirement. The request was granted. After a brief attempt at the grocery business in Fort Smith, where his wife kept the books and wrapped the customers' purchases with care, he bought an eighty-acre farm in Fayetteville, Arkansas; but Mother Nature proved as harsh a partner as the justice system, and he gave his acreage to the weeds and joined a carnival tour. There in a tent not much larger than his study, he exhibited his collection of ropes and tintypes and made his case for the certainty of punishment in a scripted speech cribbed largely from Parker's comments to the press and accepted questions from his audience. Spiritualism was in the ascendant; most of his interviewers were curious about the shades of the men he had slain. He combed his fingers through his beard and said that if any of them were disposed to return, he would simply hang them again.

Back home, his wife and son turned away reporters asking for details of human interest about the domestic life of a celebrated hangman. They said there was nothing of interest, and pressed shut their door.

V

A PROMISE TO PUNISH

That virtue is her own reward, is but a cold principle.

—Sir Thomas Browne

EIGHTEEN

"Which Cherokee Bill is this? It seems to me this court encounters one every couple of months." Judge Parker trayed his cigar to review the request for a warrant.

"The worst of the lot so far," said Colonel Crump. "His right name's Crawford Goldsby. It stands to reason 'Cherokee Crawford' didn't answer, though he could claim 'Greaser Bill' and be closer the mark. There's Mexican and Sioux in his blood, and I'm told his mother was black as Jed's boot. There's Cherokee on her side, too, but it'd bleed out if he were to nick his little toe. He looks like he ought to be butchering chickens in Nogales."

"I didn't inquire into his ancestry. He rides with the Cook brothers. I was under the impression we had them on the run." Parker paged back and forth through the record. Crump's reports were closely written and maddeningly chronological, a product of his army training.

The marshal, a second-term Cleveland appointee who had succeeded Jacob Yoes, adjusted his beard the way another man might straighten his necktie. He put more pride in his military background than in his present spoils position, and Parker considered him competent, although he had a prejudice against him for replacing George Winston, who had served the court as bailiff since before Parker's own appointment, with a Democrat. He suspected Crump distrusted Negroes, and therefore that he harbored disloyal opinions of the judge as a carpetbagger.

"Jim's in custody in Tahlequah," Crump said, "or was. The word is he escaped, but God help the white man who tries for a straight answer from the Cherokee courts when they soil their britches. Brother Bill's still at large. The posse that took Jim lost a man; Goldsby's tagged with that killing. That's neither here nor there, since he was Lighthorse and it's Indian jurisdiction, but Goldsby's a rotten little egg of eighteen. They say he shot his first man over a woman at a dance."

"In Fort Gibson, I see. The man recovered." Now came details of Goldsby's adventures with the Cooks and their band. "Chicken. Dynamite Dick. The Verdigris Kid. I wish these fellows read something other than *Ned Buntline's Own*. Why haven't I heard of Goldsby before this?"

"Up to now it's been by guess and by God. There was the man at the dance, who pulled through, and any of a half dozen Cherokee Bills might have been responsible for that Lighthorse affair. A conductor named Collins on the Katy Flyer took one through the heart because Goldsby forgot to buy a ticket, but go find a coach passenger who'll admit he saw anything if it means coming to Fort Smith. This time, though, we've got Cherokee Bill's own word for what happened in Lenapah."

Bill Cook kept a loose hitch on his brother Jim's gang. Two members, thought to be Cherokee Bill and the Verdigris Kid, cut out to rob Schufeldt & Son, a store and post office in that busy town in the Cherokee. The Kid laid down fire outside to discourage interference while Cherokee Bill ordered John Schufeldt to open the safe. When the man in the street called for shells, his partner searched the store, spotted a curious housepainter named Ernest Melton peering through a window on the alley, and shot him in the face. The bandit then filled his pockets with money from the safe and fled on horseback with the Kid.

Crump thudded a finger on a passage in his report, attributed to deputies W. C. Smith and George Lawson: *An informant in our employ, acting upon instructions, sought out "Cherokee Bill," who said, "I had to kill a man at Lenapah."*

Parker signed the warrant, and a petition calling for a reward of $1,300 from the Justice Department for the capture or death of Crawford Goldsby, *alias* Cherokee Bill. The request was granted, as he knew it would be; Crump had recently traveled to Washington to plead his case with Attorney General Richard Olney to encourage public cooperation in bringing an end to such as the Cooks, and the Department of the Interior had become involved in the interest of establishing a territorial government. A pen-and-ink likeness of the bandit drawn from witness descriptions appeared in train stations and telegraph offices throughout Arkansas, Texas, and the Nations: Cherokee Bill's broad Hispanic face and flat negroid features peered out from beneath the broad flat brim of a pinch hat.

"If these efforts fail," Olney had announced, "it is assumed that the military will be called into requisition."

Parker glowered at the suggestion. To Crump he said, "These United States have entered a new chapter: We no longer declare war on countries, only men."

"Whatever help we get is all to the good."

"The difficulty is in persuading it to leave once it's served its purpose."

The judge authorized wires enlisting the aid of the Cherokee Lighthorse and the Indian police in the Choctaw, Creek, Seminole, and Chickasaw nations and on the Osage reservation, and drafted a personal invitation to the directors of the Rock Island, Santa Fe, and Missouri, Kansas, and Texas railroads to lend their detectives to the cause. These men responded swiftly and in the affirmative. With Crump's deputies placed on alert, some five hundred men had joined the hunt. It had taken only seventeen to run Ned Christie to ground. This time, at least, there would be no cannons.

The killing in Lenapah had shifted Cherokee Bill's accomplices to the background, with $250 offered for each, dead or alive. Deputy W. C. Smith, who had helped connect the bandit to the murder through his own words, remarked to his partner, George Lawson, that the price of shooting housepainters had risen steeply since he'd come to the territory.

When a small party of manhunters crossed Bill's path and shot his horse out from under him, Bill took to the scrub on foot—and vanished. They tracked him until his trail doubled back on itself, then gave up the chase. Stories of his Sioux blood got into the newspapers, a biography ran many columns, attributing more killings to its subject than to the Doolins and Daltons combined. Writers in the East borrowed from it heavily to fill out space between garish paper covers. With all the hostile tribes subjugated, popular fiction in the 1890s turned toward road agents and guerrillas. By Christmas 1894, Cherokee Bill was nearly as well known as Kris Kringle.

A trio of Cook associates was surrounded by deputies and Indian police outside Sapulpa. Two were killed and a third was taken to Fort Smith and tried with another man captured during the robbery of a bank in Chandler. Parker sentenced them to ten to fifteen years in the Detroit House of Corrections.

The rest of the gang migrated west, away from their pursuers, but not in such haste they failed to attend to business. In the Seminole Nation, they waylaid a family of German settlers on their way to Tecumseh, robbed the father of his money and a gold watch, stole the horse from the wagon, and raped the man's daughter. The hunt for Cherokee Bill had improved communications; deputies trailing the gang from the scene of the atrocity wired the Texas Rangers, who captured three members near Wichita Falls without firing a shot and held them until the deputies arrived to remove them to Fort Smith. Parker sent one man to Detroit for thirty years and the others for twenty years apiece. Some who witnessed the proceedings muttered that the judge was mellowing.

"He's saving his teeth for Cherokee Bill," said one.

The rumor furnace was stoked and putting out heat. Cherokee Bill had raped the girl; Cherokee Bill was nowhere near the Seminole at the time of the assault, but was robbing a train at Red Ford; Cherokee Bill was taking a holiday in Nowata, openly courting a girl named Maggie Glass. It was a signal of a desperado's rise to stature that the laws of space and time presented him with no greater challenge than those of man. Few who followed his adventures could encompass the fact that neither his name nor his alias had yet appeared in print scant months earlier. The stuff of legend now traveled at the speed of Morse code.

He was, in fact, in none of the places attributed to him at the time of the Seminole incident, but sleeping long hours under the attic roof of a farmhouse near Talala. Neighbors who remembered the farm's first ownership referred to it as the Frank Daniels place. There, Bill found cartridge-loading equipment and sent his sister, Maude, who worked the farm with her husband, George Brown, into town to secure powder. Brown, a wolf-lean man several inches taller than his guest, had during their tenancy established the house as a regular stop on the local whiskey peddler's route. When Brown's store ran out before the peddler's return, he saw giant rabbits for a time, then after the shakes passed grew quiet and relatively amiable; Bill during these periods considered him better company than he'd been running with, and the pair smoked and swapped stories on the front porch evenings when the wind didn't blow from the north while Maude washed the supper things inside. It was only when the peddler had come and gone and Brown made up for lost time that the farmer lost his affability and made cutting remarks, usually at his wife's expense but sometimes at Bill's; the recurring complaint was that his brother-in-law considered him a hotelier, and slept all day "like a hog" and kept Brown up all night with his bullet-rammer chunking directly above the bedroom where the Browns rested. "How many shells does a man need to defend an attic?"

Cherokee Bill's host was not the only one to take note of his nocturnal activities. In Talala, Deputy Lawson, who knew Bill's sister lived nearby, had spread money around town against information on any change in the Browns' routine; he had aspirations regarding collateral rewards offered for the fugitive dead or alive, but found business too confining to stake out the farm. Informed of Maude's recent black-powder purchases, he wired Tahlequah for reinforcements from the Cherokee Lighthorse for a raid on the homestead.

Brown's sneering remarks seemed to have no effect on his houseguest. In the days before his infamy, Crawford Goldsby had been thought by some a typical dumb greaser, and probably a coward. The vilest insult to his face made no change in his expression and brought no retribution. These witnesses had not been present when Bill was with his sister, his confidante in the early years when his father took out his mixed-blood miseries on the only other masculine member of the household, first with his belt, then when Crawford grew too large to present his backside without protest, his fists. When Brown grew weary of trying to get a rise out of Cherokee Bill and took a horsewhip to Maude over the matter of an overcooked ham, Bill dusted the black powder from his palms, loaded his revolver with six newly minted rounds, stuck it under his belt in back, and went downstairs.

He found his sister curled into a fetal position in the corner next to the stove and Brown standing over her, panting like a hound, the whip dangling from his hand, exhausted from his exertions and sweating pure skullbender from every pore; he smelled like a still in ninety-degree heat. Streaks of blood stained Maude's dress where the lash had shredded the material.

"George, let's go out for a smoke."

Brown looked at him, his features stupid. He appeared to take a moment to recognize Bill. "I'm fresh out. You smoked everything in the house but the rat shit in the potato bin."

"I've got cigars." Bill patted his shirt pocket.

"What'd you do, steal 'em? You spent every penny you stole on whores. I ought to've put Maudie out on the line herself for all the use she is around here." But he dropped the whip and started toward the door. He had one foot on the porch when Bill drew the revolver and shot him in the back of the head.

Maude screamed and began blubbering widow's incoherencies.

Bill went to a cupboard, emptied a coffee jar of household cash, reached down to pat her shoulder, saddled up his horse in the barn, and rode hard for the Cimarron with his saddle pouches full of fresh cartridges. It really was a shame what she'd done to a fine Arkansas ham.

The new year of 1895 was barely a month old when the story, reported widely in newspapers as far east as Chicago, was retold in *Cherokee Bill's Gamble,* in which the Bandit Prince shot a stranger's cruel husband in a fair fight and upended a bank bag filled with greenbacks onto the woman's kitchen table before taking his leave.

Deputy Lawson, in the company of the Cherokee Lighthorse, had found Maude Goldsby Brown seated hollow-eyed at that same table, bare but for a worn oilcloth cover, with a dead man on the porch under a rug to discourage flies. He borrowed a shovel to bury George Brown while the Indian policemen watched, smoking and retelling old jokes in Cherokee.

Cherokee Bill's story so overshadowed that of the Cooks', the worst gang ever to plague the Nations until the coming of Rufus Buck, that when Jim Cook resurfaced, years after the capture and imprisonment of his brother Bill, journalists suffered his company only to ply him with questions about Cherokee Bill, who had joined the band too late for Jim Cook to offer any recollection of him. In the early years of the twentieth century, Jim formed an alliance with Al Jennings, an Oklahoma train robber recently released from custody, to film a series of fanciful photoplays about the wild days on the border, only to be cast out of the company for his inability to embroider upon historical fact. He passed from the record, penniless and forgotten.

Cherokee Bill, it was said, traveled with a small library of his exploits, seasoned like a cookbook with exclamation points and purple adjectives; he'd grown up reading similarly embellished accounts of Ned Christie's vendetta and took almost carnal pleasure in his own ascension into that company. In the meantime he'd taken his amusement at the expense of banks, stores, a train or two, and the odd complacent traveler, and made sport of the humorless men who gathered, heavily armed, to write his final chapter.

Judge Parker, who maintained a close watch on everything that appeared about events that took place in the Nations, expressed little outrage over the distortions in *Cherokee Bill's Gamble.* By the time he learned of them, Cherokee Bill was in the Fort Smith jail awaiting justice.

NINETEEN

The new courtroom reminded some visitors of a giant humidor, wainscoted four feet high all around, with stout rails separating the gallery from the proceedings, straightback chairs for the jury, a paneled box for witnesses beside the judge's high bench, and pews polished by the shoulder blades and backsides of those who sat to spectate, bored and mesmerized by turns by the inexorably turning gears of justice. The furlongs of polished oak smelled strongly of furniture oil, which on hot days when the slow swoop of the electric ceiling fan failed to stir the heavy air blended with sweat and the stench of mothballs from woolen suits just out of storage.

Others compared the place to a church, and the analogy was not inept. For all the men who had been removed from that insular chamber to the new federal jail, there to await their appointments with George Maledon on the old scaffold, and the men and women who had been escorted from there in manacles to trains bound for penetentiaries in Michigan, Ohio, Illinois, and Little Rock, there were nearly as many stories of innocence established, wrongs reversed, families reunited, and unions sanctified: Parker had performed weddings there and at his home. Accounts of these happy occasions found their way into the social columns of the *Elevator* and the *Evening Call*, but died on the telegraph wires between Fort Smith and the newspapers in the East, where multiple executions boosted readership far more dependably, although not so much as in the days when the engine of the law had chugged away in the old military barracks; with the escalating situation with wicked Spain in Cuba and the Philippines, America had begun to fancy itself a world power, and business was more pressing from the eastern half of the globe. The Shah of Persia was dead by an assassin's hand, the British were mired in the Sudan, the Turks were slaughtering Armenians in gross lots in Constantinople. The Hanging Judge seemed as quaint as knee breeches.

Nevertheless the scaffold was maintained in working condition. Mollie King, who with two of her lovers had murdered and buried her husband, Ed, in the Cherokee Nation, had been found guilty and scheduled to hang, but as her four female predecessors had had their sentences commuted or their cases pardoned, and J. Warren Reed had taken up her standard, Parker doubted he'd be executing a woman that season. Still other cases considered settled in Fort Smith hung like overripe fruit on the tangled branches in Washington while the dates set for final disposition came and went. His enemies in Congress and on the Supreme Court had engaged him in a war of nerves, a staring contest in which he was determined not to flinch. The gray nonentity from the staff of deputy marshals who had assumed Maledon's responsibilities upon his retirement oiled the trap, treated the ropes as prescribed by the man he'd succeeded, and dropped sandbags to stretch the hemp and test its strength, the *squee-thump!* blending as always with the other routine sounds of Fort Smith. One never knew when the men in the capital might decide the old gargoyle on the bench was right for once, and the equipment must be equal to expectations.

Parker meanwhile attended church each Sunday—sometimes twice, in deference to Mary's Catholicism, although not as frequently as when her brandy bill was not so high and her tread more steady. There were weeks when she didn't imbibe, and accompanied her husband to meetings of the Social Reading Club, of which he was president, and which met in the homes of members. They read and discussed *Uncle Tom's Cabin,* General Wallace's *Ben-Hur,* the poems of Rudyard Kipling, and *The Prisoner of Zenda,* which Mary defended with passion, but which the judge considered a cheap imitation of better works by Dumas the elder. She recited poetry—*Wet the Clay* was the favorite—and Parker, buoyed by an unexpectedly favorable finding in Washington and a saturation of Sunday bonhomie, sang "She'll be Comin' 'Round the Mountain" in a rich baritone while the organist from the Methodist church played piano. The husbands shook his hand with enthusiasm and their wives expressed surprise at the strength of his voice. They avoided the indiscreet depositions in court and had never heard him condemn a prisoner to his face with all the thunder of a damnation in the Book of Exodus. ("Old Thunder" had become a term of endearment applied to him by deputies who had been present during sentencings.)

Charlie and Jimmie Parker still attended church with their parents, but did not ride with them in their carriage on the way home or to noon dinner with friends, finding their own amusements in town; it was painfully evident that timid, pliable Jimmie had fallen victim to his older brother's sinister influence. Father and firstborn rarely spoke. Having spent his wrath in court, the judge hadn't the energy to pursue it at home, even were it still possible to change the course of events. Isaac and Mary drove in silence and separated inside the door, the judge to his study and his pile of portfolios, the wife to her sewing room and the squat bottle she kept on the shelf behind the wicker basket containing needles and spools of thread. She was as likely to take to it in the morning as in the evening, when sleep eluded her, with predictable results; she had given up baking cakes for the condemned after disastrously substituting salt for sugar on one occasion, and arranging and delivering bouquets of flowers to the new cells aboveground presented the obstacle of climbing stairs to one who could no longer trust where she put her feet. Her husband had questioned her drinking early in its course, but she had made no response other than to return the bottle to its place with the cork secure. Later from the dining room he'd heard the tiny clink of the neck touching the edge of a glass. She was the partner of his youth, the strength in his early struggles; he could not lecture her as he did the principals in the trials over which he presided. When along in the evening the light went out beneath her door and she passed to bed, Parker continued to read and smoke until the hall clock told him he had just eight hours to rest before morning session.

With little opportunity for casual discourse at home, he found congenial company in his officers, particularly deputies like Madsen, Thomas, and Tilghman, whose tirelessness and insistence upon obtaining proper warrants best exemplified his dream of justice in the Eighth District. When he encountered them in hallways, in chambers, and in the marvelous hydraulic perpendicular railway that conveyed passengers between floors in the brick courthouse, he addressed them by their Christian names, while maintaining the customary formality behind the bench. (These officers in their turn called him "Your Honor" always.) In private they discussed baseball and the county fair, and in the lift one day Parker related the amusing anecdote of the time Belle Starr treated unsuspecting deputies to a meal of fried rattlesnake. More and more he discovered that exasperating woman's record a source of pleasurable exchange, and it occurred to him that something of the heart had gone out of outlawry when she'd been blasted into legend. At such times his pallor and snowy whiskers took on the mien of an indulgent grandfather.

His listeners this time were Chris Madsen and Bill Tilghman, who chuckled good-naturedly at a story they'd heard several times before in differing versions, from a half dozen deputies who swore they were present at Belle's memorable dinner. It happened that the pair were on their way to the attic to review some items of physical evidence before testifying in the trial to which they'd been summoned, and they stayed aboard the car after the judge stepped out. The doors were not soundproof, and as the contraption continued its ascent, Parker overheard the following:

Tilghman: "How old you figure the old man is?"

Madsen: "Not sixty yet."

Tilghman: "He's started in repeating himself."

Parker grunted. Perhaps he had. That was what came of having to defend one's every decision time and again.

The room where he spent most of his life was seldom less than two-thirds filled, even during such routine events as public drunkenness and a final divorce decree, for the theater of the courthouse was the town's biggest attraction, and one never knew when a bit of drama might break out, such as the details during testimony of a romantic indiscretion or an attempt at escape; Maledon himself had ended five of those with his pistols, with which he was ambidextrous, although left-handed at table and on the scaffold. Then, too, there were the judge's impassioned soliloquies when it came time to hand down his final judgments. Before his arrival, the men and women assembled chattered happily, offering one another apples and other cold victuals from sacks in hot weather and passing around vacuum bottles filled with soup or coffee when frost nibbled at the windows, but fell silent and rose at Crier Hammersly's command when the white-haired man in black robes strode in and took his place in the leather-embossed chair. The smack of his gavel was superfluous as to establishing order and served no purpose other than overture.

Once he claimed that familiar position, Parker's humor changed, for as many cases claimed his attention as had from the start. His sphere shrank by the day, it seemed, with such business as Mollie King's held up in debate over whether it belonged to the authority of the Cherokee court and not Fort Smith, but his docket remained elephantine, the largest in the United States and its territories, and larger than the famous Assizes of Great Britain. If anything it was increasing. It was as if the jackals who had preyed upon the people of the Nations had sensed the end of days, and become ferocious in their determination to squeeze the region of its last drop of innocent blood before the curtain fell. When the unassigned lands of the Cherokee Strip opened to homestead, some fifty thousand pilgrims had swarmed in to break ground, and in so doing offered the ruthless element that many more potential victims. Robbery remained steady, a staple of the venue, while rape and murder rose in direct proportion to immigration, the details becoming more grisly; clearing the room of women was not an option, and it distressed him to observe how many genteely dressed matrons and their daughters did not abandon their seats when such things unfolded—leaning forward, in fact, lest something be missed. He thought of his loyal executioner, retired now to shopkeeping, and was grateful that he himself had sired no daughters.

It didn't help trim the schedule when sensational novels trumpeted the heroic exploits of murderers like the Daltons, Bill Doolin, and Cherokee Bill, while readers who might have benefited by Parker's efforts to protect the people he regarded as his flock had to make do with indignant editorials and the *Congressional Record.* Contributors to that journal, fusty in its appearance yet as purple in its prose as *Buffalo Bill's Leap for Life* and *Deadwood Dick, Prince of the Road,* included as many enemies as ever, as new antagonists rose in place of old ones who had retired or died. The opposition now was bipartisan: Whereas the aging Old Guard of Democratic imperialism had never forgiven him for switching sides, his tormentors now were as likely to come from his own side of the aisle. They saw in him a disgraceful relic of buccaneering days, to be flung overboard to improve the party's chances in November, and this November in particular. Cleveland's second term had been plagued by economic panic; the Republicans smelled blood.

The world, it seemed, shared those pews with the curious loiterers, waiting for something to happen, for the Old Man of Fort Smith to stumble. It made a man slow and deliberate in his movements, forced him to retard the workings of his mind, like a phonograph winding down to a guttural growl. It was no good for the cylinder, and no good for the heart. His was winding down. He knew it, and all the strength he retained would be required to keep the predators from knowing it as well.

The clock struck. He folded his spectacles, put aside his reading, and retired to prepare for fresh battle in the morning. So had it been for going on twenty-one years; but never before had he found it so difficult to rise from his bed when six o'clock came around.

He had, however, one victory left in him, won on enemy ground, and one flight of judicial oratory that would stand up to examination for a century and beyond. The old man still had all his teeth.

TWENTY

Funeral bells were breaking up that old gang of Bill Doolin's.

Early in 1894, with the Nations alive with deputies, Indian policemen, and bounty killers hoping to retire on the rewards offered for the death or apprehension of him and his companions, Doolin married Edith, a minister's daughter, and settled down to the life of a gentleman farmer in the Comanche and Kiowa Nation. There he read in the papers of the slaughter and arrest of close friends, raised horses for racing purposes, and hired hands to plant crops and string fence. His split of the plunder would not hold out long in this fashion, but with five thousand dollars on his head, Doolin thought clodbusting beneath him.

In his semiretirement he learned of the passing of old associates: of Charley Pierce and Bitter Creek Newcomb, spotted by nobodies, tracked down by wire, and slaughtered by federal men in a farmhouse. That was bad enough, but the wind from the twentieth century had brought a new indignity to death, the postmortem photograph. Doolin heard an undertaker in Guthrie had peeled down the sheets that covered their corpses for a man with a camera to record them in their nudity, hair slicked back with water and their livid multiple wounds obvious to see. Charlie had had bullets in the soles of his feet, for Christ's sake. Was ammunition as cheap as that, that the blood-crazy marshals would go on pumping lead into a man as he lay on the ground already shot to pieces? In Vinita he'd seen a cabinet photograph of Bob and Grat Dalton and Tim Evans and Dick Broadwell, propped up on a barn door with a Winchester across Bob's and Grat's laps and all their boots off. Bob's big toe stuck out of a hole in his sock. Doolin turned his head and spat when he thought how close he'd come to going along on that foolish Coffeyville job. But what of it, if any ignorant saloon swamp or nigger that swept up horse apples in the street could tag him for the reward and later spend a penny of it on a picture of him with a hole in his sock and slugs in his belly?

It was dangerous to train a contrary creature like a horse with such thoughts distracting him. He took a holiday from work and wife in Eureka Springs, Arkansas, whose Victorian gimcrackery and steaming mineral waters soothed his raveled nerves and improved his breathing; he had contracted consumption somewhere in his breakneck travels through icy downpour, sodden heat, dusty wasteland, and pox-ridden settlements where a man who rode the owl-hoot trail might find peace at the high price of his harbor. It was the coughing and the retching and the general feeling of weakness that had turned him off that trail more than fear of the law; a fit of hacking in the middle of a holdup was just what some nance of a clerk needed to give him the Dutch courage to clobber Doolin with a spitoon and hold him for the authorities.

That trail had taken him as far West as New Mexico Territory. One of his hosts there was Eugene Manlove Rhodes, a young adventurer with literary aspirations whose celebrity would come a generation later with publication of *Paso por Aqui*, the tale of a fugitive's flight to avoid arrest; Rhodes thus became the first in a long line of writers who championed desperate men in quest of personal publicity and raw material. For his part, Doolin found him unnerving company, always staring at him when he thought Doolin wasn't looking.

Only in Eureka Springs could a man be truly alone with his thoughts. Subsiding into the smoky waters that brought out prickles of sweat like fire ants on his forehead, he swigged from a bottle of Old Pepper and considered himself on the road to health. Naked, he lay out of reach of the .38 Colt in its scabbard hanging on the back of a wooden chair when Deputy U.S. Marshal Bill Tilghman kicked open the bathhouse door and threw down on him with a .44. He was outdressed and outgunned and surrendered himself without a fight.

"Where's the rest?" he asked, dressed and in shackles, when they were outside.

"I'm the shebang," Tilghman said.

"Well, hell. If I knew that I'd of put up some kind of argument."

"I wish you had."

"Where we headed, Fort Smith?"

"Guthrie. You must answer for Ingalls."

"I wasn't in on that."

"Your horse was. Lafe Shadley shot it out from under you and you gunned him down for it."

"He was a good horse, but I wasn't riding him that day. I loaned it to Little Dick West for a fresh mount and rode into Guthrie to see the elephant. I wasn't at Ingalls."

"You can tell that to the judge in Guthrie, and thank your lucky stars it ain't Parker."

"I'd as lief it was. Guthrie's a far piece to ride. I'm a sick man." He coughed for emphasis; which was a mistake. It led to a fit. The waters had not had their chance to finish the cure.

Tilghman untied Doolin's horse from the hitching rail. Everyone knew his saddle rig on sight. "You can ride sitting up or hog-tied on your belly. It don't make no difference to me either way, but one's more pleasant for you."

"What'd I ever do to you to get your back up against me? I wish it was Heck took me instead of you."

"You'd get the same from him or worse. Now step into leather."

With Parker's court in division, Guthrie held jurisdiction over Ingalls, where the Doolin Gang had slain three deputies during the siege on their hideout. Doolin was housed in the federal jail there, charged with the murder of Lafe Shadley, a deputy. He thought Tilghman unreasonable on that point. Heck Thomas had plenty of bark on him as well, but was less inclined to take such a thing as a necessary casualty personally. Doolin and Heck had always liked each other, apart from their professional differences.

That ride—long and hot, with infrequent stops to rest and frequent prodding at the point of Winchesters belonging to the officers Tilghman had recruited to help with the escort, men who shared his unreasonable attitude toward decisions made in the heat of battle—erased the progress Doolin had made in the springs. Slick with sweat and pale, wheezing and spraying pink drops on his shirt, he fell into hallucinating in the wagon they'd dumped him into to discourage any hot ideas about breaking for freedom, and struck up a conversation with Grat Dalton, dead these three years. At the jail, Dr. Smith, the resident physician, fed him spoonfuls of a black gluteant made from tamarack bark, spikenard and dandelion root, hops, and honey, with a drop of coal oil substituted for brandy, which was banned from the institution. It was a tribute to the prisoner's strength of will that he recovered from both his relapse and this treatment; but since the evidence rested upon a mass jailbreak led by his patient, Dr. Smith was not disposed to congratulate himself within anyone's hearing.

On July 5, 1896, several prisoners overpowered and disarmed a guard, opened cells, and spilled out, fourteen strong, into the countryside. The news reached the private telegraph station in the room in St. Louis of a successful contributor to the popular press; he paused while composing *Bill Doolin Pays His Debt* to decode the message that came tapping out, crumpled and threw away his pages, and began writing *Bill Doolin's Flight to Freedom.* Heck Thomas, apprised at home in the house he shared with his second wife, Matie, hitched his suspenders up over his shoulders, loaded his Winchester, and went out. His grown son, Albert, already an experienced apprentice manhunter, rode beside him. Back home in Atlanta, Albert's mother fretted. Heck had told her posse work was in the blood.

Rufe Cannon, a deputy marshal who had taken part in the Ingalls raid, joined the Thomases in their camp below the Cimarron, not far from where that bloodbath had taken place; Doolin, who ranged wide but always returned to old haunts, had set up his horse ranch in that vicinity. In the Nations, men of low character were like stubborn mule deer, seldom grazing more than a few miles from where they were born, and dying there more often than not; it was the terrain and the cooperation of their neighbors, not distance, that kept them out of custody for such long stretches. Edith Doolin was still in residence, cooking for the hands and promising to pay them when Bill came back and found a customer for his horses. Heck took advantage of his own friends in the community and greased the palms of promising strangers to keep a posting on what took place there. Slowly as erosion, personal profit and the changing population had worn away at loyalty in the face of a common enemy. Heck thought it sad to see, as he respected a hardworking criminal ahead of an opportunist, but you couldn't stop the world from turning.

After dark on August 23, a rider entered the deputies' camp to report that Doolin's wife had brought a team to the Noble brothers' blacksmith shop in Lawton to have them reshod. It was a rush order; the horses were needed by morning. Cannon and the Thomases mounted up at dawn.

Passing the Doolin spread, they spotted fresh wheel ruts turning into the road. That meant a household packed into a slow-moving wagon. They eased their pace to conserve horseflesh. Sometime past two P.M., they were met by the Noble brothers, who had sent the message. They had passed Edith Doolin's covered wagon, heaped to the sheet with furniture, a cultivator, a plow, and a wooden coop filled with squawking chickens, headed toward Old Man Ellsworth's store.

"How do you know that's where she's headed?" Heck asked.

Charlie Noble answered. "Brother Bob spotted Bill Doolin's saddle rig on a horse in the shed behind the store."

His brother, a hulking youth with a wispy fair beard like spun sugar, confirmed this.

The posse took the long way around to avoid meeting Edith Doolin on the road. Below a hill overlooking Ellsworth's store, with living quarters in back and the shed behind the building, they tethered their mounts and crawled through the grass on their bellies, then took turns peering through a pair of field glasses Heck had confiscated from Bill Cook at the time of his arrest. There was a deal of activity going on about the store, but none of the men milling around came close to Doolin's spindly build and stooped shoulders. The possemen shared plugs of tobacco and twists of jerked beef and waited for dark.

Nearing sundown, a wagon with a canvas cover hobbled in, creaking and clucking, and a woman in a bonnet and long dress stepped down from the driver's seat and stretched her back. Heck knew Edith Doolin by sight. She went into the store, leaving the horse in the care of a man who came out carrying a feed bag. He stroked the animal's neck and strapped on the bag, making no move to release the animal from its traces.

"They ain't stopping here." Rufe Cannon turned his head and spat a brown stream onto the ground.

Heck took back the glasses, looked, then gave them to Albert. He traded his Winchester for Cannon's eight-gauge shotgun and told him to work his way down behind the house. "Shout out after me," he said. "Don't make a sound till then."

Heck Thomas' report of what followed read like a story a man told the first time he told it, without colorful detail or interesting asides, and never took on any of those things all the times he told it afterward. With the moon shining bright and just off the full, Bill Doolin emerged from the shed, leading his horse with the reins wrapped loosely around his wrist and his Winchester held in front of him in both hands, ready for use. Later the manhunters learned that the people who'd been spying on Mrs. Doolin had been unsubtle and he was prepared for ambush. It was Bill for sure, skinny as a withered rail and favoring his left leg, which poor Lafe Shadley had broken when he'd shot Doolin's horse out from under him in Ingalls, and for which he'd given his own life in return.

Heck waited until Doolin was halfway between the shed and the road, then rose with the moon in front of him and behind the bandit. Albert rose with him. Heck shouted for Doolin to surrender. Rufe Cannon echoed the words from behind Doolin.

The man with the horse fired from reflex. Heck heard the bullet chug into the ground in front of him. He swung the heavy shotgun to his shoulder, but he was unfamiliar with the weapon and fumbled at the hammers. Doolin fired again. By then Cannon and Albert had him in their crossfire and his second shot went wide. Heck's palm found the hammers and raked them back. Doolin's carbine sprang from his hands as if yanked by a wire; one of Cannon's slugs had struck it. The bandit scooped a pistol from his belt. The others claimed later he squeezed the trigger, but Heck had no recollection of hearing the report or seeing the flash. The shotgun bellowed, punishing his shoulder.

". . . the fight was over," Heck concluded.

That was his account, the one that was accepted in Guthrie and by Judge Parker in Fort Smith, and he never wandered from it, not even when he was an old man and reporters and historians pressed him for a version with more color and closer risk. Another version, suggested first in Lawton near the scene of the shooting, spread rapidly through the Nations, carried in gusty whispers like an off-color joke, but found no life beyond the borders of Oklahoma until it stumbled into print in 1920, thirteen years after statehood and eight years after Heck's death at age sixty-six. It went like this:

When Heck got tired of waiting for Doolin to show himself, he posted his companions on lookout and went down to knock on Ellsworth's front door. At length it opened; he pushed his way through the store to the living quarters in back, swept past Edith Doolin when she tried to block his path, and found Bill lying stripped to the waist on a mattress stained black with sweat and hemorrhage. The desperado's arms were spread, his head was tipped back with the mouth open in mid-gasp and the eyes fixed on the ceiling. Heck felt for a pulse in his throat, which was still warm and moist to the touch. He took his hand away after a minute. Doolin's consumption had stalked him to his end.

Moments later, a shotgun blast rocked the house.

When the body reached the undertaker's parlor in Guthrie (the same one where Charley Pierce and Bitter Creek Newcomb had lain), Dr. Smith, summoned from the jail to conduct the postmortem examination for the record, counted twenty-one shotgun slugs in the chest and abdomen.

"Not much blood," he said.

"A scattergun don't give you much time to bleed," said Heck.

"Still." But Smith signed the death certificate.

The same photographer who had made immortal the remains of Pierce and Newcomb arrived with his box and tripod and case of glass plates. He had Doolin tilted forward on the wicker preparation table and struck his likeness, turkey-necked with his beard black as soot, with the round punctures vivid on his naked torso. At Edith's request he took another in a display coffin with the corpse fully dressed in his Sunday suit of clothes. She had no other photos of him for the family album. Bill had avoided flash pans throughout his career.

People streamed in from Kansas and east Texas and from as far away as Doolin's birthplace in Johnson County, Arkansas, to file past the bier where the King of the Oklahoma Outlaws lay in state. His hair was combed, his beard trimmed, and a small piece of gutta-percha had been inserted beneath his upper lip to give him a hint of a smile, as if he were dreaming of easy banks and slow-moving trains. A bouquet of blue lupine, handpicked by Edith, stood in a pot on a metal stand. Beside the registration book lay a wooden strongbox with a slot cut in the top for coins and banknotes to be deposited for the widow and Doolin's small son; it was said Mrs. Doolin had spent her last penny on the funeral arrangements. Heck Thomas, who had shared with his posse a reward in the amount of $1,435 offered by Wells, Fargo, the Missouri State Legislature, and various citizens' groups for Bill Doolin's death, never responded to the rumor that half his cut wound up in the box at Doolin's services.

TWENTY-ONE

"Where's papers?" Cherokee Bill asked.

Ike Rogers, turning from the door to follow Bill's swinging stride through his front parlor, hesitated; as always, his visitor bore with him a brimstone stench of burnt wood, leather, horse, and spent powder. He carried his Winchester in one hand and slung his bedroll into an upholstered chair with the other. Snow slid from it, thawing on contact with the red velvet seat and staining it as dark as ink. "What papers are those?" Rogers said.

"*News*papers, what you think? I ain't seen one in a month."

"I used them to start a fire."

Bill bit back a curse. Rogers had family in the house and he considered himself a gentleman bandit. "The marshals got the telegraph to tell them what I'm about. What've I got to tell me what they're about, except the papers? You knew I was coming. You sent word."

"I guess there's some in the outhouse."

Bill went out through the back. When he didn't return in two minutes, Rogers figured he'd stopped to take a shit. He wasn't fooled by any excuse Cherokee Bill might offer about his interest in the press; he just wanted to see if he was mentioned. Right now there would be three or four cheap novels with his name on the covers rolled up in his blanket and slicker.

Sitting on the icy seat with his trousers down and his flap unbuttoned, his breath curling, Bill slid his finger down the smudged columns smelling of mildew. There was a stack of them on the floor for a man to wipe his ass with when the corncobs in the bushel basket ran out. The basket was empty, and Rogers seemed to be partial to front pages. He looked in vain for his name. He read that Bill Doolin was in custody in Guthrie. With Jim Cook on the run and Bill Cook on his way from New Mexico to Fort Smith in shackles, he'd hoped to join up with that bunch, but not if Doolin was absent. The great Ned Christie was dead; Henry Starr, the latest road agent to bear that celebrated surname, had been taken in Colorado. It was up to Cherokee Bill to keep the war going against order in the Indian Nations.

It was the central tragedy of Crawford Goldsby's life that he'd been born too late to "ride the high country" during the Golden Age of frontier banditry. He'd been just seven months old when the Jameses and Youngers were shot to pieces by squareheads in Minnesota, by which time old Wild Bill, who for all his service to the law and the Yankee army had tinkered his share with the life of the road agent, had been dead barely a month, slain in cowardly fashion from behind. Give him just ten years and Crawford would have prevented Bob Ford from killing Jesse in that same yellow mode, or at least avenged him face up, with both of them armed and a bullet in Ford's black heart when he wavered, as cowards did without fail, and another in his white liver to show the world his intention.

Concealing himself from his father's wrath, behind the barn with wick turned low and his face two inches from the rough sawtooth page, young Crawford had read of these atrocities in *Beadle's Dime Library* and fantasized about "calling out" the brutal old man who had sired him, "throwing down" on him with the "hogleg" he wore high on his hip, and blasting him into hell; after which he would go "on the scout," separating high-interest banks and arrogant railroad barons from their soiled coin and distributing it among their victims, or failing that into his own pockets and saddle pouches and living the "high life" in saloons and "dance-halls," where beautiful women in brief costumes admired his straight legs and square jaw and told him of the men who had "ruined" them (he knew not just how, only that the act was disgraceful and its effects permanent), whereupon he sought the blackguards out and deprived them of their lives. There was usually profit involved; invariably the men were thieves who lived in close proximity to their "ill-gotten booty," and didn't it say somewhere in Scripture that robbing a thief was no sin? If it didn't, it should have.

The early move from Texas to Fort Gibson, on the western boundary of the Cherokee Nation, had made a showdown with his father unnecessary; but it had exposed him to the truth of his Native blood and opened his ears, at the impressionable age of ten, to whispers of Ned Christie's war against the United States. When the marshals set fire to his cabin in Rabbit Trap Canyon and shot out Ned's eye, the boy had transferred his hatred to Fort Smith, and longed to join Christie in his new fortress, defying the government in Washington with his private army and vast arsenal; when after seven triumphant years Christie fell and his body was dragged to the federal courthouse for exhibit, Crawford asked his acquaintances to address him as Cherokee

Bill and laid an elaborate plan to assassinate Judge Isaac Charles Parker. The thing seemed easy enough; it was said that in his arrogance the old murderer paraded up and down Garrison Avenue with neither weapons nor bodyguard, in full view of God and the Devil, openly inviting disaster. The bullet that sent him to hell would assure immortality to the man who fired it. Why no one else had thought of it was one of those mysteries that alienated generations.

He came across a social piece about Parker uniting a young couple in "wedded bliss," and considered the ease in which a personable young man dressed for the occasion might produce a short-barreled Colt from a shoulder rig beneath his swallow-tail coat and unite the man holding the Bible with the men he had sent to the scaffold. What a reunion that would make in the pits of Hades.

But business had become too confining for all that. (He had read *The Authentic Life of Billy, the Kid,* attributed to Bonney's slayer, Sheriff Pat F. Garrett, and consigned to memory the Kid's response to Garrett's call for surrender: "Can't do it, Pat. Business is too confining," and yearned for the day when he could make it his own.) Bill had slain a man at a dance over some little thing, and "lit a shuck" toward the outlaw life with the Cooks, as stupid a pair of brothers as had ever taken to the outlaw trail, although he'd admired the viciousness of their dedication. Notoriety had followed hard, depriving him of the anonymity necessary to stalk the streets of Fort Smith unnoticed. And so he'd taken his vengeance by proxy, preying upon the institutions the carpetbagger in the courthouse held dear. The situation carried its compensations, right enough; every ounce of gold diverted from Parker's salary spent sweetly in the brothels of the city that had sprung up around McAlester's store, where Bill experienced at firsthand the results of the "ruination" he'd read about, to his immediate satisfaction, and with each double eagle he spent toward his education scored deeper his contempt for organized society. Compromise signaled manhood as much as pubic hair and the muscles that spread a man's shoulders and strengthened his resolve. Let Parker hand down his decisions and wait timidly for confirmation on high. In the Nations the name Cherokee Bill, with weapon in hand, carried certain death, with no appeal between it and the Prince of Darkness. He saw himself the judge's dark twin.

"I thought you fell in," said Ike Rogers, when Bill reappeared in the parlor.

"Where's Maggie?"

"She'll be here directly. Her people have her on a close halter."

Maggie Glass had aroused the bandit's interest. A handsome combination of Negro and Cherokee, she was the sixteen-year-old daughter of Christian folk who placed little faith in the men who came to their door requesting her company. Ike, who was a quarter white, was a cousin who enjoyed their trust, and therefore the opportunity to open his home to *rendezvous* between her and Cherokee Bill. (Bill had first heard the term from Maggie, who read novels dolloped heavily with passages in French; he liked the sound, which if you broke it into thirds came out like Cherokee.) The bandit supposed he'd ruined the girl, although she didn't seem to hold the fact against him.

Bill appeared to consider what Rogers had said. He still had on his deerskin coat and flat-brimmed hat and was holding his Winchester. At that moment Rogers' wife, a full-blood Cherokee, came to the door that led into the kitchen and announced that supper was on the table.

"Put down your rifle, Bill," said Rogers, "and let's eat."

"That's something I never do."

Rogers wanted to say, *What, eat?*, but didn't. In their acquaintance he'd never known the highwayman to smile at a joke or tell one of his own. He wondered if he saved his humor for those he trusted. It was a source of doubtful conjecture that Bill remained unaware of Rogers' official connection with Fort Smith. He'd been commissioned a deputy marshal by Colonel Crump, with rewards attendant upon the capture or death of Judge Parker's chief object of interest that season. A peaceable man by nature, Rogers had of late taken to carrying an antique ball-and-percussion revolver beneath his clothes wherever he went, and kept loaded the Stevens ten-gauge shotgun mounted above the stone fireplace in his parlor. Reluctantly he left that dependable piece where it was and preceded his guest into the kitchen. Bill was good with that Winchester indoors and out, handled it with the ease of a pistol; Rogers couldn't hit a gallon jug at close range with anything but a scattergun.

Maggie came in while they were seated around the oilcloth-covered table. January was in full charge, rattling the frosted panes with gusts loaded with needles, and her color was high beneath the brown pigment as she untied her bonnet and removed her cape. Bill stood up quickly, nearly tipping over his chair, grasped her by the wrist, and hauled her toward the bedroom, carrying his rifle in his other hand. She made some pretty noise of outrage but offered no resistance.

Rogers accepted a bowl of potatoes from his wife and lowered his voice to a murmur. "He knows."

"If he don't, Maggie's telling him. I saw the second she came in she suspects."

Bill returned, too quickly even for a man who'd gone months without feminine companionship, and sat down in his chair. He'd removed his hat and coat, but he still had the rifle. He leaned it against the table. Rogers saw all over again how big a man he was. People who didn't know him took him for a Mexican through and through, but his size was against it. He was strong, too; Rogers had seen him hoist the carcass of a two-hundred-pound elk and hold it while Rogers finished tying it up to a limb to gut and drain. That was before the commission, before he'd gone and had that rifle grafted to the end of his arm. Rogers watched him tear a piece off a loaf of bread with his big, heavy-veined hands.

"Where's the kids?"

"In bed. It's late, Bill."

"I thought maybe you'd sent them away."

The Rogerses exchanged a look. "No, they're in bed."

Bill got up and carried the Winchester out of the room. The door to the children's bedroom squeaked. Rogers started to rise, but then Bill returned and took his place with the rifle close to hand.

Maggie came in, smoothing her skirt. When she sat down, Mrs. Rogers placed a plate of fried chicken in front of her, took a pitcher of milk from a windowsill where it kept cold, and poured her a glass. For a time the only sound was the click and scrape of flatware on crockery. Rogers pushed the food around on his plate, then shoved himself back from the table.

"Not hungry, I guess," said Bill.

"I don't eat as much as I used to."

"Stay put a bit."

Rogers rested his hands in his lap. The butt of the big pistol was gouging a hole in his back. Maggie nibbled at a chicken leg and drank some milk. Bill sopped the grease from his plate with a piece of bread and ate in silence. Outside, the wind hummed around a corner of the house.

The host leaned down from his chair. Bill stopped chewing and watched him lift a jug from the floor.

"You know I don't drink, Ike."

"I thought I'd have one myself, but I changed my mind." He returned the jug to its place. "How about a hand of cards?"

Maggie helped Mrs. Rogers clear the table while Rogers dealt from a dog-eared pack. They played several hands without any conversation unrelated to the game. Afterward they adjourned to the parlor, where Bill's bedroll had been removed from the chair and placed in a corner. Rogers sat in the chair and his wife knitted in the rocker while Bill and Maggie sat together on the settee, talking in low voices with her head on his shoulder and his arm around both of hers. His other hand rested on the Winchester leaning against his knee.

"It's a rotten night, Bill. Why don't you stay over?"

When Bill smiled, nothing moved but his lips. He had fine teeth. "Why, I believe I will, Ike. I'm obliged you asked."

Mrs. Rogers returned to the kitchen to wash the pots and pans she'd left soaking. She dropped one, making a racket. Rogers chuckled. "All thumbs, I guess."

The clock ticked on the mantel below the big ten-gauge. Outside, the wind rose and fell. Rogers patted back a yawn. "I think I'll go on to bed and leave you two to catch up."

"I'll go with you."

"To *bed*? I don't like you that way, Bill." He tried to grin. He was aware that his wife had come to the door and stood there wiping her hands with her apron.

"You only got two beds," Bill said. "Mrs. Rogers can bunk with the kids and I guess Maggie can make herself comfortable in here. This bench is too short for me."

Ike Rogers figured he would remember that night as long as

he lived. He and Bill stretched out fully clothed on the mattress, the Winchester next to Bill on the other side. Rogers lay in the dark with his eyes open, listening. When Bill's breathing became even, he slid toward the edge.

Bill sat up, his hand on his rifle. "What's the matter, Ike?"

"Just restless." He sank back.

Twice more during the night he tried again. Either Cherokee Bill was the lightest sleeper in the Nations or he'd learned to do without sleep entirely. It was no wonder he'd remained at large when so many of his fellow travelers were in jail or dead. Rogers began to ask himself what had made him think he could succeed where so many others had failed, often at the cost of their lives. He thought about his wife and children.

In the morning—the slowest in coming Rogers had ever known—Clint Scales, a big Negro who helped out around the place, joined them at breakfast. Clint, who knew the situation, took one look at his employer's exhausted face and nodded his head a quarter of an inch. Bill was filling his cup from the big two-gallon pot that stood on an iron trivet.

Rogers' boy and girl ate crisp bacon with their fingers, asking Bill questions about his life on the scout. The guest, who had had no childhood of his own, liked children. He told stories that opened their eyes wide. Any one of them was enough to hang him. He kept his gaze on Rogers as he spoke. His host began to realize the stories were meant more for him than for the little ones. Most of them seemed to have to do with the price of betrayal. When he paused between anecdotes, Rogers turned to his children and asked them if they'd like to go next door and play.

"We want to stay and talk with Uncle Bill," said the boy.

"Bill can't hang around anyplace for long." He got up, Bill's gaze following him, and took a cartwheel dollar out of the jar of household accounts. He held it out to Maggie, who had barely touched her plate; her appetite didn't seem to be any better than Rogers'. "Why don't you take the kids next door and leave them and buy two chickens? We'll have them for noon dinner."

"We had chicken last night."

"I'll stew them," Mrs. Rogers said. "We've plenty of milk for gravy."

Maggie and the children bundled up and left. Rogers saw her glance at Bill from the door. Bill made a sandwich of bacon and a biscuit and appeared not to notice.

When he finished eating, Bill stood and picked up his rifle. "I best get going. Tell Maggie I'll see her in a few days."

Rogers said, "Sit a spell. She'll be back in a minute."

"Why'd you send for me, Ike?"

Mrs. Rogers paused in the midst of scrubbing dishes.

"Why, to see Maggie," said Rogers. "Her folks are in Nowata. I knew they wouldn't miss her if she stayed the night."

Bill seemed to turn that over, standing big as a cast iron boiler in the low-ceilinged room holding the Winchester. Then he leaned it against the wall, took makings from a shirt pocket, and rolled a cigarette, twisting the ends. When he lifted a lid from the stove and set fire to a piece of kindling for a light, Clint Scales turned over his chair, scooped a chunk of hickory out of the woodbox, and swung it with both hands. It made a nasty thump when it struck Bill's temple and he fell to the floor with a crash.

TWENTY-TWO

In August 1895, an event of monolithic proportions occurred in the Eighth District. Judge Isaac Charles Parker took his first holiday in twenty years.

This decision shook the court to its soul. It was as if the stately brick building on Sixth Street had lifted its stone skirts and waded across the Arkansas to visit with the train station.

Parker's doctor, who had diagnosed him with a weakened heart as a result of a dropsical condition, had ordered the change of scenery and routine on pain of death ("You will listen to the sentence . . ."). The couple decided to visit Charlie, who had begun the practice of law in St. Louis, and left young Jimmie in charge of the brick house on Thirteenth Street, to which they'd moved from the old commissary. The younger son was studying for the bar in the State of Arkansas, and expressed eagerness to be alone with the choice legal library on the shelves in his father's study; the proprietor of the House of Lords prepared for his nightly commerce on the judge's credit. Unlike his brother, Jimmie was a morose drinker who kept to himself at the end of the bar and frequently had to be slapped awake at closing and pointed toward the exit. The bartenders who filled Mary Parker's brandy order through the ladies' entrance said he came by his habits honestly.

Citizens gathered on the platform to watch as His Honor, wearing a cinderproof cape and carrying a stick, his white leonine head covered by a soft felt hat, saw his wife aboard a Pullman car and submitted his elbow to the support of a porter to join her. They noted that his face was gray with fatigue and that he made more use of the stick than just for fashion.

They stopped to rest in Little Rock, then pressed on. Parker sat in on a case Charlie was defending in the St. Louis courthouse, where he disapproved of his son's arrogance, which brought objections from the prosecution and several admonitions from the bench, but after the habit of years chose not to criticize him personally. He remembered his own early mistakes and counted upon the legal system to shape his son. He and Mary enjoyed the comforts of the Planter's House, whose gilded dining room displayed prominently a large portrait of Charles Dickens, an early visitor, and when the judge felt energetic enough to venture out in the evening they attended a performance of *The Pirates of Penzance* at the opulent Olympic Theater. As the days passed the lines smoothed out in his features and they resumed the marble-like quality that had inspired some observers to compare them to a profile on a Roman coin. He had by this time taken to brushing his snowy hair in a dove's-wing swoop over the right side of his forehead and combed out his beard so that it was broader at the base than at the top, and others thought he resembled a minor poet. He and Mary strolled the levee; passersby, alerted by the city's social columns that the famous Hanging Judge of the

Border was visiting, made note that his linen was acceptable and he did not strike matches on the seat of his trousers. They found his wife "blowsy," wearing last season's dress, but her expression was pleasant and she was kind to street vendors no matter how aggressive. When she opened her reticule and gave a coin to a one-legged veteran, her escort frowned. He and St. Louis appeared to share the same opinion about encouraging vagabonds.

At length Parker felt rejuvenated enough to grant an interview to a local reporter, who soon learned that one did not so much ask questions of the judge as sit and record his instructions to the jury; in this case, readers of the *St. Louis Globe Democrat.* The subject was Cherokee Bill, who after two years of committing depredations against the residents of the Indian Nations was now in federal custody waiting out his appointment with the noose.

"What is the cause of such deeds, do you ask?" said Parker; although in truth the young man had not. "There are now fifty or sixty murderers in the Fort Smith jail. They have been tried by an impartial jury; they have been convicted and have been sentenced to death. But they are resting in the jail, awaiting a hearing before the Supreme Court of the United States. While crime, in a general way, has decreased very much in the last twenty years, I have no hesitation in saying that murders are largely on the increase. I attribute the increase to the reversals of the Supreme Court."

Here the reporter made so bold as to ask if His Honor did not believe in the appeals process.

Parker drew on his cigar and broke an inch of ash into the crystal tray in his suite. "I have no objection to appeal. I even favor abolition of the death penalty"—the young man's ink-pencil scratched furiously, as his subject leaned forward in his armchair—"*provided* there is a certainty of punishment, whatever the punishment may be, for in the uncertainty of punishment following crime lies the weakness of our halting justice.

"This court is but the humble instrument to aid in the execution of that divine justice which has ever decided that he who takes what he cannot return—the life of another human being—shall lose his own."

The reporter made private note of the fact that Parker seemed to carry his court with him everywhere, like a pocket flask, and uncorked it any place he found suitable; but filed the story as written, or rather as it had been dictated to him.

It ran in long paragraphs of uninterrupted monologue, with Parker's tacit endorsement of an end to capital punishment—outlawed in far-off Michigan alone in all the world—buried in its text. St. Louis society deliberated but failed to agree upon a verdict for or against the man in the *Globe Democrat*'s dock. Generations had passed since the city's unruly adolescence, and tales of lynchings and river pirates were repeated in the arch melodramatic tone usually reserved for parables from the Brothers Grimm. Its citizens were loath to surrender their perception of the ogre perched on its mountain of skulls.

Parker read the article, sensed the interpretation, and sloughed it off with a roll of his shoulders, turning to the telegraph columns for news from Washington. Mary, sipping a cordial, saw this reaction and rejoiced. She wished, without disloyalty, that Isaac's dropsy had presented itself years earlier, as nothing but the threat of death and permanent abandonment of his responsibilities would have forced him from the bench for more than a day, that day being Sunday or Christmas. They took long carriage rides, dined at the homes of local dignitaries, and watched Fort Smith fade like the details of a troubling dream, the jail and scaffold last in line. Mary Parker began to entertain the timid hope that her husband might retire. They would live in St. Louis, and Jimmie would join Charlie in his practice.

Modern communications were against her. The news that came by wire to the local papers contained new encroachments by Congress ("haggling at my jurisdiction," was Isaac's phrase) and atrocities in the Oklahoma Territory. Isaac grew restive, unresponsive to the sights and sounds that surrounded them; his temper became short, his fingers drummed. Came the morning she drew on her robe and left the bedroom to find him standing fully clothed in their sitting room with a message from Western Union spread out on the writing table, and she knew their idyll was at an end.

Back in January, Ike Rogers had found himself having the Devil's own time collecting the reward on Cherokee Bill.

Clint Scales, his hired man, had taken a mighty swing at Bill's big head; the chunk of hickory had made a thump when it connected that Rogers himself had felt in his testicles, and Bill had dropped like a turd, shaking the house and showering plaster from the kitchen ceiling. Rogers reached to catch Bill's Winchester, but missed, and before it struck the floor, Bill was up in an animal crouch, his hat gone, his hair in his eyes, and blood trickling down the side of his face. He lunged for the rifle. Rogers flung both arms around Bill's waist and Scales, who had dropped the piece of firewood, caught Bill's throat in the crook of his elbow while Mrs. Rogers, who had been watching from the sink, bent, scooped up the Winchester, and ran into the parlor.

Bill writhed and bit and straightened his legs with a snap, carrying all three men across the room and into a wall, knocking a skillet off its nail, pinning Scales backward, and emptying his lungs with a woof. Dazed, the hired man relaxed his grip. Bill raised both hands above his head, closing them into a ten-fingered fist, and brought it down onto the back of Rogers' neck with the force of a club. Rogers' knees went weak, but he held on to the bear hug despite two more blows to his head and shoulder, the second of which numbed him all down one side. He felt his hands slipping, and Bill twisted free. In so doing, he raised one foot from the floor and Scales, recovering himself, hooked Bill's other ankle with one of his own and snatched it out from under him. The three fell into a heap with the bandit on the bottom. Scales and Rogers beat at him with their fists. Bill turned over to shield his face and got both hands beneath him to shove upward and dislodge them, but Scales screwed a knee into the small of his back and forced him flat. Mrs. Rogers came running back in with a pair of manacles. The men jerked Bill's hands behind him and Rogers hooked the cuffs around his wrists, ratcheting them tight. At length the man on the bottom stopped struggling, his breath whistling in and out.

"Got him a head like a pine knot." Scales, panting also, rolled over and sat on the base of Bill's spine.

Rogers rose, wobbling. His wife asked him if he was all right. He sent her for the Winchester and told Scales to hitch up the team.

"Where we taking him?"

"Nowata. Marshal Smith and Marshal Lawson's been waiting on delivery since sunup."

Bill caught his breath, gulped, and spat. "They'll wait till hell if they're waiting for me."

Scales went out, passing Mrs. Rogers coming in with the rifle.

When the wagon was ready, Rogers prodded Cherokee Bill outside and told him to sit in the bed. Rogers then swung up and latched the tailgate and mounted his horse. He rode behind with the Winchester across the throat of his saddle and Scales driving the wagon. He slid the clumsy useless burden of the big ball-and-percussion pistol out from under his belt and stuck it in a saddle pouch.

Turning into the road—his wife, that good woman, watching from the porch—Ike Rogers felt easier than he had in days, when he'd first decided to set his snare. That night in bed with the worst killer in the Nations had nearly unmanned him, and in the kitchen he'd fought with the blind savage terror of a kit caught in the jaws of a wild boar, but in the end it was Bill's time that had run out, and Bill knew it, too; he'd gentled right down once the cuffs were on. Rogers thought if he could remember what he'd done with that badge they'd given him he'd pin it on.

The sun was out, headache bright on the snow. They crossed the Verdigris River basin, the horses stepping high to clout a path through the drifts, and climbed out of it onto the plain leading flat as a poker table to Nowata. Rogers saw Bill struggling with his shackles now, the big muscles across his shoulders bulging like pumpkins. The boar still had some piss in him after all.

"Lay off that, Bill. You'll rub yourself to the bone."

"They're too tight, Ike. You want me to get the gangrene?"

"The reward notices don't say nothing against it."

"You're a Judas son of a bitch."

"Times are hard, Bill."

The prisoner relaxed. Moments later, he started in again. His temple resumed bleeding as he strained against the short length of chain.

"Bill, you're stubborn as—"

Bill braced his feet against the tailgate, his back against the headboard, and heaved. Something snapped. Rogers thought it was the tailgate latch, but then Bill got both hands on the sideboard and threw himself over. *Jesus, he's strong.* He landed on his feet, but his momentum combined with the wagon's almost pitched him forward onto his face. He stumbled, found his footing, and broke into a sprint, the sun glinting off the broken links dangling from his manacles.

Scales hauled back hard on the lines; the team tried to rear. Rogers drew rein gently, taking his time. Three hundred yards of open plain separated the running man from the cover of the nearest cedarbrake. Rogers levered a shell into the chamber and raised the Winchester to his shoulder. The sound crackled loudly in the sharp air. The fugitive ran another couple of yards, then slowed to a stop.

"What's the matter, Bill, restless?" Rogers called out.

Cherokee Bill turned around and walked back toward the wagon. Taking his time.

Deputies Smith and Lawson listened to Ike Rogers' account, grinning all through the details of the previous night, and fitted the prisoner with irons for his legs, which were heavy enough to hobble a buffalo. After holding him for a while in the back room of a store, they took him, shuffling in his chains, to the Arkansas Valley Railroad yard and locked him in a cattle car. The train was a while leaving; people gathered around to peer through the slats at the man seated on a pile of straw. He leaned forward and cut loose with one of Ned Christie's trademark high-pitched turkey gobbles. That sent them scrambling. He sat back and closed his eyes, sore in every muscle with his head pounding and fatigue settled deep in his joints. If he'd shot Ike Rogers last night when he'd been in the mood, he could have taken his rest then and been in Rabbit Trap Canyon by now, defying the Lighthorse and marshals from the ruins of Christie's fort, where at fourteen he'd crawled over the charred logs, making popping noises with his mouth and tumbling enemies left and right.

He awoke with the train moving. He had no idea how long he'd slept or how far he'd traveled. The scenery sliding along the openings between the slats was unfamiliar. He'd never been so far east. He was freezing. He wiggled his toes to draw feeling back into them and huddled deeper into his coat, moving awkwardly in his shackles. His belly gnawed. He'd eaten breakfast at Ike's, so a fair number of hours had passed, but without knowing just when the train had begun rolling he remained disoriented as to space and time. He'd always preferred traveling by horse, which put a man closer to the earth and more in harmony with it. He wondered if someone would come to feed him and whether he'd be armed and what measures might be required to separate the man from his weapon, but the train kept going at a steady clip and no one came. It passed through low scrub and gullies spanned by shallow trestles and might have been crossing the face of the moon for all any of it signified.

Finally the wheels slowed, trash and hovels accumulated alongside the tracks, and the train belched and farted to a halt beside a low frame building with a plank sign swinging from chains stapled to the roof: CLAREMORE. The platform was jammed with people. As the steam settled they moved in and pressed their faces to the gaps between the slats. Eyes swiveled his way, jaws hung slack. For a time he enjoyed the attention, feeling like Sam Starr and Bill Doolin and the Daltons rolled into one. Then the novelty wore off and he lowered his chin to his chest, placing the brim of his hat between himself and the gawkers. He was glad when a couple of railroad men banged at the side of the car with coupling pins to back them away and the train lurched into motion.

Monotony set in. His car passed through a string of small settlements without stopping. He learned to anticipate civilization whenever rusty buckets, empty beer bottles, piles of sodden newspapers, and shacks built of mud and lath began to congregate.

At Wagoner, the train stopped again and four men gathered on the cinderbed to cover him with Winchesters while a fifth unlocked the car; this was Clint Scales, Ike Rogers' hired man, who'd brained Bill with a chunk of forewood and sat on him. One of the others ordered him to step down and change trains. He recognized Marshal Bill Smith and behind him, back a pace and to the side to shield himself behind the marshal, Rogers in the flesh, looking more weaselly than usual with his moustaches standing out in stiff bristles. Bill didn't know the other two, but their coats hung open showing stars on their waistcoats. One wore a Colt in a suspender rig under his arm.

Hobbling along with the rifles at his back, circulation needling back into his legs in their irons, he was ordered to stop when a little man came puffing across the platform hauling a camera on a tripod and a black leatherette case. As he set up his equipment, the marshals and Scales lined up on either side of Bill.

"Not by Rogers," Bill said. "I won't be photographed standing next to snake shit."

The marshals were accommodating. Bill maneuvered himself next to the man with the underarm pistol; he found out later it was Dick Crittenden, who had joined the party at Claremore with his brother Zeke. The little photographer gestured to them to press closer together. Bill threw a friendly arm across Crittenden's shoulders. Just as his fingers touched the Colt's grip, the marshal shoved him away.

Cherokee Bill shrugged and posed with his hands in his pockets. The sun was too bright for the photographer's inexperience; the picture was overexposed, and badly retouched later to bring out the men's features, but Bill never got to see it. He was in jail in Fort Smith by sundown.

August hung heavy as stink in Fort Smith. When an officer of the court met the Parkers at the station, he found little sign of recovery in the judge's face, which appeared as pouched and gray as when he'd left for St. Louis. Cherokee Bill, whom he'd sentenced to hang for the murder of Ernest Melton, the housepainter, had made a break for freedom, and slain a man in the attempt.

TWENTY-THREE

Crawford Goldsby, as he was named in his indictment, retained an attorney whose name was known across the Nations nearly as well as his own. "Cherokee Bill and J. Warren Reed," a source close to Colonel Crump was overheard to say. "No one's seen a combination like that since Frank buried Jesse."

Counsel for the defense arrived just after Bill, in leg irons but wearing the too-tight suit and cutthroat collar Reed had procured for him, was seated behind the oaken table facing the bench. The lawyer surrendered his silver-headed stick at the door but retained his shimmering silk hat, which he removed with a Vaudeville twirl and set bottomside-up on the table. He tossed his gray kid gloves inside the crown, touched his cravat, flipped up his tails like a concert pianist, and sat down beside his client. Only then did he look at Bill, turning his head just far enough to wink at him.

Parker came in, and Cherokee Bill laid eyes for the first time upon the man he'd once sworn to kill. He looked like an old lady in a black dress; Bill had known one or two in Fort Gibson who could have grown a set of whiskers just like his if they let them go long enough. He was fussy, too, just like a hag, opening his leather folder and arranging the sheets just so, wiping his pen with a little piece of stiff cloth and nodding as his clerk whispered in his ear. Then he smacked his gavel and looked at Bill while the charge was read. He hadn't appeared to take any notice of the defendant before that, and there was nothing in his expression to indicate he thought any more of him than of anyone who had wandered into the gallery to take in the show.

The pews were packed. People who'd come in less than half an hour before the proceedings stood at the back. Some of them wore stars, but mostly they looked like store clerks and day laborers, ordinary folk there for the entertainment. More than a few of the spectators were women, all dressed up in gloves and hats and little fur-trimmed jackets; they sat in a special section thought to be out of earshot of the more explicit testimony, but this segregation only called more attention to their distracting presence. The newspapers called it "Beauties' Row," and Parker was said to disapprove of it, chiefly because of the almost tangible wave of sympathy that washed the jurors' way from that direction when the defense was pleading the prisoner's case. But no loophole existed in the phrase "speedy and public trial" for the exclusion of women.

Cherokee Bill was the draw. He'd heard some of the early birds had made a day's wage in an hour by selling their seats, and someone had tried to bribe the bailiff to hold a place for him near the front. In the press section, reporters from as far away as St. Louis and Denver crowded in beside the gentlemen from the *Elevator* and the *Evening Call.* Attempts had been made by some of them to barter their way into the jail for an exclusive interview with the desperado, and when those had failed they'd filled their columns with all manner of nonsense about him to keep the story alive. Bill didn't know it, but he and Parker shared contempt for the breed, although Bill enjoyed seeing his name in print when someone from outside gave a turnkey tobacco to get a paper into the jail; it seemed half of Fort Smith's transient population was made up of friends in federal custody. Bill traded rations for a peek now and then, but the fun was going out of it. If this kept up, no one was going to give credence to the things he *had* done.

And would do yet.

Trial began at noon. A parade of witnesses appeared and identified him as the man who had robbed Schufeldt's store and shot the housepainter point blank when he'd showed his face at a window. Everyone in Lenapah, it occurred to Bill, had picked that hour to do his shopping, and a good deal more than had been present, or he'd not have had room to raise his rifle. He muttered as much to Reed, who waved off the intelligence as a thing of no consequence. Bill began to have doubts about the man he'd heard so many favorable things about from acquaintances on the scout: The road agent's friend, they'd called him. Gin blossoms on the attorney's cheeks had raised his suspicions already. Cherokee Bill had never found a taste for the stuff, and considered the "blue ruin" the flaw that had led to the demise of such as Ned Christie. When it came down to brass tacks, the fellow who chose to ride the high country had only himself to rely on.

His opinion altered not at all when the prosecution rested and Burns called the first witness for the defense: Bill's own little brother, Clarence Goldsby, whom he hadn't seen since Hector was a pup, and whom he knew rather less than the men he'd ridden with. He remembered a scrawny lad who'd wet his pants whenever their father lurched into the room, stoked high on Ginger Jake and resident evil. The slight young man who took the stand and stammered with his hand on the Bible lent no confidence to the case.

Reed rose, but made no move to stray from behind the defense table, standing with his hands in his pockets jingling his loose change. A man who had to reassure himself he had the price of a drink was no good in a crisis.

"You are the brother of the defendant," Reed said. "Where does he live?"

Clarence mumbled a response. Parker asked him to speak up. He cleared his throat, leaned forward, and said, "Fort Gibson."

"How long have you lived there?"

"About seventeen years."

"How old are you?"

"About seventeen years."

Bill's contempt calcified. He saw the gray-whiskered jasper at the prosecution table scribble a note. A man who wasn't certain about his own age could not be expected to give certain evidence of anything.

"Do you know where your brother was on the last day of November eighteen ninety-four?"

"That morning, before daylight, he was at home, as near as I can remember."

Bill started to count on his fingers the months that had passed since he'd seen Clarence last. A sharp clank of the coins in Reed's pocket made him leave off.

"How long had he been there? How many nights?"

"Two."

"Where did he stay in the daytime?"

"Somewhere up in the hills."

"When you talk about the hills, that would be the Grand River Hills where he was?"

There was some business during which the prosecution objected about leading the witness. Parker said, "Sustained," and directed Reed to rephrase the question. Reed nodded, and established through Clarence that the Grand River Hills were indeed where brother Crawford had been at the time of the robbery in Lenapah. Bill saw his course then; he couldn't believe the thing was so simple, and a glance at the men in the jurors' seats, ox-faced and likely counting their fees, told him nothing.

Bill's mother and sister were in the gallery, seated close to the rail that separated America from Judge Parker. Bill turned to look at them from time to time, putting his hand on the back of his neck as if it were stiff. They looked as if they were attending a tent service. He couldn't bring to mind just when he'd seen them last. There had been roast turkey and some stewed greens. Studying Parker he was unable to tell if he was even aware of their presence. It all seemed a waste of time and train fare. Bill would have to kick in a fat bank just to get them back home.

The prosecutor thought so little of Clarence's testimony he didn't ask him any questions of his own. Reed rested; Bill knew he'd been betrayed as surely as if he'd retained that yellow snake Ike Rogers to represent him. He'd bored holes in Ike's face all the time Ike was testifying, and taken grim satisfaction when the court laughed at his account of his night in bed with the man on trial; he'd as good as admitted he'd shit the bed. Even the old lady behind the bench had smiled. But now here Bill had gone again and built his trust on loose gravel.

The opposition's summation to the jury painted a picture of the defendant as scarlet as any cheap novel's: He was a plague, a blight, and probably a cornholer, conceived in Texas and puked out onto the unsuspecting people of the territory, and Ernest Melton a hardworking family man who farted roses and left a widow and two half orphans to fend for themselves. (Bill was prepared to concede all of that, even the roses, but a fellow with a wife and kids ought to have sense enough to keep his head down when caps are being busted and not go peeking through strange windows.) When the graybeard prosecutor finished and sat down, twelve faces cut square out of bedrock turned Bill's way.

Then Reed rose, hooking his thumbs inside the armholes of his silk waistcoat and poking out his belly, and Bill found out what he was paying him for.

Seldom raising his voice above conversation level, and balancing its timbre against the counterweight of his heavy handlebars, the gentleman from West Virginia poured honey onto his accent and proceeded to dismantle every one of the statements the United States had made against the poor Indian boy in the dock. He was a victim, not a disease, the son of a brutal father who'd deserted his family, and a sickly mother unequal to the challenge of rearing three children properly in the wicked Nations. (Mother and daughter, in bonnets, lowered their gazes to their folded hands; Clarence lifted his brave chin.) Nevertheless, Reed said, the boy was the sole support of them all. Where was counsel for the prosecution when in his desperation the lad fell in with low company? (Bill thought Reed was trying to cut the pie both ways: He wasn't there when the housepainter got it, but if he was, it wasn't his fault.) He spat words like *calumny* and *canard* at his esteemed colleague on the other side of the aisle and was generally as entertaining as any of the spellbinders with the Chautauqua; Bill hadn't always understood what they were saying either, but it was thrilling to let himself be swept along by the torrent of syllables. Finally, harboring no illusions about his chances against the combined might of the U.S. marshals and the court in Fort Smith, young Crawford had appealed to a friend for shelter, only to be betrayed, beaten with a club, and thrown into a cattle car, where he was exhibited like a beast for the thirty pieces of silver on his head.

Bill thought it a whizbang show, especially when Reed punctuated *betrayed* by jabbing an accusing finger at Ike Rogers in the gallery, reddening his face and making his whiskers twitch like a water rat's. The Beauties were moved, too; some of them sobbed aloud. But when the attorney took his seat the jurors regarded the defendant with pitiless eyes. White men in suits, the bunch, not an honest pair of overalls among them.

Parker told them how the law worked. He sounded tired, as if it were him who'd been measuring the floor of a cell for a month, and Bill, who'd heard stories of his sermonizing, was disappointed after the performance he'd just witnessed. Choking off a man's life in his prime had become a daily thing and meant no more to him than moving his bowels.

The jury left, to return twenty minutes later, hardly long enough for a hand of pinochle. Bill stood to hear the guilty verdict, and damn if the man standing next to him didn't tip him another wink.

There were cards in jail, and time enough for Bill to learn every new game. He was one of fifty-nine men waiting to hang. Sometimes he was taken from Murderers' Row, where the condemned were segregated from the general population, to sit down with Reed. The attorney had applied to the president for clemency, but Cleveland hadn't any on hand, so Reed had put in an application to the court in Washington with the claim that seven witnesses had come forward to swear that Cherokee Bill wasn't in Lenapah at the time of the Melton killing.

"Where was they when I was on trial?"

"The same place." Reed touched his temple.

"What the hell use is that?"

"Patience, boy. I save my best business for the curtain call."

His mother visited. Bill made arrangements with her to finance Reed's inquiries and some other things and took a few dollars for the comforts. He'd been too busy stealing money to spend it, and she was his bank.

Parker had set his execution for June 25. The date came and went by his order while the high court was reviewing the letter that Reed's eloquent wife had composed for him. Bill had his picture taken with Deputy Lawson, who lent him an unloaded Winchester to pose with, like a dead grizzly stuffed and set upright with its claws raised. It was a fine weapon with an action as smooth as a sewing machine's; he worked the lever rapidly several times and asked who owned it.

"Houk, the postal inspector."

"That is a waste." Bill returned it to Lawson with a sad smile and something growing inside him.

In July, a former Doolin hanger-on named Ben Howell escaped from the Fort Smith jail. He'd begun a ninety-day sentence for stealing groceries in Ingalls, and as a short-timer had been allowed to wander the yard outside the building.

In his cell, Cherokee Bill heard the row. Within minutes he had the details. He crawled under his cot, slid a broken brick from its place in the wall, removed a loaded Colt revolver from the recess, and replaced the brick, using his hands to spread out the loose mortar dust. Then he crawled back out and put the weapon in his slop bucket where the turnkey would be sure to find it.

TWENTY-FOUR

The dismal dungeon—the fetid, dripping purgatory of old Fort Smith, malarial and in a state of perpetual eclipse—still existed as a jail only in the East, where *progressive* was never a term applied to anything connected with Isaac C. Parker. Its successor was a marvel of government architecture and late nineteenth-century technology, all sandblasted brick and polished steel, with the cells stacked in tiers—a cage inside a box—and a gear-driven mechanism that secured them doubly once their doors were locked with a conventional key. A bar ran the length of each row of cells, and when a lever was thrown, the "brake" slammed into place with a reverberating bang. Officials from throughout the federal penitentiary system traveled many miles to tour the facility, and of course to see the sinister scaffold; the splendid waterworks that hydrated the city rated a poor third. They had their pictures taken with the first two, like the deputy marshals with their quarries alive and dead, shining in their reflected glow.

Veteran residents of both the old and new institutions agreed that the sanitary arrangements and ventilation were vastly improved, but there were some who said that the chuckle and squeak of the old gridiron gates did not sicken the heart nearly as much as when that pitiless shaft slammed shut like a mighty breech. It was as if the entire weight of the massive engine of U.S. justice had fallen on them from above, burying them alive. They preferred the rats and stink to the impersonal working of the machine, the measured exchange of fresh air for old breathing through the ductwork day and night as in a steam-powered lung. The coming century gleamed bright as cold steel, and thank God for Parker's Tears that they wouldn't live to see it.

Lawrence Keating had been a night guard at the jail for six years, and for three years before that in the old basement keep; the newer men lingered in the guards' quarters past their shifts to hear stories of the convicts old George Maledon had gunned down trying to escape. He liked the late hours, "when the boys are all asleep and look just like angels." One of the oldest officers in the system, he was as white-haired as Judge Parker, with a magnificent set of moustaches and four children at home he let pull on them. Charles Burns, who had presided at Fort Smith's very first hanging, had liked him, and "Uncle Dick" Berry, who had assumed Burns's duties as head jailer upon his retirement, regarded Keating as his most dependable man. The prisoners considered him a mellow old gentleman who used no weapon when he struck them for calling him "Pops." Fort Smith approved of him warmly; it was still a small town for all its modern conveniences and growing population, and a man who helped out on the pump wagon when fire broke out and tended bar in the beer tent on Independence Day was known to all.

Campbell Eoff—"Oaf" to his intimates, a garrulous Scot with

a heavy burr, altogether too foreign for popularity—worked the day side in Murderers' Row, a lower tier that discouraged suicidal leaps. He presided over the evening lockdown, securing the cell doors with a set of keys on a ring the size of a croquet ball preparatory to throwing the brake. In deference to the Caribbean heat of Arkansas in July, the hour had been pushed back from 6:00 to 7:00 P.M., and with old Larry Keating keeping pace outside the bars that lined the corridor, Eoff unbuckled and hung up his gun belt and let himself inside with his ring of keys. Keating's shift would begin when this ritual was completed.

Cherokee Bill occupied Cell No. 20, third from the far end of the corridor. Bill rested against the door with his hands through the bars and smoke scrawling from the end of a hand-rolled cigarette between his fingers. Next to him in 19, Dennis Davis, a Negro sharecropper who had shot a neighbor to death in the Creek Nation in a dispute over shares, lay on his cot singing a tune with neither lyrics nor melody. Four court-appointed attorneys had sought to have him declared not guilty on the grounds of insanity, but he'd been convicted and consigned to the scaffold.

Eoff stood before the door to Davis' cell. He turned his head to call over his shoulder to Keating. "There's something wrong here."

Keating stepped up to the bars that separated him from the corridor. Eoff was struggling with the key to No. 19, which was stuck fast in the lock.

The door to No. 20 swung around on its pivot and crashed against the bars of Davis' cell. Bill stepped into the corridor, leveled a revolver at Keating's face, and rolled back the hammer. "Throw up and give me that pistol!"

Keating jerked his sidearm from its scabbard. Bill fired twice. The guard staggered back.

The unarmed Eoff swung about and ran toward the opposite end of the row of cells, leaving his keys dangling from the lock, which had been stuffed with a wad of paper. A bullet struck sparks off a bar to his right; another went between the bars at the end of the corridor and spanked the brick wall beyond.

Eoff reached the end, grasped the bars in both hands, and rattled them. "Jesus, let me out!"

Cherokee Bill's cigarette smoldered in the corner of his mouth, stinging his eyes. He spat it out and drew careful aim between the guard's shoulder blades.

Someone jostled him hard from behind; he almost fired wide. George Pearce, a murderer awaiting execution and Bill's nearest neighbor to the gate on that end, charged out carrying a bludgeon fashioned from a table leg in his cell and advanced upon Eoff, blocking Bill's line of fire.

"Step aside, George!" Bill called out.

"Keys!"

"They're stuck in the goddamn door!"

The door in the wall beyond Eoff's end burst open and four officers came through with pistols. One was Deputy Marshal Lawson, who had taken Bill off Ike Rogers' hands and lent the prisoner a Winchester in order to have his picture taken with Cherokee Bill. The first thing he saw was Larry Keating, swinging around the corner of the cage with one hand supporting himself on a bar and the other holding his revolver. The front of his uniform was soaked and slick. Eoff was spread-eagled on the end gate, banging it in its hinges and shrieking to Jesus. Ignoring the new arrivals, Keating raised his weapon to aim between the bars at the man standing with gun leveled at the far end of the inside corridor. He hesitated; Pearce had stopped halfway down holding his useless club, blocking the guard's target. The revolver was slippery in his hand; he had no strength to grip it. It fell. He felt himself sinking. His knees were bending on their own. "I'm killed," he said.

Lawson aimed between the bars and fired at Pearce. The bullet rang off steel and Pearce flattened himself against the line of cells on the left side. Billy McConnell, one of the guards who'd entered with Lawson, shot at Cherokee Bill, who returned fire twice, snapped the hammer on an empty shell, gobbled like a turkey, and scrambled back inside his cell as the officers assembled opened a fusillade. Bullets twanged off brick and steel, spent themselves, and rattled on the floor like shelled corn. A cell door halfway down the row swung open, drawing a volley of lead and spitting sparks where it hit; the prisoner inside stayed put. Bill had thrown the lever on his end, hoping for cover when the men poured out. But they appeared contented to wait instead for the rope.

There was a lull while McConnell tried to revive Keating. Bill had shot his wad, and the officers spread out to cover his cell from all sides. Then three rapid shots fanned out from inside and they ducked for cover; he had reloads.

Now the area outside the cage filled with armed men summoned by the sound of gunfire. Deputy Marshal Heck Bruner emptied the barrel of a shotgun, the characteristic boom followed by the skittering sound of falling buckshot. The air was a blue haze.

An unspoken truce was declared while the smoke cleared.

"Hey! Hey, goddamnit!"

This was a new voice, coming from a cell near the far end from Bill's.

Bruner poked a new shell into his empty barrel and slammed shut the breech. "That you, Henry Starr?"

"Who in hell else would it be, Heck? You're the son of a bitch dropped the lid on me."

"I just thought you was a gallows grape by now."

"I'm waiting on my appeal."

"Well, good luck with that."

"What if I brung you Bill's pistol?"

Bruner remembered he had a cud in his cheek. He shifted it to the other side. "I don't draw no water in Washington, Henry. I couldn't promise a thing."

"All I ask's a word on my part."

The deputy raised his voice. "How's that set with you, Bill?"

Cell No. 20 was silent while chambers were reloaded all around. Then: "How many's out there?"

"Right around twenty."

"Start Henry, then."

"It's your funeral, Henry," Bruner said. "I'll say a kind word to the judge or at your graveside, one or the other."

Bruner's ears rang. He strained for the reply.

"Is it true Maledon's quit?" Starr asked then.

"Hanging *and* storekeeping. I hear he's put his hand to busting sod. The new man's okay, but he's been known to strangle one from time to time."

"All right, then. Bill, you go to shoot me, you make it clean, you hear?"

"Sure thing, Henry," Cherokee Bill said. "That damn wash line's took too many good men."

"Don't shoot," Starr said, and crept out into the corridor, hands above his head.

Bruner told the officers to hold their fire.

Starr walked slowly. When he passed George Pearce halfway

down, words were spoken, too low for anyone to overhear. Starr walked on without pausing.

He stopped in front of Cell 20 and lowered his hands. The men watching strained to listen, but only a stray word or two of Cherokee reached them. Starr stepped inside; they braced themselves to fire. When he turned back toward the corridor, his hands were raised again, and a heavy Colt dangled by its trigger guard from his left index finger. He went across and eased it between the bars into the hand of an officer.

Keating was dead. His body was carried out gently, and no more words were spoken until after the cage was opened by a spare set of keys, letting out a lank and spent Campbell Eoff. Cherokee Bill was in manacles, and his cell was searched for contraband beyond the handful of loose cartridges they found on the cot. They discovered the broken brick, and space behind it for two pistols, including the one Bill had put in the bucket for the guards to find when they went through the prison after Ben Howell's escape. Bruner split Bill's cheek with the butt of his shotgun, and still nothing was said. The officers were saving their words for when their kids asked the old man about the time the great Henry Starr set out to disarm Cherokee Bill.

A hundred shots had been fired, one man slain, and none wounded, which was considered some kind of record. The noise had emptied the shops, homes, and streets of Fort Smith. By the time Bill's irons were in place, the crowd outside the prison was larger than any that had gathered there since the order had come down to restrict the audience for hangings. Larry Keating's fate was common knowledge before it went out over the wires to

Judge Parker in St. Louis; within thirty minutes of the shooting, all the old man's faults had been eradicated from memory and he was reckoned to have been the best Christian the community had ever known outside of the judge himself. His best friends would fill the county fair. It was hot as hell and lynch fever spread like diphtheria.

Parker was livid. He went straight to the courthouse from the train station, leaving Mary in the carriage to go home and unpack.

He found Colonel Crump in the same humor. The mob had been broken up, and at his request the city police were enforcing the curfew an hour early to prevent unhealthy gatherings. Crawford Goldsby was confined to his cell, shackled hand and foot, with turnkeys keeping watch on him in round-the-clock shifts.

"Those last three measures should have been taken when the gun was found in his cell," Parker said. He sat facing the marshal's desk, still in his traveling cape and hat.

"I asked Jailer Berry why they weren't. He said it made the prisoners unruly in the heat. The truth is he assumed the crisis was passed when the gun was found."

"That's just what Goldsby counted on. Who smuggled it in to him?"

"Berry questioned all the trustees at the time and took away their privileges. Much good that did him."

"Lynch talk, and in Fort Smith! This is what comes of meddling in Washington. The citizens have a keen sense of justice, if they know nothing of statutes and precedents. When I came here I promised it to them, and I kept my word, in the face of a firestorm from Washington and brickbats from the press. This fellow Reed and his tribe have managed to tear down in less than seven years what it took me fourteen to build. And now here's a good man slaughtered and a peaceful population determined to string his slayer to the nearest branch while a proper scaffold gathers dust."

Crump smoothed his beard and weighed suggesting another of Parker's popular open letters when his secretary knocked, entered, and told him his presence was requested at the jail.

"Berry?" barked the judge.

The secretary hesitated. "Yes, sir. Your Honor."

Parker waggled a finger at the marshal. "Either he's gotten to the bottom of the business or he's written a letter of resignation. Accept nothing in between." He left while Crump was lifting his hat off the peg.

They reconvened in chambers. Parker had removed his hat and cloak and looked up over the tops of his spectacles from the portfolio he had flayed open on his desk.

"He didn't resign." Crump's face was flushed, either from the heat or from some other stimulant.

"Indeed."

"Goldsby's a coward once his fangs are drawn. He knows now there's nothing between him and a steep drop but that letter to the Supreme Court."

"As of Friday night it's a penny wasted."

"Even so he's a penitent. He's prepared to swear out an affidavit identifying Ben Howell as the man who smuggled in both weapons, the decoy included. Goldsby claims that idea as his own. It was pretty smart at that."

"Refresh my memory."

"There's no reason you'd place Howell. You gave him three months for pilfering tins and such from a store in the Cherokee.

He walked away from a work detail two weeks ago; there's a warrant out on him next time someone spots him from a prison wagon. We'll raise the ante on that. As I see it, he let himself get caught just to ferry those guns in to Goldsby. Berry fired the turnkey who was supposed to search him directly he found out."

"The man should be up on charges."

"Berry thinks he was careless and that's all there was to it. It was a ninety-day bit."

"Still too long for Howell; but I imagine he had money waiting for him. Who made the arrangements?"

"Goldsby isn't saying."

"Give me the benefit of your professional experience."

Crump brushed again at his beard; heat and moisture were making it curl. "Who else? His sweet, sickly mother."

Judge Parker spread out his sheets of foolscap and smoothed them in that pernickety way that had caused Cherokee Bill to mistake him for something less than Lucifer. He was a full minute at it, and Bill suspected he'd read his thoughts on the matter and was bound to twist the knife once or twice more before shoving it home. At last he rested his pink, naked hands on the bench and looked at the man who stood before him, with irons on his wrists and ankles and two feet of chain linking both sets. Then he folded his spectacles and recited the long text from memory. His blue eyes were glacial and no mercy lived in them.

"You have taken the life of a good man," he said, "who never harmed you; of a faithful citizen, a kind father, and a true husband. Your wicked act has taken from a home its head, from a family its support. You have made a weeping widow; your murderous bullet has made four little sorrowing and helpless orphans. But you are the man of crime, and you heed not the wails and shrieks of a sorrowing and mourning wife no more than you do the cries for a dead father of the poor orphans. Surely this is a case where all who are not criminals or sympathizers with crime should approve the swift and certain justice that has overtaken you.

"All that you have done has been done by you in the interest of crime, in furtherance of a wicked criminal purpose. The jury in your case has properly convicted you; they are to be commended for it, and for the promptness with which they did it. You have had a fair trial, notwithstanding the howls and shrieks to the contrary. Your case is one where justice should not walk with leaden feet. It should be swift. It should be certain. As far as this court is concerned it shall be."

The harsh voice stopped. A throat caught in Beauties' Row with a faint mew. Parker made no sign he heard it. Now he shuffled his pages, bringing one to the top, and placed the steel-rimmed spectacles astride his nose.

"You will listen to the sentence of the law, which is that you, Crawford Goldsby, *alias* Cherokee Bill, for the crime of murder committed by you, by your willfully and with malice aforethought taking the life of Lawrence Keating in the United States jail in Fort Smith, be hanged by the neck until you are dead; and that the marshal of the Western District of Arkansas, by himself or deputy or deputies, cause execution to be done in the premises upon you on Tuesday, September tenth, eighteen ninety-five, between the hours of nine o'clock in the forenoon and five o'clock in the afternoon of the same day.

"May God whose laws you have broken and before whose tribunal you must then appear, have mercy on your soul." Parker flicked his gavel and turned away.

The sharp crack broke the string that had bound the assembly into a taut bale. A woman sobbed openly, and a capacity crowd exhaled as one. Pencils scratched paper in the press section. Even the big electric fan overhead seemed to resume its slow swoop after a breathless pause. Colonel Crump stood two rows behind the defense table, near enough to hear the wet trickle when Cherokee Bill opened his throat to swallow saliva. Apart from that he showed no reaction to the damnedest example of oratory the marshal had ever witnessed, in and out of war and politics.

He watched two of his deputies conduct the man in chains out of the courtroom and opened his watch, marking the time without quite believing it. The judge had spoken exactly twice as long as J. Warren Reed had taken in summing up the case for the defense, yet that earlier address had seemed fusty and long-winded by comparison; the peacock had commenced to molt. Trust Old Thunder to use the machinery of judgment to dispatch another of his infernal open letters and save himself a penny.

TWENTY-FIVE

In 1896, following the snail's progress of appeal, and after standing idle for more than a year, the great scaffold in Fort Smith claimed the lives of nine men between the middle of March and the end of July. Not since 1876, when only God and the president had the power to challenge Parker's will, had so many capital sentences been carried out in that jurisdiction, and no other year came close. A black cloud of despair descended over Murderers' Row; it seemed to the condemned, and indeed to the nearly half million people in the Eighth District, that Washington had broken itself at last on Parker's granite shore.

The high board fence that had been erected around the place of execution strained against the turnout for each event. Colonel Crump, anticipating an escalated demand among federal employees, local luminaries, the press, and ordinary citizens for the final disposition of a case involving the murder of an officer of the court and a popular neighbor, had tripled his standard print order for passes to the hanging of Cherokee Bill; these were exhausted quickly, and he handwrote more on government stationery for late applicants who could not be turned away. Come the day, people began streaming into the compound two hours before the time appointed. By the time Deputy Lawson and Campbell Eoff, whom Goldsby had tried to kill, escorted the prisoner up the steps, the sea of hats, caps, and bonnets awakened memories of the public executions of the early years when anarchy ruled in the Nations.

Cameras were banned. However, the march of invention had replaced the cumbersome equipment employed by professional photographers with handheld Kodaks available to all, and one such item, smuggled in under a coat, captured the image of the young desperado whose two years on the scout had mobilized more officers than had skirmished with Ned Christie for seven, hatless, with arms and legs in restraints and one cheek still healing from its encounter with the butt of Heck Bruner's shotgun, the noose snug around his neck. The plate was lost, but not before an artist named Gannaway copied it in charcoal. Lithographic prints sold briskly in Fort Smith for weeks following the event.

At Cherokee Bill's request, the Reverend Father Pius of the Catholic church prayed for the soul of Crawford Goldsby. The marshal then asked if Bill had anything to say.

"I came here to die, not make a speech."

He said good-bye to an acquaintance in the crowd. Then he turned to Lawson. "The quicker it is over the better."

Lawson fitted a black hood over the prisoner's head. Eoff, who had not hesitated to volunteer for the duty, grasped the lever worn smooth as polished ivory by the hand of George Maledon and dropped Cherokee Bill into history.

Four months later, on the same day in July, the five members of the Rufus Buck Gang followed him. Small-time offenders who had all spent time in the jail, Buck, a Ute Indian, Creeks Sam Sampson, Lewis Davis, and Maomi July, and Lucky Davis, a Creek Negro, had scourged through the Cherokee Nation on a gin-driven frenzy of rape, robbery, and murder, and been brought to ground in a gun battle with one hundred deputies, Lighthorse policemen, and outraged citizens in the summer of the previous year. The Supreme Court had rejected their petition for appeal with a shudder, and with one jerk of the lever, one of the more depraved bands in the bloody chronicle of the Oklahoma Territory went to oblivion. Buck and Lucky Davis outlasted the others by several minutes, convulsing in the throes of slow strangulation. Parker turned from his window and missed Maledon.

The attendance on that occasion equaled Cherokee Bill's. By spectral telegraph, it was understood that this would be the last mass execution by the judge's order, and likely the last in the long tradition that had begun when Peter the Great took up the axe to aid in the extermination of the Streltsys; for the troubled century was drawing to a close, and Parker's ailments could no longer be concealed. His absence was noted at the Methodist service on Sundays; he was said to lie abed, conserving his energy for the Monday session. He had been seen frequently to close his eyes during testimony against the Bucks, and the language of sentencing, as wrathful as when he had consigned John Childers to his death three times over in 1875, had been read in a dreary monotone from his notes without his once looking at the wretches who stood before him. The engine of justice in Fort Smith was winding down. Old Thunder's lightning had lost its blinding white flash. Those doddering citizens who in their cynical youth had pressed in around the phaeton carrying the callow jurist whom Washington had sent to deliver them from ineptitude and corruption wandered the streets wearing figurative bands of mourning on their sleeves. The coming century promised nothing but an empty hole cut out in the shape of Judge Parker.

George Pearce, who with his brother, John, had killed a man in the Cherokee to gain possession of a mare and a colt, and who had unwittingly spoiled Cherokee Bill's shot at Campbell Eoff in the federal cage, stretched the hemp beside his brother on the last day in April, and this, too, drew a mass audience, due in part to George Pearce's connection with Cherokee Bill's desperate gamble.

James Casharago was born on a farm in Arkansas of an American mother and an Italian father, who died from a fall when Casharago was a boy; his stepfather despaired of teaching him discipline, declaring that the love of hard work that existed in the Mediterranean races had in Jimmy's case been extinguished by the American side. The boy was a petty thief who grew up to become an experienced forger of documents turned easily into cash. Unmasked and driven to flight, he was captured and jailed in Faulkner County, but escaped and went to high ground in the northern part of the state. As George Wilson, he worked as a stock clerk in a country store, where he robbed his employer of a pistol and cash. In his twentieth year, sheriff's deputies arrested him for breaking into a store in Obion County, Tennessee, for which he served three years in the state penitentiary at Nashville.

Upon his release he returned home, borrowed a mule from his stepsister, and sold it to buy a wagon, which he mortgaged to obtain a team and merchandise and turned peddler; it was remarked upon later that had he set his sights higher, his talent for swindling might have earned him the acclaim of a Vanderbilt or a Morgan and a brownstone mansion on Fifth Avenue in New York City instead of a cell in Fort Smith. He was arrested again, but broke out of jail and fled to the shelter of an uncle, in tears and declaring his intention to lead an honest life thenceforth. The uncle provided him with a letter to Zachariah Thatch, a friend in Washington County, introducing his nephew and asking Thatch to give him work on the farm.

Casharago was twenty-five, a personable young man in full possession of his health. Thatch, aged and infirm, enjoyed his company, and in April 1895 asked him to travel with him on a horse-trading expedition into the Creek Nation. Casharago loaded a wagon with camping gear, hitched up a team, and tethered the trade horses, including a splendid stallion, to the tailgate. They started out, and on May 13 reached Buck Creek near Keokuk Falls. There Casharago split open Thatch's head with an axe, weighted down the body with rocks, and threw it in the creek.

Nearly two weeks passed before the bloated corpse broke loose and floated downstream toward discovery. A search on foot ended at an old campsite where a fire had been built atop a bloodstained patch of clay. Thatch and Casharago had been seen together, and deputies matched the description to a man found driving a wagon in Sapulpa, who gave his name as Wilson and who when taken to see the body said he'd never known the man. Asked about bloodstains in the bed of his wagon, he said he'd killed a prairie chicken for supper some days before. He was taken to Fort Smith regardless, and there his story disintegrated when acquaintances identified him as James Casharago, the murdered man's hired hand. Simultaneously a neighbor of Thatch's examined a fine stallion that Wilson had sold to a breeder of racing horses in Sapulpa and declared it the property of Zachariah Thatch.

"James Casharago," Parker said, "even nature revolted against your crime. The ground cracked open and, drinking up the blood, held it in a fast embrace until the time that it should appear against you. The water, too, threw up its dead and bore upon its once chaste bosom the foul evidence of your crime."

The apparatus of justice in Fort Smith was now firmly connected to the sprawl of gears, pulleys, and plunging piston rods that stretched across civilization and ended in Washington. Automatically the Casharago case entered it, and in course of time the justices of the U.S. Supreme Court passed around the particulars, forcing Parker to order a stay of execution pending a ruling. It was at this time that he began to stay home from church, and as the days of the week lost their light to recess cases that traditionally he had tried late into the night. His face was pallid almost to the point of transparency; he appeared to be fading away like an old photograph.

The justices upheld his decision unanimously. The Fort Smith papers crowed that the gray lion had shown his teeth and the nine old men had recoiled. Parker was at home and could not be reached for comment.

On July 30, 1896, an officer of the Fort Smith jail tugged a black hood over James Casharago's head and stepped away from the trap. For twenty-one years, Judge Parker had stood at the window in his chambers to witness the execution of sentence; he was as much a fixture on the appointed day as the dread solid scaffold. When a second officer pulled the lever, many in the packed crowd turned their heads to look at the window on the third floor of the courthouse. It was empty.

Isaac Charles Parker had hanged his last man.

"Oyez! Oyez! The Honorable District and Circuit Courts of the United States for the Western District of Arkansas, having criminal jurisdiction of the Indian Territory, are now adjourned, forever. God bless the United States and the honorable courts."

J. G. Hammersly stood now with the support of a wooden cane, and the golden bell of his tenor had long since turned brazen and harsh, but it didn't crack even on this occasion. He glanced from habit toward the man behind the bench, but it was not Parker who slapped the gavel; a nobody from South Dakota had been appointed to sit in his place. Parker lay on his deathbed.

Parker lay on his deathbed, propped up with pillows, and responded animatedly to questions put to him by Ada Patterson of the *St. Louis Republic.* It was warm for September, and Mary stood beside the bed fanning him slowly with a palm leaf; Miss Patterson reflected, not for publication, that he looked like an aging sultan in his figured dressing gown. The cap of chalk-white hair—luxuriantly abundant despite his travails, as if it fed directly upon that immense legal brain, irrigated by the waters of Jordan—fit him as closely as a turban. These fanciful thoughts she kept from the record, which was demonstrably the final testament of a great man, greatly flawed. She leaned over in her chair to make shorthand notes in the light of an electric lamp on the nightstand; the curtains were drawn, creating a twilight condition at odds with the squeak and jabber of busy Fort Smith outside the window, a Fort Smith he had done more than anyone to create in his own image.

"When President Grant appointed me, I didn't expect to stay but a year or two," Parker said.

"You said that, Isaac."

"It bears repetition."

"It was the greatest mistake of your life. It has broken your heart and your health." Mrs. Parker turned to the journalist. "He's only fifty-eight."

Miss Patterson made note of the figure, ignoring the faint scent of strong spirits that drifted from the judge's wife.

"It wasn't a mistake."

"My readers want to know how it feels to have hanged so many men."

"I've never hanged a man. It is the law that has done it."

Followed one of those monologues Miss Patterson had been warned about, as Parker summed up his case before the jury of public opinion. "Do equal and exact justice," he finished. "Permit no innocent man to be punished; let no guilty man escape. No politics shall enter here. I have this motto in my court."

"But you have no court."

"No." His head leaned back, his eyes closed. Blue veins showed in the paper-thin lids. "But the court has had me."

"Please don't print that last part," said Mary as she saw the woman out through the parlor. "It will start the whole thing all over again."

"What do *you* think of capital punishment, Mrs. Parker?"

"I've never believed in it since I read *Eugene Aram.* It was the first novel I ever read."

The journalist looked for the book to read on the train, but there was not a copy to be had in town. In St. Louis she checked it out of the library, read the first chapter, and skimmed the rest, stopping here and there to read a passage. She tossed the book aside. It was a silly romance about a man on trial for his life and presented only the case for the defense.

Parker lay on his deathbed, marking time by the gong of the hall clock and the ebb and flow of traffic in the street and the passage of the filtered sunlight as it crossed the papered ceiling. The counterpane felt heavy, making breathing difficult, but he hadn't the strength to adjust it. It was hard to concentrate on anything for more than a few seconds; for him, who had listened to testimony for hours on end and noted when a small detail had changed before an attorney did and raised an objection. Charlie visited, in the middle of a busy legal season in St. Louis, and that was a certain sign. The Reverend Father Smyth, pastor of Mary's church, came; at Parker's request he kissed and put on his vestments, baptized Parker into the Catholic faith, and performed the last rites. His convert thanked him and closed his eyes. The sheet covering his chest rose and fell shallowly.

In the Fort Smith jail, the men on Murderers' Row smoked and waited. They had only the sounds of the building for distraction; the echo of a turnkey's footsteps on the iron-oak floor, the sigh of the foundation settling, the current of air passing in and out through the ventilation ducts like the tenuous breathing of a dying man. The scaffold stood idle once again; no *squee-thump!* to stand one's skin on end and make him drop ash.

Parker lay on his deathbed. He found he could center his thoughts on numbers, cold and intractible in the face of relentless arguing on the part of opposing counsels: 13,490 cases tried, not counting 4,000 petty offenses settled in preliminary. Of 9,454 convicted and pled guilty, 344 were capital in nature. One hundred sixty-five of these had ended in conviction, with 160 sentenced to hang. Upon the dissolution of the court—Parker's court, as securely his own as the British Empire belonged to Queen Victoria—seventy-eight jurisdictions had sprung up to hear complaints civil and criminal; one fewer than the number of men he had caused to suspend from the scaffold. Two others had swindled the system through natural death behind bars, five had died in escape attempts, dispatched by George Maledon's brace of pistols. The rest had been spirited away through appeal, commutation, and presidential pardon. He did not count those prisoners who had managed to escape or forfeited bond; one must make allowances for the natural will to survive. The respect and love of those wards of the United States government he had pledged himself to protect from marauders from inside and outside the Nations lay without the realm of cold mathematics, and so exceeded the grasp of the remarkable brain whose whorls had worn smooth, like the grooves on the tips of the fingers of a postal clerk through whose hands had passed many thousands of letters and circulars and memoranda from the postmasters general in Washington.

The progress of his crusade was measurable in terms of time. The James Gang had confounded the Pinkerton National Detective Agency and peace officers in five states for nearly twenty years. Ned Christie had hung on for seven, the Daltons for four. Cherokee Bill had managed two, and through the railroads and the telegraph and the iron determination of the pioneers, Rufus Buck and his assembly of perverts had faced justice after just two weeks. Decades had been distilled to days. The wheels now ground as small as at the beginning, but swiftly rather than slow.

The time was near when mere hours separated the miscreant from the inevitable. He had done his part, minuscule as it was. A footnote was preferable to blank space.

Was it?

Of course it was. A man who failed to inspire love and hate in equal measure might as well have run for public office, or taken up arms against order and the rule of law.

Isaac, we've made a terrible mistake.

No, Mary. We are faced with a great task.

You will listen to the sentence of the law . . .

George J. Crump, colonel of the Army, retired, United States marshal for the Eighth District Court, which no longer existed, sat smoking a cigar in his office in the Fort Smith courthouse and considered the task of assembling boxes in which to place his personal effects, that the man who succeeded him would not have them removed to the attic, there to gather dust among the bloodied axes, arsenal of firearms, and pair upon pair of handsome boots, each of which represented a man struck down before his time and family and friends in mourning, that a killer would not go unshod. He thought also of that jackanapes J. Warren Reed, doomed to dull his blade with no Parker to grind it against, and the junior senators in Congress deprived of their devil; for surely there was nothing so ludicrous as St. George without his dragon. Crump had disliked the old bastard, but he hadn't a friend as constant.

He thought of calling his secretary to crank up the disturbing new telephone instrument and inquire after the health of Judge Parker. Then he became aware of an unearthly groundswell of noise from the direction of the jail.

He rose, threw up the window sash, and felt the whooping from Murderers' Row like a hot wind upon his face. He'd been told the same thing had happened the first time the Supreme Court reversed Parker. If he lived to be a hundred in the service of the United States Department of Justice, he would never learn how the lowliest convict in the system became aware of momentous events ahead of the official channels.

A SUMMATION FOR THE DEFENSE

In writing *The Branch and the Scaffold,* I've departed from the example set by Sir Walter Scott and told a historical tale without any fictional characters. Coupling invented people with real events serves to heighten drama, which is unnecessary in the case of Judge Parker and his remarkable court. Every figure in this book is real.

It's the privilege of the historical novelist to make certain adjustments in the interests of animation and clarity: I've introduced manufactured dialogue into episodes the record reports only in narrative, altered the order of some events, installed bits of business where details are spotty, and in the case of Deputy U.S. Marshal George Lawson and Will Lawson, a guard in the Fort Smith jail, consolidated two minor players into one. Such measures were seldom called for; the story provides so much that's required to entertain and instruct that it's a mystery so few writers have undertaken to retell it.

Beginning in 1875 and until his death in 1896, Isaac Charles

Parker tried civil and criminal cases in the Western District of Arkansas and the Indian Nations—an area larger than today's United Kingdom—every day except Sunday, Christmas Day, and one brief period of rest ordered by his physician, made even shorter by Cherokee Bill's attempt to escape from the federal jail. During his first fourteen years on the bench, Parker's sentences were not subject to appeal except directly to the president of the United States. He hanged seventy-nine men, and an examination of the record suggests far beyond a reasonable doubt that all were guilty of murder or rape or both. Sixty-five deputy U.S. marshals were slain in the line of duty during his tenure. His charge to the jury at the end of Cherokee Bill's trial for the murder of Lawrence Keating (too long and specific to include in this book) is still cited in legal references as a model of understanding and explanation of the law as it applies to murder in the first degree.

But Parker's story is more than just a legal thriller. Any drama that employes Belle Starr, Heck Thomas, the Dalton brothers, Bill Tilghman, Ned Christie, Bill Doolin, Cherokee Bill, Chris Madsen, "Cattle Annie" McDougal, Jennie "Little Britches" Stevens, and the fascinating and sinister George Maledon—the Dr. Kevorkian of his day—ought to run on Broadway for at least as long as Parker sat in judgment. All are legends, and the real wonder of the thing is they all played out in the same geographic locale within a span of two decades.

Unlike most of the tales associated with the American West, these are closely documented, in thousands of pages of trial transcript, period newspapers, many of whose editors prided themselves on accuracy, and three volumes that are absolutely essential to the solution of the enigma that was Isaac Charles Parker:

Hell on the Border, **by S. W. Harman.** Three years after Parker's death, Harman, a defense counsel in his court, published this massive chronicle, with names, dates, and all the pertinent details attending the most notorious cases that came across the Fort Smith bench between 1856 and 1896, with photographs and tables listing defendants, charges, victims, and dates of trials and sentencings, noting commutations, pardons, retrials, and their results. The book is indispensable, and is the major source of most that has been written about Judge Parker.

He Hanged Them High, **by Homer Croy.** An anecdotal and highly entertaining account of Parker's life and work (even the index is amusing), Croy's book draws its material from Harman, long-buried transcripts, and contemporary newspaper accounts, with valuable new information gathered from interviews with surviving personnel and direct descendants of the principals, many of whom were still alive when the book appeared in 1952.

Law West of Fort Smith, **by Glenn Shirley.** A prolific and popular Old West historian, Shirley distilled information from the Harman and Croy sources with research of his own among newspapers, court records, and biographies of figures peripheral to his subject to create a chronological and highly readable history. He is, however, casual about some facts (asserting that both of the Parkers' sons were present when they first came to Fort Smith, when James had not been born yet), and the lack of an index among more than one hundred pages of appendices, notes, and bibliography is irksome to researchers.

Although to my knowledge *The Branch and the Scaffold* is the first novel to present Judge Parker as its central subject, he has played an important supporting role in a number of works of historical fiction. These are among the best:

Cherokee Bill, **by Jon and Tad Richards.** This comes closest to being a novel about Parker. The judge shares nearly equal space with Clarence Goldsby, with the rest of the volume divided more or less evenly among J. Warren Reed; his wife, Viola; and, of course, George Maledon. It's a rip-roaring read, authentic in detail, with much navel-gazing on the part of its eponymous protagonist.

Hanging Judge, **by Elmer Kelton.** Despite its title, it's mostly about Justin Moffitt, a newly sworn deputy U.S. marshal assigned to Parker's court, and his relationship with another fictional character, Marshal Sam Dark. Kelton, heir to the "King of the West" mantle that once belonged to Louis L'Amour (and a better writer than L'Amour by far), is known for his intimacy with historical detail, fully drawn characters, and compelling plots, and his subject matter here delivers in all three departments.

True Grit, **by Charles Portis.** The book is best known as the inspiration for the movie that won John Wayne his only Oscar; but the role would not have been so meaty had it come from the brain of a Hollywood screenwriter. An Ozarkian, Portis draws from primary sources and his own relationship with the locale to create a seminal work in the literature of the frontier. The early scenes in Fort Smith are worth the price of the book, but what follows is pure entertainment, and "true grit."

Winding Stair, **by Douglas C. Jones.** Jones, an Arkansawyer, hit the national bestseller list with *The Court-Martial of George Armstrong Custer,* postulating what might have happened had Custer survived the Battle of the Little Bighorn, but here he plays it straight, with a lengthy cameo by Parker and a brief but unforgettable glimpse of Maledon in a plot based loosely on the manhunt and final disposition of the Rufus Buck Gang. Eben Pay, the fictional lawyer hero, is naive and a bit prissy, but Jones' creation of Deputy U.S. Marshal Oscar Schiller is his best contribution to the pantheon of Great Western Characters Who Never Existed.

Parker has been represented in the cinema with spotty success. James Westerfield was too old and bald in the movie *True Grit,* but played the role with an admirable balance of authority and irritability; John McIntyre, another fine character actor who donned the robes in the dismal sequel, *Rooster Cogburn,* was also much older than Parker lived to be, but was closer physically; at least he had hair. The best Parker in Hollywood was Pat Hingle, who in *Hang 'Em High* bore a close resemblance to the judge during his early years on the bench, and characterized him with an Old Testament clarity of purpose tempered with conscience—rendering inexplicable the decision to change his name and even the name of Fort Smith. (Fun fact: One of the men Hingle sends to the scaffold is James Westerfield, *True Grit*'s Parker!) The film and *True Grit,* book *and* movie, borrowed heavily from *He Hanged Them High.* Dale Robertson's gunslinging Judge Parker in a TV movie, *The Dalton Gang's Last Ride,* was claptrap, although it's entertaining to see Parker shoot down bounty hunter Jack Palance in a quick-draw contest at the finish.

Bloody business connected with the Indian Nations did not end with the breakup of the Eighth District Court, and a number of mysteries that took place in its jurisdiction are still unsolved.

No one ever stood trial for the murder of Myra Belle Shirley, better known as Belle Starr. The likeliest candidate, neighbor Edgar Watson, was arrested, but released for lack of evidence, only to be shot down by a citizens' posse in his home state of Florida in 1910. Ed Reed, Starr's shiftless son, remains a strong suspect. In 1971, a man named Robinson reported that his grandmother, Nana Devena, had confessed on her deathbed to slaying Starr in a case of mistaken identity involving a feud with another neighbor.

No hard evidence supports the controversial theory that Heck Thomas did not kill Bill Doolin but peppered his tubercular corpse with buckshot in order to claim the reward and split it with Doolin's wife. Glenn Shirley, in *Heck Thomas, Frontier Marshal,* called the story "scurrilous," and in *Bill Doolin, Outlaw O.T.,* Colonel Bailey C. Hanes suggested it was fabricated by an enemy of Thomas' to discredit him, but Dennis McLoughlin, in his entry on Doolin in *Wild and Woolly: An Encyclopedia of the Old West,* asserts on the authority of his research that Thomas acted from altruistic reasons and talked Doolin's penniless widow into accepting part of the reward after the fact. Whichever account is true, in a chronicle jam-packed with stalkings and gunfights, the postmortem-shootout theory is the more intriguing, and deserves further investigation.

Emmett Dalton, youngest of the bandit brothers, recovered from severe wounds suffered during the addle-pated attempt to rob their first two banks simultaneously in their hometown of Coffeyville, and was paroled from the Kansas State Penitentiary in 1907. He became a building contractor in Hollywood, moonlighting as a writer for the silent screen. His memoirs, *When the Daltons Rode,* were filmed in 1940, three years after his death from old age, but censorship required that the man upon whose autobiography the script was based die in the robbery along with the others.

George Maledon retired after the appeals process cheated him of the satisfaction of stretching the neck of the man who'd murdered his daughter. After failing at farming and shopkeeping, he toured the country with his ropes and tintypes and a piece of the original mainbeam of the Fort Smith scaffold, lecturing on the theme that crime does not pay. He died in Johnson City, Tennessee, on May 6, 1911, a few weeks short of his eighty-first birthday.

Ike Rogers did not long outlive Cherokee Bill, with whom he'd shared a bizarre night in bed and the next day turned over to Parker's deputies for the reward. In August 1897—by chance, some said—he stepped out of a railroad coach onto the platform in Fort Gibson and was shot fatally through the neck by a revolver in the hand of Clarence Goldsby, younger brother to Cherokee Bill. Goldsby, who, incredibly, was employed as a payroll guard at the time, dove under the stopped train, sprang up on the other side, and ran away from his pursuers, who were probably not that keen to begin with; Rogers had been overheard boasting that he would kill Cherokee Bill's brother.

James Parker, the judge's second son, committed suicide in 1918. It was said he never got over the loss of his father.

Charles Parker, his firstborn, married a daughter of Prosecutor William H. H. Clayton. She left him. He hadn't many friends beyond those of the drinking variety and few turned out for his funeral when he died of cirrhosis of the liver in Durant, Oklahoma, in 1925.

Mary Parker buried her sons and returned to Fort Smith, but the generation that had grown up since her husband's death did not remember the town's former first lady. She went back to Durant, where she had lived with Charlie, and died a year later. She was interred beside her husband in the National Cemetery in Fort Smith.

J. Warren Reed lost his enthusiasm for the practice of law after the passing of his nemesis. ("Our beloved judge has fallen asleep," he told a reporter for the *Fort Smith News-Record.*) He began a book about the court, then lost interest in that too and turned his notes over to S. W. Harman, who used them for *Hell on the Border.* Then Reed lost his wife. He retired to a life of senile dementia in Muskogee. In 1912 he joined Viola in Fort Smith's Oak Cemetery.

Ned Christie presents as great a challenge to history as he did to the Eighth District Court. Depending upon the source, he was either an innocent or a fiend or remarkably stupid; and the last two are insupportable by the evidence. Slipshod sensationalists have charged him with multiple robberies and as many as eleven murders, but when pressed for details fall silent. That he was cunning is inarguable. Accused of murdering a federal officer, a crime which then as now invited swift and savage retribution, he managed to remain at large for seven years, with every deputy marshal and Indian policeman in the territory knowing where he was, and when they finally converged upon him in his self-built fortress, a cannon failed to dislodge him and his ingenuity trumped even dynamite. Did he kill Deputy Daniel Maples? The picture is murky; I introduced a canine atrocity in lieu of specifics about the "disturbance" that led to harsh words between them. The long record of skirmishes with Parker's men, several of whom Christie shot but none fatally despite ample opportunity, casts doubt on his guilt in the Maples killing. I'm inclined to believe that had Christie gone to Fort Smith to tell his side of the story, he might have been released. Popular history, of course, would have suffered.

Henry Starr, no doubt in part for volunteering to disarm Cherokee Bill in the federal jail, was allowed to plead his murder case down to manslaughter and served five years at hard labor. Paroled again in 1913 after robbing a bank in Colorado, he caught Dalton fever two years later and took a bullet through a leg while trying to rob two banks in Chandler, Oklahoma. He was sentenced to serve twenty-five years in the state penitentiary, but was granted a pardon in 1919. (By now his adventures had begun to appear in serial form in Sunday newspaper supplements, where they were devoured by little Charles Arthur Floyd, who was not yet known as "Pretty Boy.") In February 1921, Starr left his automobile running in front of the People's Bank of Harrison, Arkansas, adjusted his snap-brim hat, and with pistol in hand swaggered into a shotgun blast courtesy of the manager. He died the next day, the last of the old-time Oklahoma badmen.

Defending Isaac Charles Parker from detractors is a staple of books about him. However, modern opinion of his record is more moderate than it was in his own time, particularly in the East. The fact that as many men (counting local peace officers and Indian police) died in the court's service as were condemned by it suggests that circumstances were far from overbalanced in the court's favor, and judiciary reviews have for the most part supported Parker's rulings. Certainly the men and women he felt duty bound to protect experienced no ambiguity in the matter; they showed up in the hundreds to pay their respects at his graveside service. Wherever one stands on the thorny subject of capital punishment, it is tempting to hope that such as he will sit in judgment in a case of personal interest.

As for the Fort Smith scaffold, silent since the dissolution of the court, the suggestion that it be sent on tour with Maledon horrified the citizens, who were eager to forget it ever existed. The city council had it burned and the ashes buried. Two generations passed in near ignorance of the court and its great engine of death; then, with mock gunfights being staged in Tombstone, Arizona, and pilgrimages being made to the scene of Wild Bill Hickok's murder in Deadwood, South Dakota, the city had a change of heart and reconstructed the scaffold on its original site to draw visitors. It stands in the shadow of the courthouse, directly under Judge Parker's window.